ALL AMERICAN BOYS

JASON REYNOLDS
BRENDAN KIELY

A CAITLYN DLOUHY BOOK

Atheneum Books for Young Readers
NEW YORK · LONDON · TORONTO · SYDNEY · NEW DELHI

For my younger brother, Christian—
May you never be made to feel small.
May you always be unafraid to stand up.
—J. R.

For all the organizers and educators who live
and work with love—thank you.
—B. K.

atheneum

ATHENEUM BOOKS FOR YOUNG READERS • An imprint of Simon & Schuster Children's Publishing Division • 1230 Avenue of the Americas, New York, New York 10020 • This book is a work of fiction. Any references to historical events, real people, or real places are used fictitiously. Other names, characters, places, and events are products of the author's imagination, and any resemblance to actual events or places or persons, living or dead, is entirely coincidental. • Text copyright © 2015 by Brendan Kiely and Jason Reynolds • Jacket photograph copyright © 2015 by Jessica Koscielniak; back cover photograph copyright © 2015 Thinkstock • Author photograph of Jason Reynolds by Kia Chenelle • Author photograph of Brendan Kiely by Gary Jason Cohen • All rights reserved, including the right of reproduction in whole or in part in any form. • ATHENEUM BOOKS FOR YOUNG READERS is a registered trademark of Simon & Schuster, Inc. • Atheneum logo is a trademark of Simon & Schuster, Inc. • For information about special discounts for bulk purchases, please contact Simon & Schuster Special Sales at 1-866-506-1949 or business@simonandschuster.com. • The Simon & Schuster Speakers Bureau can bring authors to your live event. For more information or to book an event, contact the Simon & Schuster Speakers Bureau at 1-866-248-3049 or visit our website at www.simonspeakers.com. • Book design by Dan Potash • The text for this book is set in Minion Pro. • Manufactured in the United States of America •

18 20 19 17

CIP data for this book is available from the Library of Congress.
ISBN 978-1-4814-6333-1 • ISBN 978-1-4814-6335-5 (eBook)

"History can only teach its lesson if it is remembered."

—Carmelo Soto

"If I am not for myself, who will be for me?
But if I am only for myself, what am I?"

—Hillel the Elder

ZOOM IN.

ZOOM IN MORE.

A LITTLE MORE.

A BOY, GRAINY.
FACEDOWN ON THE PAVEMENT.

A MAN ABOVE HIM. FISTS RAINING LIKE STONES.

HOWLING. LIGHTS AND SIRENS.

BLOOD ON THE STREET.

THE BOY IS STILL MOVING.

AND THEN HE IS NOT.

Friday

RASHAD

Your left! Your left! Your left-right-left! Your left! Your left! Your left-right-left!

Yeah, yeah, yeah.

I left. I left. I left-left-left that wack school and that even more wack ROTC drill team because it was Friday, which to me, and basically every other person on Earth, meant it was time to party. Okay, maybe not everybody on Earth. I'm sure there was a monk somewhere on a mountain who might've been thinking of something else. But I wasn't no monk. Thank God. So for me and my friends, Friday was just another word for party. Monday, Tuesday, Hump Day (because who can resist the word "hump"?), Thursday, and Party. Or as my brother, Spoony, used to say, "Poorty." And that's all I was thinking about as I crammed into a bathroom stall after school—partying, and how I wasn't wanting to be in that stiff-ass uniform another minute.

Thankfully, we didn't have to wear it every day. Only on Fridays, which was what they called "uniform days." Fridays. Of all days. Whose dumb idea was that? Anyway, I'd been wearing it since that morning—first bell is at 8:50 a.m.—for drill practice, which is pretty much just a whole bunch of yelling and marching, which is always a great experience right before sitting in class with thirty other students and a teacher either on the verge of tears or yelling for some other kid to head down to the principal's office. Fun.

Let me make something clear: I didn't need ROTC. I didn't want to be part of no military club. Not like it was terrible or anything. As a matter of fact, it was actually just like any other class, except it was Chief Killabrew—funniest last name ever—teaching us all about life skills and being a good person and stuff like that. Better than math, and if it wasn't for the drill crap and the uniform, it really would've just been an easy *A* to offset some of my *C*s, even though I know my pop was trying to use it as some sort of gateway into the military. Not gonna happen. I didn't need ROTC. But I did it, and I did it good, because my dad was pretty much making me. He's one of those dudes who feels like there's no better opportunity for a black boy in this country than to join the army. That's literally how he always put it. Word for word.

"Let me tell you something, son," he'd say, leaning in the doorway of my room. I'd be lying on my bed, doodling in my sketch pad, doing everything physically possible to not just stop drawing and jam the pencils into my ears. He'd continue, "Two weeks after I graduated from high school, my father came to me and said, 'The only people who are going to live in this house are people I'm making love to.'"

"I know, Dad," I'd moan, fully aware of what was coming next because he said it at least once a month. My father was the president of predictability, probably something he learned when he was in the army. Or a police officer. Yep, the old man went from a green uniform, which he wore only for four years—though he talks about the military like he put in twenty—to a blue uniform, which he also only wore for four years before quitting the force to work in an office doing whatever people do in offices: get paid to be bored.

"And I knew what he was trying to tell me: to get out," Dad would drone. "But I didn't know where I was going to go or what I was going to do. I didn't really do that well in school, and well, college just wasn't in the cards."

"And so you joined the army, and it saved your life," I'd finish the story for him, trying to water down my voice, take some of the sting out of it.

"Don't be smart," he'd say, pointing at me with the finger of fury. I never managed to take enough bite out of my tone.

And trust me, I knew not to push it too far. I was just so tired of hearing the same thing over and over again.

"I'm not trying to be smart," I'd reply, calming him down. "I'm just saying."

"Just saying what? You don't need discipline? You don't need to travel the world?"

"Dad—" I'd start, but he would shut me down and barrel on.

"You don't need a free education? You don't need to fight for your country? Huh?"

"Dad, I—" Again, he'd cut me off.

"What is it, Rashad? You don't wanna take after your father? Look around." His voice would lift way higher than necessary and he'd fling his arms all over the place temper-tantrum style, pointing to the walls and windows and pretty much everything else in my room. "I don't think I've done that bad. You and your brother have never had a care in the world!" Then came his favorite saying; it wouldn't have surprised me if he had it tattooed across his chest. "Listen to me. There's no better opportunity for a black boy in this country than to join the army."

"David." My mother's voice would come sweeping down the hallway with just enough spice in it to let the old man know that once again, he'd pushed too hard. "Leave him alone. He stays out of trouble and he's a decent student." *A decent student.* I could've had straight *A*s if I wasn't always so busy sketching and doodling. Some call it a distraction. I call it dedication. But hey, decent was . . . decent.

Then my father's face would soften, made mush by my mother's tone. "Look, can you just try it for me, Rashad? Just in high school. That's all I ask. I begged your brother to do it, and he needed it even more than you do. But he wouldn't listen, and now he's stuck working down at UPS." The way he said it was as if the lack of ROTC had a direct connection to why my older brother worked at UPS. As if only green and blue uniforms were okay, but brown ones meant failure.

"That's a good job. The boy takes care of himself, and him and his girlfriend have their own apartment. Plus he's got all that volunteer work he does with the boys at the rec center. So Spoony's fine," my mother argued. She pushed my father out of the way so she could share the space in the doorway. So I could see her. "And Rashad will be too." Dad shook his head and left the room.

That exact same conversation happened at least twenty times, just like that. So when I got to high school, I just did it. I joined ROTC. Really it's called JROTC, but nobody says the J. It stands for the Junior Reserve Officer Training Corps. I joined to get my dad off my back. To make him happy. Whatever.

The point is, it was Friday, "uniform day," and right after

the final bell rang I ran to the bathroom with my duffel bag full of clothes to change out of everything green.

Springfield Central High School bathrooms were never empty. There was always somebody in there at the mirror studying whatever facial hair was finally coming in, or sitting on a sink checking their cell phone, skipping class. And after school, especially on a Friday, everybody popped in to make sure plans hadn't been made without them knowing. The bathroom was pretty much like an extension of the locker room, where even the students like me, the ones with no athletic skill whatsoever, could come and talk about the same thing athletes talked about, without all the ass slapping—which, to me, made it an even better place to be.

"Whaddup, 'Shad?" said English Jones, making a way-too-romantic face in the mirror. Model face to the left. Model face to the right. Brush hairline with hand, then come down the face and trace the space where hopefully, one day, a mustache and beard will be. That's how you do it. Mirror-Looking 101, and English was a master at it. English was pretty much a master at everything. He was the stereotypical green-eyed pretty boy with parents who spoiled him, so he had fly clothes and tattoos. Plus his name—his real name—was English, so he pretty much had his pick when it came to the girls. It was like he was born to be the man. Like his parents planned it that way. But, unstereotypically, he wasn't cocky about it like you would think, which of course made the ladies and the teachers and the principal and the parents and even the basketball coach even more crazy about him. That's right, English was also on the basketball team. The captain. The best player. Because why the hell wouldn't he be?

"What's good, E?" I said, giving him the chin-up nod while pushing my way into a stall. English and I have been close since we were kids, even though he was a year older than me. We were two pieces of a three-piece meal. Shannon Pushcart was the third wing, and the fries—the extra-salty add-on— was Carlos Greene. Carlos and Shannon were also in the bathroom, both leaning into the urinals but looking back at me, which, by the way, is a weird thing to do. Don't ever look at someone else while you're taking a piss. Doesn't matter how well you know a person, it gets weird.

"You partying tonight at Jill's, soldier-boy?" Carlos asked, clowning me about the ROTC thing.

"Of course I'm going. What about you? Or you got basketball practice?" I asked from inside the stall. Then I quickly followed with, "Oh, that's right. You ain't make the team. Again."

"Ohhhhhhhhhhh!" Shannon gassed the joke up like he always did whenever it wasn't about him. A urinal flushed and I knew it was him who flushed it, because Shannon was the only person who ever flushed the urinals. "I swear that's never gonna get old," Shannon said, laughter in his voice.

I unbuttoned my jacket—a polyester Christmas tree covered in ornaments—and threw it over the stall door.

"Whatever," Carlos said.

"Yeah, whatever," I shot back.

"Don't y'all ever get tired of cracking the same jokes on each other every day?" English's voice cut in.

"Don't you ever get tired of stroking your own face in the mirror, English?" Carlos clapped back.

Shannon spit-laughed. "Got 'im!"

"Shut up, Shan," English snapped. "And anyway, it's called 'stimulating the follicles.' But y'all wouldn't know nothin' about that."

"But E, seriously, it ain't workin'!" from Shannon.

"Yeah, maybe your follicles just ain't that into you!" Carlos came right behind him. By this point I was doubled over in the stall, laughing.

"But your girlfriend is," English said, with impeccable timing. A snuff shot, straight to the gut.

"Ohhhhhhhh!" Of course, from Shannon again.

"I don't even have no girlfriend," Carlos said. But that didn't matter. Cracking a joke about somebody's girlfriend—real or imaginary—is just a great comeback. At all times. It's just classic, like "your mother" jokes. Carlos sucked his teeth, then shook the joke off like a champ and continued, "That's why we gotta get to this party, so I can see what these ladies lookin' like."

"I'm with you on that one," English agreed. "Smartest thing you've said all day."

Off went the greenish-blue, short-sleeved, button-up shirt, which I also flung across the top of the door.

"Exactly. That's what I'm talkin' 'bout," Shannon said, way too eager. "'See what these ladies lookin' like,'" he mimicked Carlos, the slightest bit of sarcasm still in his voice. If I picked up on it, I knew Carlos did too.

"I can't tell you what they'll be lookin' like, but I can tell you who they won't be lookin' at . . . you!" Carlos razzed, still on get-back from Shannon being slick and for laughing at my basketball crack. It had been at least three minutes since I made that joke, and he was still holding on to it. So petty.

"Shut up, 'Los. Everybody in here know I got more game than you. In every way," Shannon replied, totally serious.

I kicked my foot up onto the toilet to untie my patent leather shoes. Just so you know, patent leather shoes should only be for men who are getting married. Nothing about patent leather says "war."

"Argue about all this at the party. Just make sure y'all there. It's supposed to be live," English said, the sound of his footsteps moving toward the door. He and Shannon didn't have mandatory basketball practice like usual, but were still going to the gym to shoot around because, well, that's what they did every day. For those guys, especially English, basketball was life. English knocked on my stall twice. "Look for me when you get there, dude."

"Bet."

"Later, 'Shad," from Shannon.

"Aight, 'Shad, hit me when you on your way over," Carlos called as the door closed behind them. Carlos grew up right down the street from me, and, like English, was a senior and therefore could drive, and therefore (again) was always my ride to the party. We smoked him with the jokes all the time because he'd tried out for the basketball team every single year, and got cut every single year, because he just wasn't very good. But if you asked him, he was the *nicest* dude to ever touch a ball. What he actually *was* good at, though, was art, which is also why he and I got along. He wasn't into drawing or painting, at least not in the traditional sense. He was into graffiti. A "writer." His tag was LOS(T), and they were all over the school, and our neighborhood, and even the East Side. Whenever we were heading to a party, for him it was just another opportunity to speed around the city in his clunker, the backseat covered in paint markers and spray cans, while he pointed out some of his masterpieces.

Really they were more like *our* masterpieces, because I was the one who gave him some of the concepts for where and how to write his tag. For instance, on the side of the neighborhood bank, I told him he should bomb it in money-green block letters. And on the door of the homeless shelter I suggested gold regal letters. And on the backboard of a basketball hoop at the West Side court, I suggested he write it in gang script. I never had the heart to do any actual tagging. I mentioned how my father was, right? Right. Plus Carlos was a pro at it. He knew how to control the nozzle and minimize the drip to get clean tags. Like, perfect. I never really told him, just because that wasn't something we did, but I loved them. All of them.

When I walked out of that stall a few minutes later, I was a different person. It was like the reverse of Clark Kent running into the phone booth and becoming Superman, and instead was like Superman running into the booth and becoming a hopefully much cooler Clark Kent, even though I guess Superman might've been more comfortable in the cape and tight-ass red underwear than an ROTC uniform. But not me. No cape (and for the record, no tight-ass red underwear). I stepped out as regular Rashad Butler: T-shirt, sneakers that I had to perform a quick spit-clean on, and jeans that I pulled up, then sagged down just low enough to complete the look.

My brother had given me this sweet leather jacket that he had outgrown, so I threw that on, and *bam!* I was ready for whatever Friday had in store for me. Hopefully, a little rub-a-dub on Tiffany Watts, the baddest girl in the eleventh grade. At least to me. Carlos always said she looked like a cartoon character. Like he could ever get her. A *cartoon character*? Really? Please. A cartoon character from my *dreams*.

But before I could get to Jill's and get all up on Tiffany, I had a few stops to make. It was still early, and I had a couple bucks, so I could get me some chips and a pack of gum to kill the chip-breath. Can't get girls with the dragon in your mouth. But other than that I was flat broke, and it was never cool to party without cash, just because you always had to have something for the pizza spot—Mother's Pizza—which everyone went to either after the party was over or when the party got shut down early, which happened most of the time. Plus, you had to have money to chip in for whoever's gas tank was going to be getting you to and from the party, like, for instance, Carlos. So I caught a bus over to the West Side to first pick up my snacks, then meet Spoony at UPS, just a few blocks from home, so he could spot me a twenty.

The bus took forever, like it always did on Fridays. Forever. So at Fourth Street, I got off and walked the last few blocks toward Jerry's Corner Mart, the day darkening around me— crazy how early it gets dark in the fall. Jerry's was pretty much the everything store. They sold it all. Incense, bomber jackets, beanies, snacks, beer, umbrellas, and whatever else you needed. It was named after some dude named Jerry, even though nobody named Jerry ever worked there. Jerry was probably some rich old white dude, chillin' on the East Side, doing his thing with some young supermodel with fake everything on a mattress made of real money. Lotto-ticket money. Cheap-forty-ounce money. Bootleg-DVD money. My money.

I pushed the door to Jerry's open. It chimed like it always did, and the guy behind the counter looked up like he always did, then stepped out from behind the counter, like he always did.

"Wassup, man," I said. He nodded suspiciously. Like he always did. There were only two other people in the store. A policeman and one other customer, back by the beer fridge. The cop wasn't a security guard, the weaponless kind with the iron-on badges. The kind my dad tried to get my brother to apply for because they pay decent money. Nah. This cop was a cop. A real cop. And that wasn't weird because Jerry's was pretty much known for being an easy come-up for a lot of people. You walk in, grab what you want, and walk out. No money spent. But I never stole nothing from anywhere. Again, too scared of what my pops would do to me. Knowing him, he'd probably send me right to military school or some kind of boot camp, like Scared Straight. He'd probably say something to my mother about how my problem is that I need more push-ups in my life. Luckily, I'm just not the stealing type. But I know a lot of people who are, and there was no better playground for a thief than Jerry's. I guess, though, after a string of hits, Jerry (whoever he is) finally decided to keep a cop on deck.

I bopped down the magazine aisle toward the back of the store, where the chips were. Right by the drinks. Grab your chips, then turn around and hit the fridge for a soda or a beer. Boom. I looked at the chip selection. Like I said, Jerry's had everything. All the stank-breath flavors. Barbecue, sour cream and onion, salt and vinegar, cheddar ranch, flaming hot, and I tried to figure out which would be the one that could be most easily beaten by a stick of gum. But plain wasn't an option. Seriously, who eats plain chips?

While I was trying to figure this out—decisions, decisions— the other person in the store, a white lady who looked like she'd left her office job early—navy-blue skirt, matching blazer, white sneakers—seemed to be dealing with the same dilemma, but with the beer right behind me. And I couldn't blame her. Jerry's had every kind of beer you could think of. At least it seemed that way to me. I didn't really pay her too much mind, though. I figured she was just somebody who probably had a long week at work, and wanted to crack a cold brew to get her weekend started. My mother did that sometimes. She'd pop the cap off a beer and pour it in a wineglass so she could feel better about all the burping, as if there's a classy way to belch. This lady looked like the type who would do something like that. The type of lady who would treat herself to beer and nachos when her kids were gone to their father's for the weekend.

Now, here's what happened. Pay attention.

I finally picked out my bag of chips—barbecue, tasty, and easily beatable by mint. That settled, I reached in my back pocket for my cell phone to let Spoony know I was on my way. Damn. Left it in my ROTC uniform. So I set my duffel bag on the floor, squatted down to unzip it, the bag of chips tucked under my arm. At the moment the duffel was open, the lady with the beer stepped backward, accidentally bumping me, knocking me off balance. Actually, she didn't really bump me. She tripped over me. I thrust one hand down on the floor to save myself from a nasty face-plant, sending the bag of chips up the aisle, while she toppled over, slowly, trying to catch her balance, but failing and falling half on me and half on the floor. The bottle she was holding shattered, sudsy beer splattering everywhere.

"Oh my God, I'm so sorry!" the lady cried.

And before I could get myself together, and tell her that it was okay and that I was okay, and to make sure she was okay, the guy who worked at Jerry's who everyone knew wasn't Jerry, shouted, "Hey!" making it clear things were not okay. At first, I thought he was yelling at the lady on some you-broke-it-you-bought-it mess, and I was about to tell him to chill out, but then I realized that he was looking at my open duffel and the bag of chips lying in the aisle. "Hey, what are you doing?"

"Me?" I put my finger to my chest, confused.

The cop perked up, slipping between me and the clerk to get a better look. But he wasn't looking at me at all. Not at first. He was looking at the lady, who was now on one knee dusting off her hands.

"Ma'am, are you okay?" the officer asked, concerned.

"Yes, yes, I'm—"

And before she could finish her sentence, the sentence that would've explained that she had tripped and fell over me, the cop cut her off. "Did he do something to you?"

Again, "Me?" What the hell was he talking about? I zipped my duffel bag halfway because I knew that I would have to leave the store very soon.

"No, no, I—" The lady was now standing, clearly perplexed by the question.

"Yeah, he was trying to steal those chips!" the clerk interrupted, shouting over the cop's shoulder. Then, fixing his scowl back on me, he said, "Isn't that right? Isn't that what you were trying to do? Isn't that what you put in your bag?"

Whaaaaa? What was going on? He was accusing me of things that hadn't even happened! Like, he couldn't have been talking to *me*. I wanted to turn around to check and make sure there wasn't some other kid standing behind me, stuffing chips in his backpack or something, but I knew there wasn't. I knew this asshole was talking to . . . at . . . about . . . me. It felt like some kind of bad prank.

"In my bag? Man, ain't nobody stealing nothing," I explained, getting back to my feet. My hands were already up, a reflex from seeing a cop coming toward me. I glanced over at the lady, who was now slowly moving away, toward the cookies and snack cake aisle. "I was just trying to get my phone out my bag when she fell over me—" I tried to explain, but the policeman shut me down quick.

"Shut up," he barked, coming closer.

"Wait, wait, I—"

"I said shut up!" he roared, now rushing me, grabbing me by the arm. "Did you not hear me? You deaf or something?" He led me toward the door while walkie-talkie-ing that he needed backup. Backup? For what? For who?

"No, you don't understand," I pleaded, unsure of what was

happening. "I have money right here!" With my free hand, I reached into my pocket to grab the dollar I had designated to pay for those stupid chips. But before I could even get my fingers on the money, the cop had me knotted up in a submission hold, my arms twisted behind me, pain searing up to my shoulders. He shoved me through the door and slammed me to the ground. Face-first. Hurt so bad the pain was a color—white, a crunching sound in my ear as bones in my nose cracked. After he slapped the cuffs on me, the metal cutting into my wrists, he yanked at my shirt and pants, searching me. I let out a wail, a sound that came from somewhere deep inside. One I had never made before, coming from a feeling I had never felt before.

My initial reaction to the terrible pain was to move. Not to try to escape, or resist, but just . . . move. It's like when you stub your toe. The first thing you do is throw yourself on the bed or jump around. It was that same reflex. I just needed to move to hopefully calm the pain. But moving wasn't a good idea because every time I flipped and flapped on the pavement, with every natural jerk, the cuffs seemed to tighten, and worse, I caught another blow. A fist in the kidney. A knee in the back. A forearm to the back of the neck.

"Oh, you wanna resist? *You wanna resist?*" the cop kept saying, pounding me. He asked as if he expected me to answer. But I couldn't. And if I could've, I would've told him that I didn't want to resist. Plus, I was already in cuffs. I was already . . . stuck. The people on the street watching, their faint murmurs of "Leave him alone" becoming white noise—they knew I didn't want to resist. I really, really didn't. I just wanted him to stop beating me. I just wanted to live. Each blow earthquaked my insides, crushing parts of me I had never seen, parts of me I never knew were there. "Fuckin' thugs can't just do what you're told. Need to learn how to respect authority. And I'm gonna teach you," he taunted, almost whispering in my ear.

There was blood pooling in my mouth—tasted like metal. There were tears pooling in my eyes. I could see someone looking at me, quickly fading into a watery blur. Everything was sideways. Wrong. My ears were clogged, plugged by the pressure. All I could make out was the washed-out grunts of the man leaning over me, hurting me, telling me to stop fighting, even though I wasn't fighting, and then the piercing sound of sirens pulling up.

My brain exploded into a million thoughts and only one thought at the same time—

please

don't

kill me.

QUINN

On Friday nights there were always only two things on my mind: getting the hell out of the house and finding the party. But before I could get my buzz on with Guzzo and Dwyer, I had to take care of Willy. Ma used to want me to stay home with him, but thank God that didn't last long, because the Cambis, our family friends a few blocks away, came to the rescue and invited Willy for their spaghetti-and-movie nights. So Friday afternoons I just needed to get his bag packed and get him over there. He could do it all himself—he was in seventh grade, for God's sake— but Ma hammered me with: "Quinn, you need to take some responsibility." If she wasn't actually in my face, or over my shoulder, across the room, sour-frowning as she said it, then she was a voice in my head making sure I knew she was there.

As usual, Willy beat me home. He left the door open. He was too old to act like a frigging wild animal, but he was the baby of the family and we still treated him like one. He was in the living room with the PlayStation. His life's major achievement was the mastery of all games and how quickly he beat them. His latest was the new version of Grand Theft Auto. Ma hated the game, but when Willy agreed to play soccer, the deal he cut, the little prince, was that he could play GTA as often as he wanted. Whatever. Willy was all charm. He got what he wanted. Whenever he smiled I was sure he put tears in Mrs. Cambi's eyes, which was why they adopted him every Friday night.

"Fuck yeah!" Willy yelled, because he knew it was me walking into the living room, not Ma. On the screen, he blasted someone away with a handgun. He'd stolen a cop car and was cruising through the streets. I knew this part. Soon he'd find the helicopter and go blow up more shit in his virtual world. I hated to admit it, but the game kind of freaked me out.

"Hey!" I shouted. "Turn that down. People'll think I'm beating you or something. You packed?"

He bobbed his head to the soundtrack and ignored me.

"Willy."

"Will, now. It sounds tougher."

"Tough Will, I will kick your ass if you don't get your bag packed now."

"No, you won't." He still had his back to me and I snuck up behind him slowly. "No, you won't, because if you do, I'll tell Ma, and she will kick *your* ass!"

"Maybe," I said, pretzeling his arm behind his head. "But it will be worth it!"

He whined and kicked at my shins, but I lifted him from the floor by the TV and dragged him like that across the room until we were by the couch, where I dropped him face-first. I got a knee on his back. "You had enough?" His face reddened. "Enough?" I pressed harder. He wasn't in pain, smooshed into the cushions of the couch like that. He was just pissed he couldn't free himself. He wanted me to hurt him—he was that stubborn. If I hurt him, he could hurt me with a week's deep shit with Ma.

Thing is, I tackled him once, two years earlier. He was in fifth grade and I was in tenth. I misjudged the distance and as we fell, his head hit the corner of the coffee table. I called the ambulance myself. I got him to the hospital myself. He needed stitches. It was after dinner, so Ma was already at work. I didn't want to call her. I didn't want to bother her. I just wanted to take care of my brother and fix everything before she came home the next morning. But they called her as soon as we got to the hospital, and when she got there, she gave me the third degree right there in front of everybody. Hell of a bawling. I didn't blame her. We all have our roles to play since Dad died.

Plus, now it was a story Willy'd bring up at the kitchen table if he wanted to get out of what I told him he needed to do. For example:

"Eat your green beans."

"Why?"

"You have to. It's healthy."

"What if I don't? You going to smash my face again? You're not my dad."

No. I wasn't a stand-in for Dad. Nobody could be that. When the IED got him in Afghanistan, he became an instant saint in Springfield. I wasn't him. I'd never be him. But I was still supposed to try. That was my role: the dutiful son, the All-American boy with an All-American fifteen-foot deadeye jump shot and an All-American 3.5 GPA.

But sometimes trying to get Willy ready and out the door was an All-American pain in the ass. I got my knee off his back and lifted him from the couch. "Come on, Will," I said. "Please. I gotta get going. Get your bag packed."

He made a big production of catching his breath and calming down and then he stomped off to our room. As soon as I heard him banging drawers and looking for his uniform for his soccer game, I went to the kitchen for my own bit of packing. That was another part of the Friday night routine: I always swiped a flaskful of Ma's bourbon. She needed it to fall asleep when she got back from her shift over at the Uline

Warehouse—twelve hours straight, so who could blame her? I took it to ignite my Friday night buzz. Me, Guzzo, and Dwyer. We got our drink on to get our party on—weekend warriors to the end.

But I always stole the booze without Willy knowing either, and I got the flask in my jacket pocket while he searched for his shin pads in our room. He couldn't see me taking the booze. His eyes were Ma's eyes were the eyes of all the jackholes in Springfield who looked at me and thought of Dad.

Apparently, I had his eyes. His build. His "All-American" looks. All-American? What the hell was that? I hated that shit. What did it even mean?

I doubled back into the living room and turned off the game and the TV. I checked the house and the lights and all that. Responsible. That's me. "Ready?" I yelled.

"Yeah," Willy said.

"You good, Tough Will?"

"Don't call me that."

"I thought you wanted to be called that—"

"Asshole."

"All right. Let's go."

Once we were outside and I locked up and we were heading down the sidewalk, I threw my arm over his shoulder. He didn't shrug it off, which surprised me, but I was glad for it. I wasn't his dad or any dad, but I did love being a brother, and I did love the little pain in my ass.

But I didn't love having to walk him to the Cambis'. *Take some responsibility!* Ma never said that to him. He could walk his own damn self! He was twelve, not five. It wasn't far, either, but Ma and the Cambis were paranoid about the two-block stretch between our houses. Supposedly, the neighborhood was going to shit, and supposedly Sal Cambi got chased by a few kids all the way home one day after school and Mrs. Cambi had to threaten to call the police to get them off her front porch. Frankly, I'd seen Sal acting like an ass so many times with Willy, he probably said something and was so dumb about it that he didn't realize it'd get him chased in the first place. The kid was an idiot sometimes, but whatever, I was glad he was friends with Willy, because the Cambis were nice as hell—they fed Willy every Friday night and made him part of their family, and all that kindness got me off the hook from babysitting so I could hang out, like everybody else I knew did.

Everyone in this neighborhood lives in multifamily buildings. We live on the second floor of ours, above old Mr. and Mrs. Langone, for a good rent, Ma says, but the Cambis own their entire building, which, they said, was why they stayed. Otherwise they would have moved a long time ago.

I didn't have to be a parent worrying about rent and electric bills and all that shit to know that when you live in a neighborhood where they don't fix the streetlights very often, where cops set up one of those elevated lookout stations around the corner and patrol the streets a lot more than they used to when I was little, the neighborhood was on the decline. But I loved the West Side. I'd lived here my whole life. What the hell did people really mean when they said the West Side was on the decline? What'd that say about the people who lived here, like me, or all the damn people who were moving here now?

When we got to the Cambis, Willy sprinted up the front steps. I hung back. He rang the bell and Mrs. Cambi answered the door. Willy dashed past her and Mrs. Cambi waved to me from the doorway. She wore slippers. I stayed right where I was on the sidewalk, not wanting to get too close. Not wanting to get roped into staying longer than I had to. Just wanting to get the hell out and get the party started for the night.

But Mrs. Cambi beckoned me, like usual. "You know you're always welcome too." She leaned against the frame and held the door open. I could smell the sizzling garlic and onions from the street. I didn't remember the last time Ma had cooked for us.

"Thanks," I said. "I'm good. I have things to do."

"Busy man. Of course you do."

"And I wouldn't want to crash Willy's time with his friends."

"It's never crashing when either of you are at our place, Quinn. You know that."

"Thanks again, Mrs. Cambi."

"Regina. Call me Regina. Mrs. Cambi was Joe's mother." She smiled, and it was that smile I saw too often. That proud pity for Saint Springfield's two sons. "You're a good kid, Quinn," she told me.

I nodded and made my way.

That stuff just pissed me off. The world was shitty, and I didn't care if that sounded melodramatic. It was. Yeah, yeah, I was a good kid. A model kid. My dad had been the model man: the guy who, when he was on leave, stood there behind the table at St. Mary's soup kitchen in his pressed Class A blues serving ladle after ladle of chicken soup he'd helped make. Yeah, yeah, model man when he lived, model man after he died. The model man and the model family he left behind.

My dad got blown up in Afghanistan, and Ma and everybody we knew and plenty of people we didn't know but knew his name, all reminded me—he sacrificed for all of us. He sacrificed for the good of our country. He died in the name of freedom. He died to prove to the wackos of the world who didn't believe in democracy, liberal economy, civil rights, and all that shit, that we were right and they were wrong. But for me, my dad was dead, so the frigging wackos won. And, seriously, who are the frigging wackos, anyway? I sure as hell didn't feel sane all the time.

Dwyer and Guzzo had been texting me since I got home, and I knew they were waiting for me in the alley near Jerry's corner store. When I was a block away, I took a quick swig of bourbon and stuffed the flask in my ass pocket, so they'd know I had it. So they'd know I wanted to get the party started too, but I'd had shit to do. I took a swig because I was taking responsibility!

By the time I got to them they were pissed, and they looked like a couple of old ladies bent over and gossiping. Dwyer with his hands thrust in his pockets, shuffling back and forth on his two feet, his skinny arms and legs all fidgety, trying to hide his big-ass head beneath a green hoodie, and typical Guzzo. Guy's built like a bear, but he stood there, with his hands on his hips, thumbs forward, kicking at the edge of the Dumpster like he was checking a tire for air. He threw his hand up when he noticed me. "What the hell?" he said.

"Dude! We've just been sitting here," Dwyer said, wiping at the buzz-cut stubble around his head. "Someone's going to get suspicious."

"No one's going to get suspicious," I told them. "We've scored beer here more times than I can count."

"Whatever," Guzzo said. "This is our last night out for months. Next week, it's back to hell."

"It's not hell," Dwyer said.

"Dude, I hate forced fun," Guzzo continued. "Coach isn't

fooling anyone with his team-building shit. Basketball meetings every Friday and Saturday night mean one thing: no goddamn partying. That's it."

"Man," Dwyer said, giving Guzzo that face that said *You dumb or what?* "You kill me. This is serious. When that scout from Duke shows up, you're going to be the first in line, squeezing his palm. All stupid smiles and clean-cut."

"No, he won't," I said. I bounced in between them and boxed Guzzo back into the Dumpster, keeping my ass low, legs spread. "I'll get there first. 'Hey, man,' I'll tell him. 'People tell me I look good in blue.'" I flashed a big fake smile, and Dwyer laughed.

Guzzo pushed at me, and I held my ground, keeping him pinned, but he's huge, and it didn't take long for him to toss me aside. He swung around in front of me. Frowned. "Fuck that," he said. "You know damn well English is going to be first in line, because everybody's going to talk to him first."

"Not if you step in there," Dwyer told Guzzo. He bounced Guzzo with his shoulder and they went at it for a few seconds, trying to get position on each other, get a leg in front, and box the other one's back. Dwyer's tall but he's all sticks, and Guzzo popped Dwyer's leg with his knee and got in front. He grinned. "Whose house?" he said to me. I laughed. I started bobbing in front of him, like I was going to shake and move past him to some hoop behind him.

"Oh, yeah," I said, dribbling my pretend basketball.

"Falcons all the way, baby!" Dwyer yelled from behind Guzzo. "Whose house? OUR house!" His cheeks were already so red his freckles seemed to gather all together.

Guzzo, squatting, his arms spread out, and keeping Dwyer behind him, nodded. "Hell, yeah," he said. Then he stopped and stood up and let Dwyer rush past him. Dwyer came at me so quickly, I thought he was going to knock me over. He dipped, pivoted, and swung around me like he was going up for an easy layup behind me. Classic Dwyer. He loved banging in the paint like a giant pinball and fighting for the rim. Guzzo wasn't as much of a fighter. He was just massive; people bounced off him more than he tried to send them flying.

Still, we laughed, but it was because it was all we thought about. It was all everybody was thinking about. It was mid-November. State rankings came out in two weeks. If we were number one, it was only going to get harder.

"Listen," I said. "If this is our last big night, let's make it worth it."

"That's what I'm talking about," Guzzo said, slapping my hand in the air. He pulled a short key on a ring from his pocket and held it in the air like a cartoon superhero. "Shotgun, baby!" he yelled.

He was so loud, Dwyer looked around to see if anybody was watching us from the top of the alley.

"Seriously," Guzzo continued. "How much are we going to

get? I'm shotgunning like ten beers tonight."

By "we," Guzzo meant me, because I usually had more cash than either of them, so I almost always bought the beer, which pissed me off, but I knew they felt bad I paid for their fun more than they paid for mine. And fuck it, we were tight, and that was most important. I'd been friends with Guzzo forever, and when Dwyer had joined us in middle school, everything had only gotten better.

"I have this," I said, patting my back pocket, knowing they could smell it on my breath. "And I don't want to be wasted when I get to Jill's, and you can't be either. You promised me. Seriously."

And that was the other reason I didn't mind buying Guzzo beer. Jill was Guzzo's cousin, and he kept promising he was going to put in a good word for me with her. I'd always liked her. Gearing up for the basketball season, I would go on these epic runs all around town, and I—okay, I admit it— I'd run by her house more than once. You know how it is. Sometimes you just want to cross paths with that one person, on the bus, on the street, wherever, just so you can nod, and say "Wassup," and hope to hell that something more comes of it. Anyway, the last time I'd seen her, she was dragging her younger brother across the street. She'd been wearing these stupid gray sweatpants rolled at the waist, rolled at the ankles, too. She walked barefoot along the walkway. I waved to her, she waved back, and all I could think was, *How does she make even a stupid pair of sweatpants look so good?*

Everybody knew she threw mad parties, so I was psyched for the night. Everybody'd be hands-up dancing on the first floor, and I'd see if Jill was down with some alone time. And if not, that was cool too, because then I'd be ripping shots with Guz and Dwyer in the kitchen, like we did at most parties anyway.

"Well, let's do this," Guzzo said. "Jerry's, beer, a couple slices at Mother's, and we're good. The party's gonna be a shitshow—Frankie brought over a frigging trunkful." Frankie was another one of Guzzo's cousins, and this was another reason being friends with Guzzo was a good thing. He had an army of cousins around the city, and if you were in the shit and you were tight with Guzzo, you didn't have to look far for help.

Basically, we always got started at Jerry's, because it was the dirtiest little corner store I knew, and the easiest place for us to get beer. Guzzo had lifted a bottle once. I had too. But we didn't try that anymore. And we never bought it ourselves. The clerks behind the counter would never risk selling to underage dudes. But one night I asked a guy on the sidewalk outside if he'd buy us a twelve-pack of tall boys, he agreed, and that had become our weekly routine. It was the safest plan anyway, and we always seemed to find someone who'd buy the beer for us.

The only problem was always this: Whoever we found to buy us the beer would only do it if we paid him extra. There weren't any Good Samaritan beer angels floating around waiting to gift us our weekly Friday buzz. So beer cost double for us, but whatever, we were seventeen. And I made mint at my summer job and it gave me play money for the year. Plus, Ma was a frigging workhorse, always doing the night shift at Uline so she could get paid more. It meant the money I made was just for me, and whatever I wanted to spend on Willy. But mostly, it went for beer and Friday night dinners at the back window of Mother's Pizza.

We had to hang around for a while, but soon after it was actually dark out, I left Guzzo and Dwyer in the alley and leaned up against the brick wall down the block from Jerry's until I saw a guy making his way up Fourth Street toward us. I recognized him; he'd helped us out before. He was a skinny white dude, who was a little strung out. I told myself that the guy looked like he could use my money to buy himself some food, but he's going to buy more beer anyway. And while I'm fucking judging the guy like that, I'm also digging in my pocket for the money I'm about to give him to buy me and the guys our beer at five thirty in the goddamn afternoon. See what I mean? Who's the sane one now? I'm thinking all this, but on the outside, I was all smiles and handshakes—All-American.

And I was about to hand him my money when the front door to Jerry's whacked open and a cop pushed a younger guy out in front of him. It was only a matter of seconds before the cop had thrown the guy to the sidewalk and pressed him face-first into the concrete. I was barely twenty feet away. The guy on the ground was black and he looked like he was around my age, and I wasn't sure, but I thought he was looking at me. He was vaguely familiar, but I couldn't place him. Did he go to our school? All I could really see was the cop over him, shouting. The cop was white and it took me a second to recognize him, because his face was angled down the whole time, but then, when he raised his head for a second, I realized right away it was Guzzo's older brother, Paul.

Holy shit! Paul! Paul was hitting the other guy, again, and again, smashing his face into the sidewalk. The blood kept coming. I wanted to move; my gut wanted me to rush to help Paul. But I knew enough to know that you stayed out of police business, plus Paul didn't need my help because he was pummeling the guy. So I just stood there, sorta frozen, just watching, transfixed. With one knee and a forearm pinning the guy beneath him, Paul bent low and said something into the guy's ear. I couldn't look away; I didn't even want to. I didn't know what the hell was going on and my own pulse jackhammered through me. I heard sirens coming up the street, and I swear I would have stayed staring if it hadn't been for the cop car that pulled up onto the sidewalk between us. When car doors swung open, I turned and ducked back down the alley to find Guzzo and Dwyer.

They were waiting near the back and I ran toward them.

"Oh shit," Guzzo said.

Another cop car raced past the entrance to the alley behind me.

"Oh shit," Guzzo said again.

"We have to get out of here now," I hissed.

"What the hell happened?" Guzzo asked.

I looked up at the chain-link fence behind us. It was higher than a basketball rim, maybe fifteen feet. But climbable. On the other side were the tracks to the commuter rail. "Dude," I said, putting my hands on the fence. "It's your brother. He busted some guy in the store. It's fucking ugly and we need to get the hell out of here. Now!"

I started to climb.

"The tracks?" Dwyer asked. "Are you crazy?"

When I got to the top, I looked both ways. No trains. Still, it was probably a high traffic time, so that wouldn't last for long. I dropped one leg on the other side of the fence, swung myself over, and began to climb down.

"What the fuck, man?" Guzzo shouted.

"No one saw me," I said when I hit the ground. "If we get out of here right now, maybe nobody will, and we can all just pretend like we weren't here. Like it didn't happen."

"What happened?" Guzzo asked, one hand on the fence, but hesitating. "Is Paul okay?"

"Yeah, man," I said. "But he just beat the piss out of some kid on the sidewalk and we don't want to be around to have to answer any questions—it was fucking ugly. Now get over here before a train comes."

They hauled ass over the fence, and we ran along the pebble embankment of the railway until we came to the Fourth Street bridge, and then we slid down the embankment to the fence along Fourth Street and climbed over that one. I heard a whistle in the distance, but we all made it over and away from the tracks in plenty of time.

"Paul?" Guzzo said again, his voice cracking.

"It was bad," I admitted.

"What the hell do you think the kid did?" Guzzo asked.

"I don't know," I said. "But whatever he did, your brother just put him in the hospital for it."

"You know what?" Dwyer said. "Let's just get a slice and chill. Seriously."

It was a good plan, but when we got there, I couldn't stop thinking about what I had seen. I swear I thought about the guy on the ground, but mostly I thought about Paul, because Paul was Guzzo's older brother, and after my own father died, Paul had basically been my older brother too. And I couldn't shake that look of rage I'd seen on the face of a man I knew and thought of as family.

Saturday

RASHAD

*C*ustody. That's the one word I kept hearing over and over again as I drifted in and out of a painkiller coma, which by the way, might've been the best sleep I'd had in I don't even know how long. And that's with a broken nose and a few fractured ribs.

Custody. They brought me into the hospital, handcuffs still on, blood still pouring from my nose like a faucet with rusty pipes. My head pounding. Every breath hurt. My jacket, the one my brother gave me, now torn.

Custody. The doctors sent me through X-rays, administered pain drugs, fiddled with my nose until it was set back in its original place, even though they made sure to tell me that it would never look the same. That it would always look broken. But once it healed I would, at least, be able to breathe normally. They applied ice packs to my ribs, which were super uncomfortable because after a while the cold makes your skin feel like it's burning. But after that, it all goes numb.

Custody. A police officer—not the one who did this to me, but a different one, the one who fingerprinted me—stood outside the hospital room on guard, making sure I didn't run. As if I could. As if I were a real criminal. As if I were a criminal at all. He stood watch at the door until my parents arrived.

Custody. The police officer explained to my folks that I had been caught stealing. Not only that, but that I had also been charged with resisting arrest and public nuisance. There was no point trying to explain. I could barely breathe. I could barely keep my eyes open. The officer read the citations and explained that even though they were all misdemeanors, I had been processed and would still have to appear in court. Then, because I'm a minor, my folks had to fill out paperwork so that I could be signed over and returned to their custody. After that, the police officer left.

The next morning, when I woke up from it all, there was my mother, sitting in a chair on the other side of my hospital room, staring out the window.

"Ma," I said, instantly wincing. I could feel the gauze taped to my face, to my nose. It's that same tight feeling my skin gets after swimming, after the chlorine has turned me into

cardboard. I cleared my throat and called out for her again.

She whipped toward me, sprang from the chair, and dashed over to my bedside as if I was about to deliver my last words.

"Rashad," she said, her voice full of all the motherly stuff. Worry and love and hope and fear. "Oh, baby," she repeated, rubbing her hand on my forehead gently, her voice cracking. "How you feelin'?"

The truth was, I was feeling two ways. Physically, I obviously didn't feel great, that's for sure. But not terrible. Not like I thought I'd feel. But maybe that was the drugs doing their thing. I did feel some soreness, though. My breathing was weird and uncomfortable. Every breath felt like a hundred tiny needles sticking me in the chest. And that was breathing through my mouth. Breathing through my nose wasn't an option. Not yet, at least. But I was okay. Hell, I was alive. And so the other stuff—well, the alternative was way worse.

The other way I was feeling was just . . . confused. I mean, I hadn't done anything. Nothing at all. So why was I hooked up to all these machines, lying in this uncomfortable bed? Why was I arrested? Why was my mother waiting there for me to wake up, dried tears crusted on her face, prayer on her breath?

"I'm okay," I said.

She sat on the side of the bed. "Listen, I need you to tell me what happened, Rashad. And I need you to be honest with me, okay?" But before I could answer, my father came into the room, making a not-so-grand entrance. He had two cups of coffee, and even though one was for my mother, my dad's face looked like he could've used them both. And maybe a third. But him being tired didn't stop him from preaching.

"He up?" my dad asked my mom, handing her a cup. He hadn't even looked at me yet. If he had, just for a second, he would've noticed my eyes were open, a sure sign of me being awake. My mother nodded, almost as if she were giving him the green light to acknowledge me.

"Rashad." He said my name the same way he said it every other day when he was waking me up for school. As if nothing was wrong. As if he wasn't broken up by the sight of me lying in bed, black and blue and taped and bandaged and tubed and connected to machines monitoring whether or not I was actually still breathing.

"Hmm," I grunted.

"Help me out here, son," he said in his normal voice, which was his asshole voice. "I need to know what the hell you were thinking, shoplifting. Shoplifting? And from Jerry's of all places?" Dad had that disappointed look on his face—the same face he used to give me before I joined ROTC, the same face he made whenever he talked about Spoony.

"I didn't steal nothin'," I said, suddenly feeling too tired to explain, even though I just woke up.

"Well then, why did the cops say you did?" Dad replied, narrowing his eyes and taking a sip of his coffee. A slurp.

"I don't know."

"You don't know?" Dad scoffed. "Really, Rashad? You don't know?"

I felt a cough coming on and did everything I could to pinch it back, knowing that if I let it out, my entire body would feel like it was being hit by a million tiny hammers on the inside. I managed to get it down to a single, closed-mouth grunt, and guess what? It didn't matter. Every bone still seemed to tremble, and my head suddenly felt full of helium.

"No, I don't know," I repeated after getting through the cough.

"Look, baby, just tell us what happened," my mother said, calming my father down as usual. "From the beginning."

I started the story but didn't get very far before the nurse came in, interrupting everything with breakfast.

"Good morning," she said in a singsongy way after a light knock on the door. My mother greeted her pleasantly. My father forced a hello.

"Got you some oatmeal, and some orange juice, and a little bit of fruit cocktail." The nurse set the food on the tray by my bed. "Is everything else okay?"

"What's your name, hon?" my mother asked.

"Clarissa."

"Clarissa, everything is fine, thank you," Ma said. "But do you think we can raise the back of the bed up just a little, so he's not lying so flat?"

"Of course," Clarissa said, sliding the tray away and coming to my side. She pulled out a remote that was wedged between the mattress and the frame. With the push of a button, the bed started to reposition, which meant my body started to reposition, which meant . . . *ooooouch!*

"Is that good?" Clarissa asked. I just nodded, which was hard to do because now my chin was smashed into my chest. I had literally been folded up.

She moved the food tray back so that it was close enough for me to reach, and after telling us that the doctor would be in shortly, she left, and my mother helped me situate myself on the bed so that I could look and feel normal. As normal as possible. Normal enough for my father to get back to business.

"So walk me through this, son. You got to the store . . ."

"I got to the store, just to get gum and chips. I picked the bag of chips I wanted, and then I bent down and dug in my bag to try to get my phone so I could call Spoony. This lady didn't see me squatting behind her, and tripped over me. Then I lost my balance, and the bag of chips went flying. The cop assumed I had done something to the lady, which I didn't. The dude who works the register looks up and thinks

I'm trying to put the chips in my bag, but I wasn't. Then the cop rushed me and yoked me up all crazy." I paused, then added, "And that's it."

My mother sat quietly and my father paced back and forth, from the door to the window. Ma was clearly horrified. But Dad, he had on that *Son, you aren't telling me everything* look. It was clear that to him, I had to have done something wrong to bring this on.

"Were your pants sagging?" Dad interrogated, now back over by the door.

"Were my pants sagging?" I repeated, shocked by the question. "What does that have to do with anything?"

"Oh, it matters. If it walks like a duck, and it talks like a duck . . ."

My mother glared at him. "David! This is your son we're talking about. The boy's never even been suspended."

"But they don't know that," Dad said. "What they see is what he presents. And it sounds like he presented himself as just another—"

"Another what?" Ma cut in again, this time her voice spiking to that *Don't start* level. Dad swallowed the rest of his statement.

"Well, they said you resisted arrest," he continued in another direction. "If you didn't do anything wrong, why would you resist arrest?" His voice began to rise. "And how many times have I told you and Spoony, I mean, since y'all were young we've been going over this. Never fight back. Never talk back. Keep your hands up. Keep your mouth shut. Just do what they ask you to do, and you'll be fine."

That was another one of those way-too-familiar songs Spoony and I were forced to sing when we were kids. Every time Dad said it, it was always the same. Just like the army talk. But this one was even worse, because it had a rhythm to it, like a poem, or a chant. Never fight back. Never talk back. Keep your hands up. Keep your mouth shut. Just do what they ask you to do, and you'll be fine.

"I know, I know. And I did all that," I said, running through the scenario in my head again. "I didn't fight back; I couldn't. And I didn't say jack besides trying to explain that I hadn't done nothing wrong, but before I could even get a word out, he was all over me."

"You couldn't have," Dad said, matter-of-fact. He looked at me as if he didn't know me and shook his head. As if he was disappointed. As if I asked for this. That really pissed me off. That really, really got me going, because I was being blamed for something I didn't do, not just by that stupid store clerk and that asshole cop, but also by my father. A burning sensation rose in my chest and stomach, the fractured ribs sizzling. My eyes began to water with frustration.

"I did." My voice shattered in my throat and came out

pitchy and emotional. "You don't gotta believe me. But I did."
I turned my head away.

You know who did believe me? My brother Spoony. He
showed up a few minutes later, after working an overnight
shift at UPS and catching a quick nap. And let me tell you,
when he arrived, he was full of fire.

First was the obligatory mother hug. Spoony ran over to
our mom and gave her a hug and a kiss on the cheek. Made
sure she was all right. Then came the "Dad." That's all Spoony
said to him. Just an acknowledgment of his presence. It's not
that he was beefing with our father or that they didn't get
along—I take that back. They really didn't get along. They
just couldn't see eye to eye on most things. Dad was all about
discipline and believed that if you work hard, good things
happen to you no matter what. Of course, part of working
hard, to him, was looking the part, dressing the part, and
speaking the part, which Spoony didn't really vibe with.

Spoony had, I don't know, maybe eight or nine locs
sprouting from his head like antennae. Thick and matted like
strips of carpet, but I always thought they looked pretty cool.
Dad . . . not so much. *They'll think you're doing drugs,* he'd say.
Spoony's clothes were always two (or three or four) sizes too
big. That was just his style. That was pretty much his whole
generation's style. Nineties hip-hop, gritty, realness. Wu-
Tang. Biggie. Hoodies and unlaced boots. *They'll think you're*

selling drugs, Dad would say. *Why can't you get a haircut? Why can't you dress like a respectable adult? Why can't you set an example for your brother? Huh, son? Why?* And because Spoony was tired of explaining himself, and Dad was tired of asking him to change, they kept their conversations short and sweet. Like Spoony greeting him, "Dad," head nod. Followed by Dad saying, "Spoony," head nod. And that was that.

Spoony came over to my bed.

"Li'l bruh, you good?" he said, something grape-flavored on his breath.

"I'm good."

"What happened?"

I started running the story down and got about halfway through, just up to when the cop pressed me, when Spoony lost it.

"See?" he said, looking around to our parents. "See? This is that bullshit! I'm so sick of them treating us like we animals. Like we America's disobedient dogs!"

"Calm down, Spoony," Ma said, which only made it worse.

"Calm down? *Calm down?*" Spoony's voice got significantly less calm. "Haven't we been a little too calm? They get to do whatever they want to us, to him—to your son—and we're supposed to just calm down?" He put his hands on his head, flattening his locs, rocking back and forth in that way people do right before they punch a wall.

"Spoony—"

"And he was unarmed! Calm down? Do you know the stats? It's something like black people are twice as likely to have no weapons on them when they're killed by cops. Twice as likely! Should I run down the list of the people this has happened to? Calm down? Let's paint their names on the walls and watch, there'll be enough to give the entire hospital a fresh new look. Then tell me to calm down. He could've been killed!"

"But he wasn't," Dad said, deadpan. He seemed totally unimpressed by Spoony's outburst, and probably wrote it off as theatrics. He was always calling Spoony a rebel without a cause.

"But he could've been! For a bag of chips that he was gonna pay for! For having brown skin and wearing his jeans a certain way. And guess what, Dad, that ROTC uniform was right there in that bag. The bag was open so that cop probably saw it. But did it matter?" Spoony's voice fanned, the anger breaking him down.

"That's enough!" Ma said firmly.

Dad and Spoony glared at each other until finally Dad turned away and looked out the window. Ma just sat on the bed, rubbing my hand, her eyes wet from it all. Spoony leaned against the wall. And I sat there thinking about what was going to happen to me. I know my father and brother were arguing about what *had* happened, but all I could think about in that moment was what was going to happen next. Would the charges stick? Would they follow me around, a smudge on my record until I was eighteen when it would finally disappear? Does anything actually disappear these days?

The silence was much worse than the yelling, so I fiddled with the remote. The same one that controlled my bed controlled the television. I turned it on. Too bad TV sucks on Saturday morning unless you're a little kid or a politician. And politics are painful to watch. Boring. So the sound of helium-pitched cartoon characters had to be the life raft for this sinking ship of awkwardness. Thankfully, the doctor came in to save us from the equally awkward distraction of cartoons.

"Good morning, folks," he said, full of cheer, which was weird because this was not a cheerful occasion. But I guess doctors always have to try to lift the mood. "I'm Dr. Barnes."

"David Butler," my father said, shaking his hand.

"Jessica," my mother said, doing the same.

"Randolph," Spoony said, introducing himself with his government name. He got the nickname Spoony because when he was young, he refused to eat with a fork. He was always scared he'd poke himself in the tongue, so he only ever used spoons. But that's not something you tell a doctor.

"And Rashad," the doctor said, pointing at me. I nodded.

"Nice to meet all of you. I just want to give you all an update on what's happening and what's ahead of us."

"Sounds good," Dad said.

"Okay, so Rashad's nose was broken, but we've already set it, so as long as he doesn't bump it or knock it, it'll heal just fine. The same goes for his ribs. There's really nothing we can do about them except make sure that Rashad isn't in any pain, but as long as they're fairly stable, they'll heal up as well. We did do an X-ray just to make sure there were no lacerations to any of his organs, and there weren't, so we're pretty much in the clear with that."

"So when can he come home?" Ma asked, starting to beam.

"Well, that's the thing. Under normal circumstances I would say that Rashad could go home tonight." Ma stopped rubbing my hand. The doctor continued. "But this isn't a normal circumstance. He has some internal bleeding—hemothorax, it's called—which just means there are some torn blood vessels around his lungs due, I'm sure, to the impact. Usually, this fixes itself, but we'll need to monitor him for a few days in case it doesn't."

"And if it doesn't . . . ," my mother began.

"Then he'll need surgery," the doctor told us.

Surgery. That's one of those words that no matter how many times you hear it, it always freaks you out. *Surgery.* My mother's face tightened as she did everything she could to hold it together, but she couldn't keep her leg from bouncing like she always does when she's trying keep her emotions tucked in. Spoony bit down on his bottom lip. My father just seemed to be taking it all in, not particularly bothered.

"Sound good?" the doctor asked.

"Sounds good," Dad replied, shaking the doctor's hand once more. Dr. Barnes said he'd be in to check on me in a few hours, and left.

I reached for the remote and turned the channel.

I wish there were more interesting things to tell you about the rest of the day, but the truth is that most of it I spent dozing in and out of sleep, while my family sat around watching me doze in and out of sleep. Well, at least, Ma and Dad did. Spoony was in and out of the room, making and taking phone calls, and whenever he was in the room he was texting. I didn't know who all the texts were going to, but I knew at least some of them were going to his girlfriend, Berry. And, funny enough, Berry's little brother was my homeboy, English. English Jones. The athlete, pretty boy, non-asshole who everybody loved. Yep, that guy. So I knew that if Berry knew what happened to me, English knew. And if English knew, Carlos and Shannon knew. And if those two dudes knew, then by Monday, half the school would know.

And then I was asleep. And then I was awake again. And Clarissa brought lunch in. I had barely touched breakfast. The oatmeal. Maybe a spoonful or two. It wasn't so bad, but after my father acted like . . . my father, I had pretty much lost my appetite. I offered it to my mother, but she couldn't eat either. Spoony ate the fruit cocktail and said it reminded him of elementary school.

"I used to love the grapes, but there was never enough of them," he said, holding the cup up to his face and slurping the fruit out.

For lunch, Central Hospital served up its finest turkey club sandwich with vegetable soup. I ate half the sandwich after my mother pretty much forced me to eat something, and I have to say, it was pretty good. All these years I had been hearing about how nasty hospital food was, and now that I finally got a chance to taste it, it wasn't half-bad. Better than school lunch, that's for damn sure.

Still nothing on TV except for an overly dramatic Lifetime movie that my mother was totally into. A cliché stalker story. A woman meets a man on a bus on her way home from work. They exchange numbers. Go out on a first date. He's perfect: attractive, smart, and he has a good job as an audio engineer for television shows. She's excited until she finds out he's wired her whole house so that he can hear everything she does when he's not around. He can hear her shower, and cook, and talk to her friends about how crazy he is. And he listens to the feed while he watches TV, on mute, in the attic of the house next door, where he lives (she doesn't know this, though). Total stalker. Shittiest actors on Earth meets the shittiest story on Earth, which makes for the perfect Saturday afternoon movie. For my mom.

And then I was asleep. And then I was awake again. But this time, my folks were knocked out. Dad in the chair, his head bent at a painful-looking angle, his mouth wide open. As usual. My mother, small, had tucked her knees to her chest and nestled into her chair—the only cushioned one—like a child. She looked so peaceful. So calm. It was nice to see her get some rest. The only person who wasn't asleep was Spoony. He was still sitting there. Still fooling with his phone. Still texting.

"Spoon," I called out softly—I didn't want to wake my parents. It was nice to have the room quiet for a moment. It was nice to not see their eyes, my father's disappointed, my mother's all sad and worried.

Spoony looked up and rushed to my bed. "Wassup, man, you okay?"

"I'm fine, I'm fine," I said, calming him down.

"Okay," he said, glancing down at his phone. "Look, I talked to Berry and told her what happened. She's been all over the internet, checking to see if anything has been posted—you know, some live footage or something."

"And?"

"And so far, nothing. But something's gotta pop up. And I don't care what Dad says, this ain't right." He bit down on his bottom lip. "It just ain't right. And you know me. You know I'm not gonna sit here and let them sweep this under the rug, like this is okay."

"I know."

I gotta admit, there was a part of me that, even though I felt abused, wanted to tell him to let it go. To just let me heal, let me leave the hospital, let me go to court, let me do whatever stupid community service they wanted me to do, and let me go back to normal. I mean, I had seen this happen so many times. Not personally, but on TV. In the news. People getting beaten, and sometimes killed, by the cops, and then there's all this fuss about it, only to build up to a big heartbreak when nothing happens. The cops get off. And everybody cries and waits for the next dead kid, to do it all over again. That's the way the story goes. A different kind of Lifetime movie. I didn't want all that. Didn't need it.

But I knew not to even bother saying it. Not to Spoony. No point. Because he'd agree that this was normal, and that that was the problem. Spoony had been dealing with this kind of crap for years. He'd never been beaten up, but he'd been stopped on the street several times, questioned by cops, asked to turn his pockets out and lift his shirt up, for no reason. He'd been followed around stores, and stared at on buses by women who clutched their purses tight enough to poke holes in the leather. He was always a suspect. And I knew, without him saying a word, that the one thing he never wanted, but was sure would eventually happen, was for his little brother—the ROTC art kid—to become one too. So there was nothing that was going to stop him from fighting this. There was nothing I could do to calm him down. This was not going away. This was not getting swept under the rug of "oh well." Not if Spoony had anything to do with it.

QUINN

In our town, it really isn't shocking to see a fight go down. I've seen kids with house keys tucked between their knuckles throwing punches at each other. I've seen ten guys from our school chasing four dudes from another school down a block and a stranger step into the melee with a bat to protect the guys who were outnumbered. And Guzzo, Dwyer, and I spent most of Jill's party telling ourselves we were tough as balls and that what happened outside Jerry's was nothing. It wasn't on our minds, we kept telling each other. No big deal. NBD, Dwyer wrote in beer on the wooden slats of the back porch with the nozzle from the keg.

In fact, we spent most of the party on that back porch, ignoring everyone else. Guzzo never said a word to Jill for me, and through the window, I saw English moving through the room like the frigging king he is, getting up close to girls and making them laugh and giggle. I was sure if he found Jill, it'd be the same. I was out there in the darkness of the back porch, looking in through the window to the bright kitchen, like I was watching the whole damn party unfold on TV.

I gave Guzzo my flask at some point and when I eventually got it back it was empty, but I didn't bug him about it. Because even though what happened at Jerry's was NBD, it was really all we talked about that night. "My brother has to deal with that shit every day," Guzzo kept saying. "And he just does it, no complaints. He's amazing."

But what had always amazed me most about Guzzo's brother, Paul, was how he had made time for me. I was ten when my father died, and it was Paul who'd taken me down to Gooch to practice. Gooch was the neighborhood park, but Paul'd get us down there so early, we'd have the whole court to ourselves. He showed me how to do the spider drill, how to dribble with two balls, how to tuck my elbows when I shot. But the man I'd watched grind a kid into the sidewalk—I don't know—was like someone else. Someone I couldn't place, some hulking animal stalking the shadows of my mind all night. I could hear his voice, and yet it wasn't him. I could see his face, and yet it wasn't him.

Dwyer and Guzzo drank much more than I did, and they stood around the keg shouting out the lyrics of all the hip-hop songs blasting from the living room inside. Earlier that day, I'd imagined myself dancing with Jill, hands in the air and then down along her back to her hips, as she draped hers around my neck, but I spent most of the night still stuck on that sidewalk outside Jerry's, my heart pumping fiercely in my throat, and when someone at Jill's yelled that the cops had arrived, I almost thought I'd called them there with my mind.

I slept terribly, but no matter how much or how little I sleep, I begin almost every day the same way: Ma's voice in my head, telling me what I needed to do, what I needed to think about, how I needed to act. But on mornings like this one—or if Coach Carney was making us do suicides up and down the court for fifteen minutes, or when Dwyer dropped another five-pounder on either side of the bar on my last rep in the weight room—it was Dad's voice in my head, or at least what I thought was his voice. I hadn't heard it in so long, I couldn't even tell if it was his or if I was making it up. Whatever it was, it got me to where I needed to get.

PUSH! If you don't, someone else will. LIFT! If you don't, someone else will. Faster, faster, faster, faster, FASTER!

I was in the living room, my feet tucked under the lip of the couch, firing through a set of fifty crunches when I heard

Ma's actual sleepy voice drift up and over the room.

"Don't kill yourself," she said. I'd been so into my push-ups and sit-ups and all that I hadn't even heard her come home. "Where's the mat?" she continued.

I kept at it in my head. *Push 25, 2, 3. Push 26, 2, 3. Push.* Ma sighed. "Boys," she said. I heard her slough into the kitchen and open the fridge. I finished my set, sprang to my feet, and felt the room spin. Black dots popped across my vision, and before I passed out, I dropped to the couch and sat there catching my breath.

"Water?" Ma asked from the kitchen.

"Yes," I whisper-shouted, but she was already on her way to give it to me.

Ma sat down next to me and put her head on my shoulder. She was so much smaller than me now, and I liked the way she sometimes leaned into me or hugged me, like she was excited. Not in a weird way, but with something I think might have been pride. She'd already kicked off her shoes, and she'd already changed into one of the three T-shirts she always wore around the house.

I drank my water in two long gulps.

"Honey, you stink," Ma said, pulling away from me.

"Sorry. Gotta do my workouts, though. Every morning."

She rolled to the other side of the couch. "Get off! You're going to make the cushions stink."

"Ma!"

"I'm serious." She pushed my shoulder and laughed and I rolled onto the floor. "Come on," she continued. "You'll ruin the rug." She leaned back on the arm of the couch and crossed one leg over the other. She could have fallen asleep right there. The bags under her eyes were prunes. Loose strands of hair sprang from her head like she'd pulled a wool hat off and the static electricity still hung in the air around her. But, despite her exhaustion, somehow she still always found a smile for me.

"What's the matter with you?" she said, yawning. "You look strange."

"Nothing," I said.

She rubbed her face and squinted at me and I knew her mind was working to put it all together. But she was so tired. "I can trust you, right?" she asked, still slouched in the corner of the couch. "You'd tell me if something was the matter?"

"Of course," I said quickly, even though there was a helluva lot on my mind. But I didn't feel like telling her about any of it. "I'm just going to rinse off," I said. It was going to be a two-shower day. "Then I got to hit the court. Coach is picking the starters this week."

"You'll make it," she said, as if fighting for a starting spot was NBD. As if it'd just come to me because I wanted it, not because I had to fight for it.

I left Ma slumped against the armrest and went straight to the bathroom. I got the water running hot first, then switched it to cold, just to fire up the senses and wake up. I still felt a little groggy from last night and I was pissed at myself, because after my workout I wanted to get right to the court. I thought I had a real shot at being a starter, but next week was too important to coast through. I had to hit more three-pointers when we went around the world. I had to have the higher free-throw percentage. English was so good, he didn't have to give up the ball, so if he did, I had to make sure he felt more comfortable giving *me* the ball—and that meant working harder to get open, and more importantly, making the shot when I got the ball. Because the scouts were coming. Of course the stands were going to be filled, but a few of those seats at every game were the seats we were all playing for. Full ride to Michigan State. Full ride to UNC. My dad had college paid for because he'd gone through ROTC at City College, but I had to do even better. Butler, Notre Dame, Villanova. Wisconsin, Arizona, Duke. Saint Springfield's son needed to go full ride too. Scouts paved the way—and I had to show them who I was. I had to be a starter.

And, as I was trying to psych myself up for a day of drills down at Gooch, I stepped out of the bathroom, wrapped only in a towel, holding my stank-ass clothes in a wad, and nearly ran right into Ma. She held my jeans in one hand and my flask in the other. She jutted her chin at me.

"Quinn Marshall Collins. You tell me the truth this minute and you start from the very beginning." She pinched her lips tight. "Is this how you want the world to know you? Some kind of derelict who doesn't give a damn about his actions?"

I stuttered. It was the strangest thing. I'd never been caught before. It was like there was regular me, the one Ma smiled at and loved, the one I'd always been, and then this new guy, the one shivering in the hallway outside the bathroom, standing in his towel, wondering why Ma had gone looking through my room while I was in the shower.

"Can I just get dressed?"

Ma sniffed. "You have thirty seconds." Then she turned and marched to the kitchen. I broke the world's record for throwing on sweats and busting back to the kitchen. She sat on one side of the little Formica table, steam from her mug of tea rising up to her face as she stared out the window to the Barrows' house next door. The flask lay askew beside the mug. She ran her hand over her eyes, and then up over her forehead like a visor.

"You know," she said slowly, "this stuff can kill you. I know you don't think so, but it can."

"Ma—" I said, sitting in the chair across from her.

"Listen," she interrupted. "When you act like this—when you sit around, breaking the law, thinking it is okay—

you embarrass me, you embarrass your brother, and you embarrass yourself. You have more important things to worry about, young man." The flask sat on the table between us and she picked it up. She waved it gently. "This is going in the garbage."

"Okay." Then I had to add, flat-out lying, "It was Guzzo's idea."

"But you took it from our house. I just checked."

She'd never done that before. Plus, I only took a flaskful after she'd emptied a glass or two from the bottle, and there was always a new bottle to replace the old one.

"And even if it was." She waved the flask again.

"Guzzo drank nearly the whole thing."

"Guzzo drank the alcohol. It was Guzzo's idea. You make it sound like you weren't there, Quinn. But you were. You were there."

Maybe it was the alcohol still in my blood, but the way she said it, I was there, in the night, that hollowed-out gutted feeling, making me nervous and stupider than usual, like I couldn't find the simplest words. I saw Paul.

"I'm sorry."

"Not good enough."

"I'm sorry I stole the bourbon. I'm sorry I drank it with Guzzo and Dwyer."

"You talk about wanting to be somebody, you talk about

basketball, you talk about making your family proud, but then you act like this. What do you think people are going to think of you now?"

"Jesus, Ma," I said. "It's not that big a deal. It was only one night. It won't happen again."

She tapped the flask with her finger. "Remember you said that. That it was only this one time. Don't let it happen again. And don't 'Jesus, Ma' me."

I looked out the window. "I'm just saying that I know it was dumb, and I'm sorry. I didn't even have that much to drink. I swear."

"It's not about that, Quinn." Ma leaned forward and grabbed my hands. She waited until I stopped looking out the window and looked at her. "It's about how the world looks at you and when they do, who do you want them to see? What kind of a person do you want to be? Who do you think you are? You're the one your brother looks up to. You're a senior, Quinn. This is the year everyone looks to see what kind of man you want to become."

I pulled my lips tight against my teeth to try to keep calm and not tear up like a baby. I didn't want to be a baby. I didn't want to be a jerk-off.

"I'm doing the best I can here," Ma continued. "I'm on my own, honey, and I'm doing the best I can to help you, but I need your help to help your brother."

She sipped her tea and watched me. I sat there like a mute because I didn't know what to say. I felt like an idiot.

She sighed. "I was going to ask you, but now I'm just telling you. Pick up Willy from his game today. The Cambis are bringing him. In fact, go see your brother's game. It means more to him if you're there than me anyway, so go see his game." She reached for her purse that hung on the back of her chair and pulled a few bills from her wallet. "He looks up to you. Spend some time with him. Take him out for pizza after. Once basketball starts we'll never see you. Take him out for lunch."

So I did what I was told, and I put on some clean jeans and my light hoodie and took the bus over to the East Side for Willy's game. Tough Will. Tough Will, who was known to sit down in the middle of his own soccer game, right there on the field, until his coach gave up and called in the sub. Tough Will spent most of his games sitting on the sidelines eating orange slices.

When I got there, both teams were already warming up on either end of the field. I'd played soccer before I was in high school and loved it. For Tough Will, it was another story. It was only the warm-ups and I could see him dragging his feet, not chasing anything or anyone anywhere—just standing around and waiting for someone to pass him the ball.

"Get in there, man!" I shouted. "Will! Will! Get in there, man."

He looked over at me and waved, totally oblivious to the rest of the players and balls around him. Still, I guess I inspired him, because he turned and chased down a red-and-white ball and dribbled it a bit before taking a shot on net. It went wide left, but at least he ran after the ball.

My phone started blowing up with texts, but Regina Cambi had set up a folding chair beside a cooler, and she was waving me over, so I had to ignore the texts because I sure as hell couldn't ignore her. She sat with a few other moms, and the dads who'd come to the game stood around in a circle a little ways behind them, under the boughs of the one large oak tree that gave this park its name. I chatted with Mrs. Cambi at first, but then the game began, and I started cheering Willy and his team on, using that as an excuse to pull away as if I wanted to walk down the sidelines and see the action more clearly, because my phone kept buzzing and buzzing in my pocket and I wanted to see what was going on.

Guzzo had texted "wassup" ten times.

SATURDAY 12:53 p.m. to Guzzo
HOWS UR HEAD?

SATURDAY 12:53 p.m. from Guzzo
FCKING AWFUL

SATURDAY 12:54 p.m. to Guzzo
BANANAS & GATORADE, MAN

SATURDAY 12:54 p.m. from Guzzo
IM PUKING WATER IF I DRINK IT

SATURDAY 12:55 p.m. to Guzzo
DAMN. U BUSTED?

SATURDAY 12:55 p.m. from Guzzo
NO

SATURDAY 12:55 p.m. to Guzzo
FCK I AM & IM NOT EVEN HUNGOVER

SATURDAY 12:57 p.m. from Guzzo
ITS A SHITSHOW HERE

SATURDAY 12:57 p.m. to Guzzo
WHA?

73

SATURDAY 12:58 p.m. from Guzzo
PAULS HOME. ITS A BIG DEAL

SATURDAY 12:58 p.m. to Guzzo
IS IT ABOUT YESTERDAY? AT JERRYS?

SATURDAY 12:59 p.m. from Guzzo
I DONT KNO. UM YEAH.

SATURDAY 1:00 p.m. to Guzzo
DAMN

SATURDAY 1:02 p.m. from Guzzo
I GUESS WE R HAVIN A BBQ 2MRRW

SATURDAY 1:02 p.m. to Guzzo
WHA?

SATURDAY 1:03 p.m. from Guzzo
YUP. C U THEN. TELL UR MOM TO BRING THAT
MARSHMALLOW PIE

SATURDAY 1:03 p.m. to Guzzo

SHE HAS 2 WORK I THINK

SATURDAY 1:04 p.m. from Guzzo
NOPE. I ALRDY KNO SHES COMIN

I hesitated, and he wrote again.

SATURDAY 1:06 p.m. from Guzzo
EVRYBDY COMIN. GOTTA BUST. C U 2MRRW

So something had to be up, because the Galluzzo family
never had people over. Or rather, they never invited people
over. There were so many people coming and going from
the house that it always seemed like a party. But they never
"officially" organized anything. I tried him a few more times,
but he didn't text back, so I gave up. I'd see him at the BBQ
anyway, because of course I'd go. I always went, and wound
up wolfing down Paul's famous burgers—but now I saw that
face, Paul's, burning, a bloodred mask of rage. He'd been so
focused on kicking the shit out of that guy. I'd seen him. Had
he seen me? What if he had? I'd never felt nervous around
Paul, and suddenly, just thinking about him made me sweat.

As I was going through all this, I tried to watch the game,
but it was slow as all hell and Will's team was terrible. Still,
Will was playing left back and he was actually running

around and chasing the ball. Near the end of the first half, one of the players on the other team got around a couple guys just over midfield and seemed like he had a clean break for a shot, but Will came out of nowhere and nailed a sweet slide tackle. The parents on the other side of the field started screaming like crazy, but Will's tackle had been legal, at least as I could see it, and that's what the referees thought too, and so when the first half ended, Will was the momentary hero, keeping the game more respectable because his team was only down one to zero. I found him and slapped him five over the heads of a few teammates in the huddle with his coach, and then I backed off. People always felt bad for me at games because of Dad, and Ma was always working, but I liked being on my own. I liked figuring out what I had to do and doing it. No one seemed to get that, and I didn't want to crowd Will, either, so I let him be. His coach was thrilled and put him back in for the second half.

Guzzo still didn't text back, and I went back and forth with Dwyer a few times, but eventually, I put the phone away because it really was more fun to check out the game—and check out Will especially. This might sound dumb to some people, but it's actually pretty cool having a little brother. I mean, he was a pain in the ass, and that I was here and not practicing over at Gooch pissed me off, but watching him smash into the guys on the other team, watching the way he shook off his own pain, made me realize that I did the same thing—twirl my fist like I was revving myself up. He had the same crooked smile. And once, when there was a pause in the action, and he was close to me on the sidelines, and he was hunched over, with his hands on his knees, he looked over at me and nodded. And I knew he was saying thank you. Not because I'd shown up to watch him, but because I had shown up to watch him he was playing harder—and he was loving it.

And after the game, I didn't mind taking Tough Will over to Mother's Pizza. On the bus back to the West Side, he kept asking me about the game and what his team could have done better. "Scored a goal," I said. "That would have helped."

He rolled his eyes. "Yeah, I know, but how?"

"Your striker. He couldn't run. That was his problem. And when he had a shot, he hesitated. Can't hesitate. Like you, man. You were awesome today." I shook his shoulder and felt bad it was the only game I'd made it to all season. I wanted to be the guy who showed up, not the one who didn't.

When we got to Mother's it was slammed like always. Mother's sits on a corner and the front door faces Spring Street and the to-go window faces Twentieth Street, and while I usually just hit the to-go window, especially when I swung by at night, the line was jammed inside and outside. So I stuck Willy on the end of one of the two picnic tables and went inside to see if it moved any faster. It still took awhile, and while I waited, I had to try to look everywhere else around the room except the one spot where I felt those eyes always watching me. That's why I preferred the to-go window; I couldn't see those eyes blazing into me. Those eyes. My eyes. My dad's eyes—in the photo the pizza guys had up on the wall, two guys in greasy T-shirts with their arms up around my dad's shoulders. Dad, a pillar of stone, dressed like usual in his Class A blues. The rest of the photos were of people in the pizza shop, but not the one with Dad. He'd gotten the guys to make pizzas for the soup kitchen at St. Mary's. His photo looked down on me.

When I was finally up near the front, I felt a tug at my arm. I was about to turn back to Willy to tell him that he might have lost our seats, but it wasn't Willy at my arm. It was Jill.

She pulled close to me, so the people behind us couldn't hear. "Hey, Quinn, you mind getting an extra slice?" she asked. Her hair fell in two blond-brown curtains around her face, and I could smell her shampoo as she looked up at me conspiratorially, and when a girl looks at you like that, all you can say is, *Whatever you want—I'll do anything for you—is there anything else you want?* "Yeah," I somehow managed to say instead.

"Yeah, you mind?" She grinned.

"No. Yeah. No." I laughed. Like a moron.

The thing about slices at Mother's is that they are huge, so she stuck around to help carry it all outside. She offered some money but I waved her off. Because I had it good at Mother's. I'd grabbed us all Cokes, too, because the guys at Mother's always gave Saint Springfield's son a major discount, and yeah, well, I was the kind of guy who just kept taking those free Cokes, no questions asked, like I actually deserved them or something.

"How were you planning on carrying this all out there on your own, anyway?" she asked.

I had two giant slices and two Cokes by the necks of the bottles; she had two slices and a Coke. "Guess I was just waiting for you," I said.

She frowned, but in a cute way, like it was really a smile. "Oh, yeah. I bet you were."

Willy had managed to save two seats, but when he saw us, he got up and offered Jill his. "Please," he said. She tried to protest, but he wouldn't let her. He stood at the end of the picnic table and glanced back and forth at us while he shoved pizza into his face.

"One of us is what you'd call a gentleman," he informed us.

"He's hilarious," Jill said to me. Now what kind of world did I live in where my twelve-year-old brother was the cooler flirt than me?

"Yeah," I said. "I'm supposed to be his role model. But maybe it's the other way around."

"Nah," she said. "I bet he learned all this from someone. But this someone needs to sit down today, huh?"

"I'm old and broken. He's got his whole life ahead of him."

"Yeah," Jill said. "And you're hungover, right?"

"I knew it!" Willy yelped. "I knew you were going to a party last night."

"Oops," Jill said.

I pointed at Willy. "Between us. Got me?"

"Oh, yeah," Willy said. "Until I need the ammo."

"Willy—"

"Will, please."

Jill laughed. She put her hand on Willy's wrist, and his face changed. His whole body probably blushed as deep red as his face. He gave her the dopiest smile. Had I looked like that when she'd asked me to get her a slice? Jesus. But Jill didn't mind. "Will," she said. "Don't get him in trouble, because then it will be my fault, and he'll never speak to me again."

I stared at Will, and he knew exactly what I was saying with my eyebrows: *Don't fuck this up, dude.*

"Whatever," Willy said. "I'm only kidding."

Willy and I shared the extra slice as Jill and I talked about the party. I tried to get a sense of whether or not she and English had hooked up, but I wasn't going to ask outright because it really was none of my damn business. She was being super flirty, but not in the way I wanted her to mean it. This had happened before. Sometimes I got the feeling she thought of me more as a brother, but no dude wants to be thought of as a brother when he is sitting across from a girl who is not his sister and who makes his stomach flip when she says his name.

While we were talking, though, things were getting a little heated over by the corner. A couple of guys had walked up to two other guys in line and started barking. They kept at it to the point where the rest of us outside couldn't even hear ourselves. People started yelling around them, and when one of the guys pushed one of the guys in line, they broke into punches. I jumped up and stuffed Willy into the seat behind me. People yanked out their phones, calling the cops, but somebody must have called the cops already, because the berry lights flashed down the block. The guys in the fight tried to swing a few more punches, but people in the crowd had pulled them apart and locked them in arm holds. One cop car pulled up and then another and everything happened so quickly, we all just stood around watching like dumb idiots until the cops had grabbed the four guys who'd been fighting, pinned them to the hoods of the two cars, and cuffed them.

I, of course, was back at the night before, when I'd seen Paul arrest the kid outside Jerry's. But this was different. Another cop car pulled up and then another, then all eight cops started asking the crowd to disperse, only holding a few people back to ask questions. This kind of thing happened all the time at Mother's; it sat right between neighborhoods, and kids from one block might beef with kids from another or some other shit, and while I tried to stay out of it, it was impossible not to watch it explode right in front of you.

The crowd outside Mother's was white, black, Latino, Asian, just like Springfield. The four guys being cuffed were white. The cops, almost all of them were white, but two of them were black. It was impossible not to think about this as Paul slamming that black kid into the sidewalk the night before replayed in my mind. It wasn't like watching one of my brother's video games or a movie. You hear bone. You see real blood. And you taste the rust of it and it makes you sick.

I broke into a sweat like I might puke. I turned to Willy and Jill. "Should we get out of here?" More people began to shout at the cops from the crowd. I was done with this. "We'll walk you home," I told Jill.

We busted back down the street away from the scene and took the long way around the neighborhood to Jill's house. I could tell Jill was as distracted as I was, as if we both had private conversations going on in the back of our minds, and we used Willy, sandwiched between us, as the focal point of conversation. But when we got to her house, she said over Willy's head, "There's a barbecue at my cousin's tomorrow. You must be going."

"Yeah," I said.

"Weird, right? The sudden party?" She looked at me, and I realized we might not have been having private conversations in our minds the whole way home. They might have been the same one.

"Yeah," I said. "I don't know, but I think I have an idea what this is about."

"Me too," she said.

As she jogged up her front steps, something ugly and awful was forming in my mind, but I couldn't quite find the right words for it—or I didn't want to. I wasn't sure.

Sunday

RASHAD

Sunday. I slept late and woke up to an empty room. Silence. No one. So nice.

Sunday TV is just as bad as Saturday TV, so I left it off and laid there in the cold space, staring at the wall, thinking about everything.

I was supposed to have been at Jill's party on Friday. Me, English, Shannon, and Carlos—three-piece and fries. I was supposed to be all up on Tiffany Watts, giving her the business because even though I was soldier-boy when I was in school, everybody knew I was nice with the moves. Rhythm ain't never been an issue for me. I was the kid Spoony made dance in front of his friends when we were younger. Show them the latest steps that I picked up from music videos. I *owned* the block party dance contests. So Jill's party, like every party, was my time to two-step without it being a march. My time to be at ease, and let the soul seep back into this soldier. Damn shame I didn't make it. Instead some big-ass cop decided to have a fist party on my face. Y'know, normal stuff. No biggie. I'm just a punk-ass kid. I have no rights. Just got body slammed for no reason. Just got my life threatened, while lying flat on the sidewalk. A broken nose, broken ribs, and a knee in the back is way more exciting than fine-ass girls checking for me (after they finished checking for English).

Fuck.

Knock, knock. The door opened and there was Clarissa pushing my lunch cart in.

"Good afternoon, Rashad," she said. She had one of those voices that no matter what, was nice. Like, it could never sound mean. You know how some people have those voices? Like kindergarten teachers or librarians? "How we feelin'?" she asked, and I was momentarily confused by the "we" she was referring to.

"I'm fine," I said, forcing a small smile.

"Good. Make sure you try to get yourself up today. You can't just lie there on your back. Also, I need you to blow into this, as hard as you can." She held up a strange-looking plastic thing with a hose sticking out of it.

"What is it?"

"It's called an incentive spirometer. Because of your ribs,

you're going to do everything you can to not cough. But you *need* to cough. You gotta make sure you're getting all the nasty stuff out of your lungs, because if it all stays in, it might turn into pneumonia and we don't want that." Then she broke it all down to me as if I was a child, which I appreciated because I had never heard of a spirometer before. Luckily, it was a simpler process than the name suggests. All I had to do, a few times every hour, was breathe in through the tube slowly, hold it, and then breathe out.

As she set the spirometer on the side table by my bed, she announced, "For lunch today we've got chicken tenders, and fries, and a small salad," while setting the tray down. Then she went through the routine of checking my vitals. Blood pressure, and whatever else. Who ever really knows what all those machines and stuff are anyway? I just know the one they put on my arm is for my blood pressure, but who, besides old people, even knows what blood pressure is? *Just make sure I ain't dying,* was what I was thinking as the cuff tightened around my arm.

Once she left, I got myself up, which was way more painful than I thought it would be. Who the hell knew broken ribs could make *everything* hurt? Or maybe it was that everything I did made the broken ribs hurt. Seemed like even blinking was painful.

I waddled slowly to the bathroom so I could handle my

business—the post-sleep pee—which was interrupted by another knock at the door. This time, it was my family. Of course.

"Rashad?" my mother called through a crack in the door before pushing it open. I had just flushed and washed my hands while performing the strange task of looking at my bruised and broken face, but only in glimpses. That's all I could take. A few seconds at a time. Three seconds, then back to the sink. Then back to the mirror for three more seconds before darting my eyes over to the paper towels. Anything longer than that made me . . . uncomfortable. Anyway, I was making my way back to the bed when my mother and father came in dressed in their Sunday spiffs. Behind them, even more Sunday. As in, Sunday himself. As in, Jerome Johnson. As in, Pastor Jerome Johnson.

"Son, Pastor's here to see you," my father said as I eased back into bed, flashing my ashy butt at everybody, including God.

They brought the *pastor*? I sort of fell quickly onto the mattress and whipped my legs around until they were on the bed. Pathetic. My mother helped me adjust, fluffing the pillow behind my head and pulling the sheet over me, up to my chin, which was way too far. She kissed my forehead and stared at me as if she was trying to recognize the kid beneath the bruises and bandages. "You okay?"

"I'm fine," I said, short. She nodded, then glanced at the food tray. She lifted the plate cover, the condensation dripping all over my chicken tenders. Damn. Soggy chicken tenders suck. "You haven't eaten?"

"It just got here. I just woke up." I said in a *take it easy* tone.

She kissed my forehead again, then leaned back so I could get a clear shot of my father, three-piece suited and shiny-shoed. And the minister, Pastor Johnson, dressed in an oversize suit, a gold chain with a gold cross lying perfectly in the middle of his fat satin tie. In his hand, the Bible. What else.

"How you feelin', Rashad?" the pastor asked. Everybody was asking that, as if I was ever going to tell them the truth. Nobody wanted to hear the truth, even though everybody already knew what it was. I felt . . . violated. That's the only way I can put it. Straight-up violated. And now, to make it worse, I had to have church. Well, sorta church. I had to have prayer.

Now don't get me wrong. I don't have a problem with a good prayer. I mean, I believe in God. At least I think I do. I just wondered where God was when I was being mopped by that cop. And I knew that's what the pastor had come to tell me. That God was there. That God was always there. Which, to me, is the wrong thing to say, because if he or it or whatever was there and didn't do nothing, then that would make God my enemy. Because he let it happen. I would much rather Pastor Johnson say that God *wasn't* there. That he was busy. That he turned his back, just for a second, to check on somebody else, and that asshole officer snuck right by him and got me. But . . . nope.

"Son, I just stopped by to tell you that God is with you. He's always with you," the pastor started, predictably. "And everything happens for a reason."

Reason? This felt like a good time for me to grab my spirometer, because I was in need of a deep breath. I mean, seriously, what reason could there have been for this? Let me guess, I was too good-lookin' and needed an extra bump on my nose, a reminder that only English Jones runs the school?

"Now we're going to offer up a prayer for your healing, son, believing that God's gon' mend you," the pastor said. "Let's all bow our heads and look to the Lord."

My mother and father lowered their heads and closed their eyes. I didn't do either. Kept mine open, and my head up, looking at the three of them, wondering if any of this mattered. I knew it mattered to them, my parents, and maybe that should've been enough for me to participate, but did it matter to me? I'm not so sure. The prayer was long and dramatic, full of the preachy punches in between each point. The pastor mentioned how Jesus was persecuted (*heh*) and Saul was made blind (*heh*) and Job was tested (*heh*) and David beat Goliath (*heh*). My mother followed right behind the pastor, accompanying his rhythmic prayer with *hallelujah* whispers, and my father's manly but, I guess, godly grunts, all eventually—finally—leading to an amen.

"Amen." Spoony stood in the doorway, nodding his head, and clapping his hands, a sarcastic look on his face. Man, was I happy to see him. Ma was too. Dad, well, not so much.

"Pastor, you remember my oldest son, Randolph," he said, caught off guard.

"Yes, yes, of course I do." The pastor reached out and shook Spoony's hand. "Ain't seen you down at the church in a while."

"That's 'cause I can't afford to come."

"Spoony!" my mother gasped.

"Sorry," he said, shrugging and smirking at me.

"No, no, that's okay," Pastor Johnson said kindly. "Nothing wrong with the boy having a mind of his own. God gave him that." Spoony just looked at Dad like, *See?* "Well, listen, I better be going. But we're gonna keep you lifted up in prayer, Rashad. And we're going to add you to the blessing list for the sick and shut-in."

But I'm not sick or shut-in. I'm beat down. Is there a list for that? But I didn't say that. I was hoping Spoony would do some kind of big brother ESP thing and say it for me.

"Thank you so much for coming, Pastor," my mother said, clenching Pastor Johnson's hand. My dad gave him a firm shake and a tight-lipped nod, and the churchman headed out.

Five seconds couldn't have gone by before Spoony sat gingerly on the side of the bed and grabbed the remote.

"Come on, man. It's Sunday. Ain't nothing on but reruns of what we just experienced," I joked.

"Oh, there's something else on. Trust me," Spoony said pointedly.

"You know, you don't always have to be so damn disrespectful!" Dad started in on Spoony with a bark, settling into a chair on the other side of the room. Cursing right after the pastor left, tsk, tsk, tsk.

Spoony ignored him and turned the TV on. He nodded up to the screen. "Check it out."

I looked up at the glowing screen. And there it was. There *I* was. On the freakin' news.

"Again, this is footage that was taken from a smartphone Friday night, of a police officer shoving a young man through the door of Jerry's Corner Mart on Fourth Street. As you can see, the officer already has the young man subdued. He doesn't seem to be resisting, but is still slammed to the ground, where the officer proceeds with what looks to be unnecessary force. Jerry's has experienced a string of robberies, but as of now we are uncertain as to whether or not this was another one of those cases. We attempted to contact Jerry's management for a comment but to no avail. The Springfield PD has also declined

making a statement at this time. What we do know is that the young man in this video is sixteen-year-old Rashad Butler of West Springfield. We'll keep you updated as we learn more."

My mother's mouth gaped. "What? I mean, how . . ."

"Spoony, how'd they get my name?" I stared at the TV in disbelief.

"I told you, li'l bruh, there are always witnesses. Berry kept checking online all night, YouTube, Facebook, everything, and eventually, the video surfaced. So we sent it to the news. Told them who you were."

At this, my dad lost it. "I mean, seriously, have you lost your damn mind? Are them things on your head affecting your thinking? Rashad doesn't need this kind of attention, Spoony. He doesn't need all this craziness. None of us do."

Spoony jumped to his feet. "You think *me* sending it to the *news* is crazy? The crazy part is what happened to 'Shad. What's happening all over this country. You of all people should know that!"

My father glared at Spoony and I mean he held it there, as if there was, in fact, some kind of father-son ESP thing, and he was beaming the cuss-out of the century straight to my brother's brain. Then, like he always did, Dad stormed out of the room, followed by Spoony throwing words at his back. "Yeah, run away, as usual."

"Spoony!" Ma shouted.

My throat dried. My stomach boiled. I couldn't believe what I was seeing. I mean, it was me, but it wasn't. But . . . it *was*. I didn't know how or what to feel. Like, how could I be that boy—a victim. Me. It was just . . . I don't know . . . surreal. But we kept watching as the story looped. Sunday, aside from being a wack TV show day, is also apparently a slow news day. Every few minutes, the footage of me being crushed under the weight of the cop played, the newsperson talking about the "string of robberies" and not being able to get a comment from Jerry's management or the police department. Then a picture of me dressed in my ROTC uniform flashed across the screen.

I glared at Spoony. "Where'd they get *that?*" I asked, already knowing the answer.

"Man, listen, I had to make sure we controlled as much of the narrative as possible. If I ain't send that photo in, they would've dug all through the Internet for some picture of you looking crazy," Spoony said. "Trust me, man. I've seen it time and time again."

I was pissed about the photo, and to be honest, a little embarrassed by it, but I knew Spoony had a point. I would've hated for them to put up some picture of me hanging with

Carlos, posing with my middle fingers up. Even though . . . well . . . never mind.

The story played over and over and over again, like watching a movie in virtual reality where it doesn't really seem like you—like it's real—but you can feel every blow, every break. You can taste blood. You can smell the officer's breath. And that was hard for me. To see myself, like that. They kept saying it was a *developing story. As more unfolds. As we learn more.*

"Cut it off," I finally said.

"We need to keep up with how it develops," Spoony said.

"Cut it off, Spoon!" I reached for the remote myself and was instantly reminded that my ribs were broken. "Argkk!" My mother lifted off her seat, ready to spring into mommy mode. Spoony quickly handed me the clicker.

"Okay, okay," he said apologetically. "Take it easy. My bad, man. It's just . . ."

"I'm fine," I said hard, shooting down whatever reason he was about to deliver. I turned the TV off. "I just don't want to watch it no more."

The truth is, I wasn't mad at Spoony. I wasn't. As a matter of fact, he did exactly what I expected him to do. I just didn't want to keep watching it.

My mother, trying to cut the tension, began digging in her church bag, which was way bigger than her normal bag. The church bag had to be big enough to fit her Sunday service survival kit. Her Bible, some candy, and all the sins of our family. "Oh, Rashad, I forgot, I brought the stuff you asked for."

The stuff I asked for was my phone and phone charger—my mother was given the duffel bag with my ROTC uniform and phone after I, and it, were released into her custody. But more importantly, I wanted my art supplies—sketchbook and pencils. That's all I really needed. That was my hospital survival kit.

She plugged my phone in the wall and put the sketchbook and pencils on the roller tray-table next to the chicken tenders I now wasn't going to be eating. And as soon as my phone had enough juice to power on, the damn dog started barking. Nonstop.

Let me explain.

Me and Carlos had this stupid joke that whenever we were going to a party, we would set our text message alerts to a crazy sound effect. Not for any real reason. I mean, originally it was so we'd always know where each other was, or be able to find a phone if any of us lost one. But at a party, who would be able to hear it over the music? See, stupid. But we kept doing it because it was our thing. A tradition. Like, good luck, or something.

This week Carlos picked a dog bark, just because he thought it would be funny, or dare I say, cool, to tell a girl that there was something in his pants, barking. I mean, it was kind of funny. But also, so wack. Then he challenged me and said that he could get a girl with that bark line before I could. Truth is, I wasn't even going to try. But I played along and changed my alert anyway. And now that my phone had enough battery to turn on, the dog was barking crazy.

"Hand me that," I said to Spoony, who was frowning at all the stupid noise.

I checked my messages.

FRIDAY 4:43 p.m. from Spoony
SHAD YOU STILL COMIN TO GET $$?

FRIDAY 5:13 p.m. from Spoony
??? WTF

FRIDAY 5:21 p.m. from Los
YO BE AT MY CRIB BY 7

FRIDAY 5:22 p.m. from Los
AND WATCH HOW MANY GIRLS I GET WITH
THAT DOG JOKE

FRIDAY 5:23 p.m. from Los
U KNO GIRLS LUV DOGS DUDE!

FRIDAY 5:35 p.m. from Los
WHERE U AT?

FRIDAY 5:51 p.m. from Spoony
WHERE U AT?

FRIDAY 6:05 p.m. from Ma
HEY, SPOONY AND CARLOS CALLED HERE
LOOKING FOR YOU. I CALLED BUT IT KEEPS
GOING TO VOICE MAIL. CALL ME.

FRIDAY 7:00 p.m. from Los
DUDE UR KILLIN' ME. WHERE THE FUCK ARE U?

FRIDAY 8:47 p.m. from Los
I DONT KNOW WHERE U ARE BUT IM OUT. IF U
CAUGHT A RIDE WITH SOMEBODY ELSE YOU
COULDA TOLD ME BRO. DAMN. UNLESS YOU
WITH A GIRL. THEN I UNDERSTAND. BUT I KNO
U NOT. I'LL CATCH YOU AT THE PARTY. BRING
YOUR BEST GAME.

FRIDAY 10:03 p.m. from English
SHAD YOU HERE? ME SHAN AND LOS LOOKIN

FOR U. LOS TRIPPIN! LMAO

SATURDAY 1:01 p.m. from Los
WHERE WERE U? OF COURSE IT GOT SHUT
DOWN. SHIT WAS BANANAS!

SATURDAY 4:26 p.m. from Shan
YO, LOS IS TIRED OF TEXTN U SO NOW IM
TEXTN U. U GOOD?

SATURDAY 4:41 p.m. from Shan
WHERE ARE U?

SATURDAY 4:49 p.m. from Los
ENGLISH JUST TOLD ME BERRY SAID U IN THE
HOSPITAL!

SATURDAY 4:51 p.m. from English
U IN THE HOSPITAL? WTF

SATURDAY 4:52 p.m. from Shan
YO YOU IN THE HOSPITAL BRO? ENGLISH SAID
SOME SHIT ABOUT THE COPS?

SUNDAY 12:11 p.m. from Los
YO YOU ON THE NEWS! CRAZY!

Crazy, indeed. I scrolled through, reading them all before sending quick responses to the three of them—Shannon, Carlos, and English—letting them know that I was okay. Well, I said a little more than that.

SUNDAY 12:17 p.m. to Los, Shan, English
IM GOOD FELLAS. GOT ACCUSED OF STEALING
FROM JERRY'S AND THE COP ON DUTY
ROUGHED ME UP. BROKE MY NOSE AND SOME
RIBS. BUT IM OK.

"I see he's got his lifeline back," Dad grumbled, coming back into the room, looking calmer than when he'd left.

"Yeah, so he should be back to normal in no time," Ma said, trying to be positive.

"I don't know about that," Spoony muttered. Thankfully my father didn't hear him, because I wasn't sure I could take another blowup. So I turned the TV back on quick. A risk, I know. But I had to do something as it looked like my folks were settling in for the afternoon. And guess what saved the day? Football.

"Ah. Football," Spoony said. "Another one of America's favorite pastimes, besides baseball, and beating the brains out of—"

"Chill," I ordered. Honestly, I just wanted to take it easy for the rest of the day. I didn't want to hear Spoony preach about how hard it is to be black, or my father preach about how young people lack pride and integrity, making us easy targets. I didn't even want to think about the preacher preaching about how God is in control of it all, or my mother, my sweet, sweet mother caught in the middle of it all. The referee who blows the whistle but is way too nice to call foul on anyone. That's her. She just wants me to be okay. That's it and that's all. So if football was going to be the thing that took our minds off the mess for at least a few hours, then fine with me. Let's cheer and scream and cuss at the TV. Not at each other.

When the game was over, my family left. And at that moment, I thanked the God I hoped was there. Back to an empty, peaceful room. Just me and my spirometer, which, by the way, was also pretty painful to use. I mean, to inhale slowly felt like sucking in shards of glass. Yeah—not awesome.

After the game, the news came on. The first story was about a kid accused of stealing from a store on the West Side. The footage of me being thrown to the ground. Again. Again. Again. My picture. My name. Again. And now, a new development. The officer's name. Officer Paul Galluzzo. And his face on the screen.

QUINN

I stayed home with Willy Saturday night and we watched *World War Z* and then had a Mario Kart marathon until I felt bug-eyed and useless. It was good to escape into his world for a while, because after we walked Jill home, I was still stuck in my head and it wasn't fair to Willy. But Sunday was different. Ma came home, napped for a couple hours, made her marshmallow pie that everyone in the world loves but me—because marshmallows taste like little chunks of chewy soap!—and then the three of us went down the block to the Galluzzos'.

We arrived late; the house was already packed. A couple of the younger neighborhood kids sat on the stairs that overlooked the front hall and the living room. Each one had a hyper-colored plastic gun, and they pretended to shoot the group of guys in the living room watching the Pats play the Broncos on TV. It was the afternoon game, but it was already in the second quarter. They were screaming at what should have been a pass interference that hadn't been called.

"Boys!" Ma yelled into the room.

I almost laughed at how quickly the roomful of grown men snapped to attention when they heard Ma.

A moment passed, then Guzzo's dad shouted back, "Marshmallow pie!" Everyone cheered.

"Nice to see you too, Richie," Ma said. We walked into the kitchen and she put the pie on the counter, Mrs. Galluzzo hugging us all hello. Out the window, I could see the small backyard, the porch. It was packed too. It looked like half the neighborhood had shown up. Willy scrambled off to find some kids his age down in the basement, where they usually played video games, and I headed outside. But I gotta admit, I felt weird. The Galluzzos' had always been my second home, but as I moved through the kitchen toward the back porch, I felt oddly slow and awkward, like I was wading through a pool of water.

As soon as I stepped onto the porch I saw him. Paul. My stomach clenched. He was flipping burgers at the grill. A red bandanna tied up over his head. Ratty T-shirt, even in this cool November weather. Guzzo stood right beside him. Two brothers side by side. Man, I'd never really taken in how huge they were, like, they could have squatted, pitched forward, and put their knuckles in the dirt, and they'd be the linemen I just saw wearing Pats and Broncos uniforms. They waved, and I waved back, but was instantly wondering if Guzzo had said anything to his brother about the other night. It bugged me not knowing. I wasn't sure if I was supposed to keep quiet about it, or if I was supposed to head over and slap Paul on the back. It did feel like this party was thrown together all of a sudden for him. Why else were we all there? Paul didn't live here, and yet he stood there at the grill, like he was at the helm or something, and the whole party radiated out in front of him.

Paul prodded the burgers and I saw that Jill was on the porch too. She was sitting on the railing, leaning against the post in the corner, watching Dwyer shoot hoops in the driveway. I joined her in the corner, sitting on the other railing, facing her and the yard behind her, where I could see Guzzo nudging Paul and pointing at me.

"You think you all really have a chance this year?" Jill asked me, nodding toward the basketball.

Of course she'd go there first—that was all anybody wanted to talk about.

"Everyone else does," I said.

She turned and looked at me. "That make you nervous?"

"I keep hearing this voice in the back of my head," I said,

hoping I didn't sound like a frigging crazy person. "It's pushing me, you know, like, 'go, go, go,' but what I really hear is 'Don't fuck it up.'"

"Coach putting pressure on you?" she asked.

That wasn't even half of it! Coach Carney and his plans were drilled into me. We'd had our warm-up practices the week before. The first serious preseason practices began on Monday. Everyone knew we had a great team this year. People were even talking about it in the press, wanting to know how far we'd go—semifinals, finals—but all *we* cared about was who was going to be a starter. That's who the scouts would focus on—the guys with serious playing time.

But it wasn't the team that bothered me, it was the press. I'd already seen Coach Carney doing interviews left and right, getting all excited like some clown at the carnival. I was sure we'd see more of them too. It had been a long time since we'd had a team with a shot at being ranked number one in the state, and even though there were only fifteen players, three coaches, and a part-time trainer, it felt like we were chasing the trophy for thousands of people.

But right then, I decided I was only going to concentrate on one person. Jill. So I just said, "Not too bad," and she nodded, and it was kind of impossible not watch the light shift in the highlights in her hair. There were other people on the porch, but nobody was listening to us.

"So here's something, I don't know, weird. You know how the cops came to the party the other night?" she said.

"Yeah."

"Well, no one got busted. The cops broke up the party, shook a few guys down, looking for pot, but not finding any, and they just made me send everyone away, made *me* stand there in the hall and watch everyone leave. They made me call my parents. It was so embarrassing." She leaned in closer. "But what was worse, they stood there in the front hall looking at me, waiting for my folks to come home, after everyone else had left, and one of them, I don't even know his name, but he obviously knew I was Paulie's cousin, he kept looking at me like he was disgusted. Finally, he pointed at me and said, 'Don't fuck this up for your family.'"

"Did you get in any kind of trouble?"

"No," Jill said skeptically. "I thought he was going to call Paulie, but he didn't. He just said that, waited for my parents, and when they got home, he left. Nothing else happened. It was just . . . like I said, weird."

Mr. Galluzzo pushed open the screen door to yell out to Paul. "Hey, it's almost halftime. We got a roomful o' guys gonna come running out here for burgers soon."

Just his dad shouting to him seemed to pull the whole yard closer—pulled me closer to him. I looked past Jill's shoulder to Guzzo and Paul. They were still at the grill, Paul with the spatula in one hand. "I get a day off and all you do is put me to work?" he yelled back to his dad. He laughed. "Don't worry," he said, raising his hand in the air, the spatula his scepter, "I got this." Paul was famous for his burgers. He made them himself and even while the burger itself was still juicy, the bits of onion inside stayed nice and crunchy. They were my favorite, better than anything Ma ever made. Mr. Galluzzo poked his head back in the house to tell folks that the burgers would be ready in a minute, but someone shouted to him to come see some play Brady made, and he left the porch and let the door slam behind him.

"I think I know why they couldn't call Paul," I said to Jill.

She gave me a *go on* look, then added carefully, "Yeah, I saw something on the news."

"I saw it happen."

"What?" Jill bent forward and grabbed my wrist.

I could hear the rubbery echo of the ball pounding in the driveway, the chatter from some of the neighbors in the backyard, the rattle of a bag filled with bottles being moved through the kitchen inside. I shifted closer to her on the railing. "Me and Guzzo and Dwyer were at Jerry's before your party," I told her, voice low. "I saw it. I saw Paul and that kid."

"It was *Rashad*, Quinn. That's who Paul arrested. You know Rashad. He goes to our school. He's tight with English and those guys."

"Fuck," I said. In fact, as soon as she said it, I could picture him, hanging with English in the halls. "ROTC dude, right? Shit."

I felt like such an ass. I'd quickly convinced myself I had no idea who that kid with Paul was that night. And yeah, there were like a thousand kids in each grade at school, or whatever, but I did know him. Or know *of* him, really. I'd seen him—Rashad—in that uniform, and it'd made me think of my dad wearing his own at college. How my dad had looked proud in all those pictures.

Jill cocked her head in disbelief. "You all just watched it go down?"

"Guzzo and Dwyer were waiting in the alley. But I was there." I glanced around, all paranoid, making my voice even lower. "It was ugly. I don't know what Rashad did, but Paul kicked the shit out of him."

"I heard someone talking about it earlier," Jill said, scooching closer. "They said he was resisting arrest."

"I guess."

"Did Paul, like, see you, or anything?"

I hesitated. "I don't know," I said. It felt weird to talk about any of this, as if by mentioning it at all, I was betraying Paul. I looked over to him and Guzzo as if reading their faces might tell me what they were thinking, or whether Guzzo had said anything.

"I don't think he saw me," I said, turning back to Jill. "I doubt it."

"Did Guzzo?"

"What?"

"Tell him?"

We were hunched so close together at this point that when I heard my name shouted out, it felt like someone dropped an ice cube down the back of my shirt.

"Hey, Quinn!" It was Paul. "Why don't you quit hitting on my cousin and come help me serve these burgers?"

I froze. The timing scared the hell out of me—it was as if he knew I'd just been talking about him! Jill spun around and yelled, "Go flip your own burgers, Paul!"

"What does that even mean?" he asked. He and Guzzo laughed.

"I don't know," Jill said, turning back to me. "But better than saying nothing."

Jill never took shit, never let anyone get the jump on her. I always figured it was because she was used to being the only girl in a huge group of guys—there were eleven Galluzzo cousins, and she was the only female—and she just wouldn't let them tease her, or if they did, she decided long ago that she sure as hell was going to make it through the gauntlet regardless.

I, however, wasn't as used to it. In fact, I must have looked stupid with nerves because her eyes stayed glued to me as I got up and told her I'd catch up with her later, and as I turned, she smiled and I felt the air leave me in a rush, because I wanted to take her by the hand and get the hell out of there, but I couldn't.

"Quinn!" Paul again.

Then Guzzo. "Quinn!"

Then Guzzo began a slow clap, and he and Paul chanted my name louder and louder as I crossed over to them, and I was sure even folks in the neighborhood who weren't already at the party could hear them.

"Dude," Guzzo said when I reached them. "You have no chance."

"Like you know anything about chances."

"Damn right," Paul said, grinning at me.

"Shut up," Guzzo said.

Paul ignored him. He had a bottle of beer in his left hand, and he held out that fist to bump knuckles with me, and I did. "What's up, Quinn?" he said. "You don't say hello anymore?" He took a swig of beer and wiped his mouth on the sleeve of his T-shirt. That's when I noticed his right fist was stuffed into a bucket of ice water on the grill shelf beside him, all casual—*frigging hell, he had scabs all over his knuckles*—like nursing his wounds from Friday night right there in front of everybody at the BBQ was NBD!

"What's up?" I asked.

He tossed the empty beer bottle into a cardboard box near his feet. "Hold this," he said, handing me a faded plastic tray. He squeezed the juice from a couple of burgers with the spatula, sending flames up and around them. "I know the O'Rileys like 'em dried out," he said. He pressed again, charring them more. "Make sure they know which ones are theirs." He pulled his swollen fist from the ice bucket, flexed the fingers, then stuck it back in. "Seriously, man," he said to me. "Were you ever going to get your ass over here?"

"It's a party," I said. "People mingle. I just got here. Jesus. What's the matter with you?"

"Nothing's the matter," Guzzo snapped. "Why are you getting defensive?"

"What are you talking about?"

"Look," Paul interrupted. He cut the air between us with the spatula, a drop of grease landed on my T-shirt. He pulled his wet hand from the bucket and pinched at the spot, pulling off as much of the grease as he could. "What the hell's the matter with you two?"

"Nothing," I said, but I wasn't sure. I kept trying to read his face or Guzzo's for some sign. Still not knowing if Guzzo had said anything to Paul was starting to eat away at me. Guzzo wouldn't meet my eyes.

But Paul did. "Listen," he said. "I'm not kidding. You guys

need to have a mind meld or something. If you keep bitching at each other like this into the season, you aren't going to play well. You're going to suck. So strap on a pair and get your shit together."

I nodded and Guzzo did too. It was always like that—Paul'd give us marching orders and we'd march—especially with basketball.

"Way I see it," Paul continued, "if the whole team moves off the ball more, and if you can get English to give it up more, you all have a real shot. Everyone else relies on two, maybe three players at most. You've got eight or nine solid players, right?"

"English's been working on his range," I said. "He's going to shoot all he can. He's going to break his record from last year."

"You *all* should," Paul said. "That's my point."

He started scraping burgers up off the grill and dropping them on the platter.

"They better have the fixings ready in the kitchen," Guzzo said.

"Why don't you go find out?" Paul said. Guzzo was about to protest, but Paul spoke over him. "Seriously," Paul said before shouting out, "Burgers up!"

Guzzo jogged ahead while I waited for Paul to slide the last burgers onto the pile. As soon as he did, I started to follow Guzzo, but Paul grabbed my arm. His blue eyes were red-rimmed and tired. "I'm going to have a few days free," he told me. "We should work on your footwork. We'll get a little in today. You come by after practice tomorrow too. I'll be here."

"Yeah," I said. But he kept holding my arm longer than he needed to until it was obviously awkward.

"You all right?" he asked. "You seem a little uptight. What's up?"

"Burgers," I said, way too chipper. "Nobody wants them cold."

I could feel his eyes on me as I carried them up to the kitchen, and I could still feel the pressure of his fingertips like a ring around my elbow. I made a point of eating in the living room with the guys watching the game. The game was a good distraction, a way to pay attention to something else, to try to take my mind off Paul squinting at me, his gauging me as he'd been talking to me at the grill. He'd been all smiles, all business-as-usual, and despite the swollen hand in the bucket and the shredded knuckles, he'd been waving to people across the yard like there wasn't a damn thing on his mind other than serving them their burgers.

And while I kept seeing Paul's Popeye arms at the back of Rashad's neck, nobody else seemed to be wondering about why the Galluzzos felt the sudden need for a party. No one else was talking about the fact that Paul was in the news. Instead they all yelled at the TV when the Pats blew a twenty-five-yard pass with another flag for holding. They yelled again after the Pats recovered from a sack and, on third and eighteen, scored a touchdown. I yelled along with them. It was just easier. Guzzo came in and out of the room a few times, but it felt like he was keeping his distance from me, hovering around his brother, when Paul would come in to check on the score.

But the game wasn't distracting enough—when I tried to swallow the burger down, it felt like I had an animal trying to crawl up and out of my throat, so after a while, I wandered into the kitchen, wondering where Jill was, and I found her there fighting with her mom in the corner. They were going at it about Friday night's party, right there in front of everyone.

"I'm not kidding, young lady!" Jill's mom said, cramping a cigarette between two fingers and waving it in front of Jill. "This is serious. The Rowells are still screaming at us because of the last party. This is it; you've really blown it this time."

"All right. All right. I got it," Jill said, standing like she was ready to fight or run, whichever she needed. "Can we not do this here?"

Her mother leaned back and drew a big breath, as if to collect herself. "And one more thing," she finally said. "You can't expect Paulie to just be there to save you all the time."

"Oh my God. I *don't*."

Mrs. Galluzzo had been halfheartedly rinsing off a few of

the now empty platters with my mother, but when she heard Paul's name, she swung around.

"You *do*," Jill's mom continued. "And he's got bigger and better things to worry about than his little cousins screwing around."

"You're right—he does," Jill said under her breath, but everyone heard her.

"Hey," Mrs. Galluzzo interrupted, her face going all tight and pissed. "You watch what you say next." She stepped away from the sink. Everyone else in the room went quiet, and Jill had gone deep red. "You might have a little respect. Today. In my house. *To-day!*" The platter in her hand shook, and my mother put a hand on Mrs. Galluzzo's back to calm her.

"That's what I was trying to say," Jill's mom said, stepping closer to Mrs. Galluzzo. "I mean, you know. He has an important job." She fumbled for more words, then turned back to Jill. "See what you've done? You apologize to your aunt Rita right now."

"I'm sorry," Jill said automatically.

"You're always sorry," her mom added bitterly, before sucking on her cigarette.

"Honey," Mrs. Galluzzo said to Jill, her face softening. "Paul has a hard job, and sometimes he has to make tough decisions. All I'm saying is, please respect that, and who he is."

"Yes," Jill said, but she wasn't looking at Mrs. Galluzzo. She was looking at Paul, Paul who was looking in through the screen door.

"Thanks, Ma," he said.

"Oh, Paulie," Mrs. Galluzzo said, whirling around. She looked like she wanted to say more, but didn't have the words for it.

And as we were all waiting to hear what she would say next, we heard something else. The TV. It was turned up so loud for the game that when there was a break, and the news anchor's voice set up the teaser for the evening news, we all heard it in the kitchen: *Tune in tonight for the latest updates to this developing story as our experts analyze the shocking video released today of Officer Paul Galluzzo's arrest of Rashad Butler.*

Suddenly the TV went mute. Someone in the living room must have found the remote, but it didn't matter. It was too late.

The kitchen was so silent I could hear my pulse in my ears, pumping red-hot burning blood into my face. I couldn't say anything. I couldn't move. But I wasn't alone—no one did.

We might have stayed like that, frozen in time, but Mr. Galluzzo busted into the kitchen from the living room in a kind of frantic waddle, holding a spread of dirty paper plates in his hands. "Hey, m-maybe we need to get some m-more burgers going," he sort of stuttered, more nervous than I'd ever heard him, but he stopped short as he looked around the shocked crowd in the kitchen.

"Well, I'm not making any more right now," Paul said from the doorway, staring back at his dad.

"Yeah. No. Yes. Of course. I just mean—"

"Look," Paul told his dad, interrupting him. "Take it easy." He sighed, but then he lifted his head and glanced around the kitchen through the screen door. "Let's just say it. There's going to be more of this press. It's going to look ugly. But everything's going to be just fine. This just comes with the job. I'll be all right." He remained on the porch, but he leaned forward, his thick arms going up on either side of the door frame. "But yeah," he added. "I do need everyone to stick by me. Especially family."

Everyone immediately started saying how they supported him, and he nodded and smiled, but was looking past all the women to me. "You too, Quinn," he added. "Right now, I need your ass out here on the court for a little two-on-two."

I was so freaked out it was a frigging relief just to be given an order.

"Okay," I said dumbly, and I swear there were a few faces in the room, including my own ma's and Mrs. Galluzzo's, who looked at me with a swelling pride, as if he'd just asked me to saddle up and join the posse on the hunt for some ruthless criminal, and I was putting down my farming tools to go join the greater cause. I passed Jill on my way to the porch, and I tapped her elbow as I walked by. She could hold her own better than anyone I knew, but I wanted to let her know she wasn't alone, because at least Jill was strong enough to actually say what I was only thinking. Maybe everyone else at the party was nervous for Paul, but I was nervous *about* him—especially as I followed him down to the driveway.

"Two-on-two," Paul said. "All rebounds are offensive. After a basket, you gotta make three passes before you take another shot. Got it?" He waved his thumb between Guzzo and himself. "Galluzzos against you two dumbasses." The dumbasses were me and Dwyer, of course.

They gave us the ball first, and from the first drive, I knew it was going to be a physical game. I didn't shoot. I just dribbled and kept Paul slapping at my forearm and side. He'd taught me to dribble, a little too well. Guzzo's too big to try to take him to the hoop, but he took my bait, so I got the lane plugged with both Galluzzos and Dwyer popped out back by the top of the key. I got him the ball with a no-look pass and he made the shot.

"Get your ass in action," Paul told his brother.

This went on for a while and the game got rougher. The score stayed close, but none of us could hope to out-rebound Guzzo, so they made more points off our missed shots than they could make on their own. Their driveway is narrow, and the rest of the time, Paul and Guzzo bumped us until we were backed up against one of the houses on either side. But while Paul's arms were as thick as my neck, I beat him off the dribble, and twice in a row I got a foot around him and nailed fadeaway jumpers Guzzo couldn't block.

"What? You think you're English now?" Paul said to me.

"No."

Paul put his hand in the air for us to stop. "Wait. Was that even three passes?"

"Yeah," Dwyer said.

"You losing count," I laughed, trying to keep it light.

But Paul didn't. We checked, and he came up all over me. If we'd had the full space of a real court, this would have made it easier to get around him, but in the driveway, he just kept bumping me back and back, until I was almost out to the sidewalk. The driveway sloped down, and I was in the street when Paul finally eased up.

"Where the hell are you going?"

I didn't answer. I just chucked the ball from the street. It wasn't a real shot, and I didn't think I could actually make it. I just wanted to watch it hit the rim and see what would happen. It hit the top of the backboard and bounced into the yard near the grill.

"What's up with that?" Guzzo yelled.

"You got to be tougher than that," Paul said to me. "You

can't give up. I'm just trying to help you, Quinn. You got to keep your head in the game and nowhere else. You got that?"

"Man," I said. "This isn't a game." I brushed past him and walked up the driveway. "I'm done," I said.

Dwyer and Guzzo started to complain, but Paul's voice rose up over theirs. "I'm just trying to help you, Quinn. Like I always have. You remember that."

How could I forget? I collected the ball from the yard and tossed it to Dwyer, then went inside. I said a quick good-bye to Mrs. Galluzzo and told Ma I'd meet her at home, then left through the front door, taking the steps two at a time, half expecting Paul to be there, blocking my path, reminding me how many times he'd been the one working with me in that same driveway, the one cheering me on from the stands of my middle school, JV, and now varsity basketball games. The one who taught me how to angle the blade beneath my chin when I shaved. But he wasn't there. He was back under the basket with Guzzo and Dwyer, showing Dwyer how to get a leg around a man bigger than him—the same move I'd used on him moments before.

Monday

QUINN

If I thought walking away from Paul would make me not think about him, or what he had done for me over the years, I was an idiot. At school on Monday it felt like everyone was talking about Rashad. Who'd seen him? What was going on? Was he coming back to school? How bad was he hurt? Was he gonna die? When you go to a school as large as ours, it's impossible to know everyone, but even in a school as large as ours you definitely know someone who was friends with Rashad. And of course, it worked the other way around too—especially when the cop involved was the older brother of your oldest friend.

But what was worse was that everyone—*everyone*—was talking about the video. The clip that had made the rounds on the Sunday morning news shows, and then went viral.

The video everyone had seen but me, because there was no way in hell I was putting myself back there, back at Friday night, watching that happen all over again.

I'd gotten texts all night from Dwyer and a couple of other guys on the team, other kids too, but I'd ignored them. I'd clicked my phone to mute. No way was I watching that video. I wanted to erase the whole damn memory from my mind, but I couldn't because it was like the whole damn high school had been there on the street with me—everybody had seen it.

It was nonstop *Rashad buzz* all day, and by fourth period, as I was making my way up the stairs and Nam yelled to me from behind, I already knew what he was going to say.

"Quinn, man. Wait up." Nam was another one of the guys on the team, our point guard when English needed a break, and he dodged around a few people to catch up with me. "Yo, all that shit that went down with Rashad on Friday, right?"

"Yeah, man."

There were a couple of other people in the stairwell watching us. Listening.

"The cop, that's Guzzo's brother, right?"

"Yeah, man."

"But like, that's got to be weird, right?"

"Yeah, man. It is. It's weird."

"I mean, you wonder why he did it?"

"What? Steal something from Jerry's? Are you kidding?"

"No, man. Not Rashad. I'm talking about Paul Galluzzo. Why'd he do it?"

We pushed open the doors to the third floor and walked down to trig. A couple guys I'd seen at Jill's on Friday nodded to me. I nodded back. "What the hell, Nam?" I said. "He was just doing his job."

"You kidding? You've seen the video, right?"

"No."

"What? You kidding?"

We walked into trig together and sat down in our usual seats. Mrs. Erlich sat us in alphabetical order, which put me in the last row, but Nam sat in the middle, next to English. I flashed a peace sign to English and he nodded, but only briefly, then he and Nam started talking quietly. Nam looked back at me once, and I was certain they were talking about Paul and Guzzo, and therefore me too.

Why did it feel like everyone was looking at me? Wanting answers to all those questions from me? Plus, what the hell was wrong with me, anyway? Why was *I* the paranoid one? Shouldn't they all be looking at Guzzo instead?

Then it hit me. *The video!* Was I on it? Had anyone seen me on it? That must have been why everyone was staring at me like I had four heads. They were looking at the dude who just stood there like a pants-shitting five-year-old watching everything happen in front of him instead of doing anything about it.

After class, Nam and English busted out before I could catch up with them, and I was sure it was going to be a long day—and practice was going to suck. If nothing else, English and I would usually swap a few words about a party or a game from the weekend, something, anything, but today he was clearly avoiding me. I made my way downstairs, hoping not to get caught in another conversation I didn't want to have, and when I pushed open the door to the second floor, I was surprised to see Jill by my locker. She was waiting for me! And she was about the only person I wanted to talk to.

"Hey," she said as we hugged hello. "Do you want to grab lunch?"

Of course, I'd have had lunch with her any damn day and every damn day, and after we both dumped our books in my locker, we skipped the cafeteria and went around the corner to Burger King.

"Back-to-back burger days," I said when we found some seats.

"Salad. Seriously. Does anybody actually like it? Multi-colored Styrofoam. No thanks. I'm a burger girl."

"Hell yeah," I said. "But these aren't half as good as Paul's."

"Yeah . . ." She trailed off and we were quiet for a moment while we ate. But then she finally got to it. "Have you seen Guzzo today?"

"No." In fact, honestly, I'd actually been *avoiding* him. We weren't in any classes together, so we usually found each other by one of our lockers or in the hallway to the gym. But not today. Of course, he hadn't come looking for me, either.

"Whatever. After you left yesterday, everybody was talking about how it was unfair the media had to make such a big deal of the situation. 'How are cops supposed to do their jobs if they're always under the microscope?' Rita kept saying. 'It's just backward,' she kept saying. She might be my aunt, but it bugged the hell out of me."

"Yeah, but then look at today," I said, more mopey than I wanted to sound. "All anybody's talking about is that stupid video."

"Well, duh."

I didn't say anything. I just took another bite of my burger. Jill watched me as I chewed.

"What?" I finally said with my cheek still full.

"You haven't watched it, have you?"

I took a sip of soda. "No," I admitted.

"You should," she said. She sounded almost a little pissed at me.

"I was there. I don't want to see it again," I argued. "I just keep thinking about how extreme it all was. I mean, I don't know what Rashad did, but whatever it was, I can't imagine he needed to get beaten like that. I mean, as far as I know, he's a guy looking to stay out of trouble."

"Yeah. Exactly." She paused. "And did you hear?" she asked with more concern. "He has internal bleeding."

"Jesus."

"He has to stay in the hospital for like days."

"*Jesus.*"

"Yeah. It's awful."

I was silent again.

"And you were there," Jill continued. "I can't believe you were there."

"I was," I said. But as I was freaking out that she might have been saying she'd seen me in the video, my pulse suddenly quickened because—oh, my God!—I'd been there with Paul before. Or, sort of been there. Years and years ago. How had I forgotten about that? Paul, with another kid. Marc Blair. "Oh, Jesus," I said.

Jill nibbled on a fry and waited for me to continue.

"It was almost like that time he kicked the shit out of Marc Blair," I said. "I mean, that was different. But this thing with Rashad. That thing with Marc. They're like side by side in my mind right now."

"Oh my God," she said, scrunching up her nose. "I forgot all about that. Paulie killed that guy."

Not literally. But it was bad. I hadn't actually seen it. But I'd seen the aftermath. And here's the thing—Paul'd done it for *me*. I felt sick.

Jill tapped the empty plastic Coke bottle against the table nervously. "You think those are the only two times?"

"I don't know. I mean, it's Paul. This is the same guy I've seen carrying my mom up the front steps, for God's sake." I was thinking about that time Ma got trashed because it was her first wedding anniversary without Dad. Paul had been so gentle. He'd taken the frigging day off just so she didn't have to spend it alone. "She was tanked," I said to Jill. "And he helped her home. I remember him putting her down on the couch and pulling the afghan over her."

"Paulie's always been the good guy."

"That's what I want to think."

"That's what my mother kept saying last night after the party, after she was done yelling at me for being the world's most ungrateful daughter for the hundredth time. 'Paulie's the good guy,' she kept saying. 'Why is anyone giving him a hard time?' But people *are* giving him a hard time. I don't know. I was watching some of the news online. It's kind of hard not to wonder. I mean, I wasn't there, but . . ."

"You've seen the video," I said, flat. The fear that I was in it kept buzzing through me.

"Yeah, Quinn. Everyone's seen it. It's crazy."

I swallowed hard and finally asked. "Am I in it?"

"What?" Jill said. "No. You must have been too far away. Different angle. I don't know."

I couldn't help it. I sighed with relief. "Jesus. Thank God."

Jill narrowed her eyes. "This is not about you, dumbass."

I took a deep breath through my nose and just held it. She was right. I'd been all worked up about whether or not I was on the video. Rashad was in the video and he was in the hospital. Paul was in the video too. Where was he now? Sitting at his parents' house watching all the news about himself on TV? Was he hiding?

"Look," Jill went on. "I get why you're worried, but when you see it, well, it's just crazy." She hesitated. "I feel so stupid saying this, but I don't know. It just changes things for me."

"Yeah," I said quietly.

We finished the last few fries and had to get back to school. But before we got up, I reached across the table and put my hand on Jill's. "I know this sounds weird, but I kind of feel like you are the only person I can talk to about this right now."

She turned her hand beneath mine and squeezed back. "I know. Me too."

As we walked back to school, we tried to joke a little about the party on Friday, but we both knew we were just putting on a show and really thinking about Paul and Rashad. Because as Jill was telling me about the guy who spent half the night puking in the upstairs bathroom because he'd done a keg stand right before I'd gotten there, I was thinking more about how I spent all this time playing basketball with a bunch of guys who were friends with Rashad and I didn't know jack-all about him—which made me feel all kinds of asshole-ish.

When we got back, Jill had to rush to get all the way over to the physics lab, but I had econ with Ms. Webber, so I took my time at my locker, playing with my phone, but really, now I was stuck on that time Paul had beaten up Marc Blair.

When I'd been much younger, and I first started going down to Gooch on my own, there was a guy who lived right next to the park who was a few years older than me, Marc Blair. Compared to my scrawny ass, he was all muscle—if it didn't get too cold in the winter, he'd have played shirtless year round, a pit bull charging up and down the court on these squat, beefy legs. I was too young, and he never let me onto the court when he was there. I hated it. He didn't like me, or any of the kids younger than him either, but he didn't like me in particular, because while most kids my age played mute around him, I sometimes mouthed off. Finally, after I'd called him an asshole one too many times, he grabbed me by the collar, dragged me across the court to the chain-link fence, and pressed my face into the wire so hard it left a crisscross hatch of red indented on my cheek and forehead. When he let go, I cried on the spot like a goddamn baby, falling to my hands and knees. He stood back and pointed at me, and I was so scared I puked near the base of the fence. And after that, I was always afraid of him.

And I began to imagine what it would be like for Paul to beat him up. Take care of him. I thought about it with a kind of freaky hunger. Paul wasn't a cop yet. He was just the tough guy who took me under his wing. I wanted to see Marc pay. I wanted him to feel a kind of pain that matched my own level of fear whenever I was near him.

And that was the part that was tripping me up now. The fear. I was making leaps in my mind now, but once I'd hung on that word "fear," I remembered the time I was a freshman and I saw a senior walking down the hall. He was black, and I didn't know his name, but he was wearing an old-school Public Enemy T-shirt: *Fear of a Black Planet*—the bull's-eye logo poised to eclipse the Earth. Fear. The T-shirt was right. Like the way Mrs. Cambi talked about our neighborhood now. Fear. Like the way Ma told me to cross the street to the other side of the sidewalk if I was walking home alone and I saw a group of guys walking toward me. Guys. That wasn't the word she used. Thugs. Fear of thugs. Just like what some people were saying on the news. Rashad looked like a thug.

"Thug" was the word Paul used when I told him about Marc. It was two weeks after Marc had pushed me into the fence. I finally told Paul, and Paul found him later that same night. Beat the hell out of him. Paul was banged up too, but he said he'd won. *Fucking thug won't bug you anymore, for real.*

I never found out if Marc had needed to go to the hospital that night. But if Paul's bruises and split lip were the signs of the winner, I had to image that Marc was a whole lot worse.

And now, six years later, I felt as sick as if it had happened yesterday: I was the one who could have put another kid in the hospital all those years ago, just by asking someone to take care of him. It was no different than ordering a hit. Didn't that make *me* a thug? Christ sake, I'd wanted to see someone else's blood. To see him bleed.

And so I was thinking about all that when I got to Ms. Webber's class. After she got us settled, she explained that she had a change of plan for the day. We'd get back to our study of marginal utility another day. Today we were just going to sit quietly and work on a practice section for the next test. Quietly. She emphasized that. *Quietly.* But as we got started, it was all too easy to see Ms. Webber twitching, smiling like she was reminding herself to, and anybody could tell she was nervous and just wanted a silent and nonteaching day of class.

Only about five minutes into it, though, Molly leaned over and asked EJ if he'd been to Jill's party. Before he even had time to answer, Ms. Webber looked up from the pile of papers she was grading and pointed to EJ.

"Every time, EJ," she said abruptly, so loud that she seemed to surprise even herself.

"What?" he asked.

"You." Ms. Webber's eyes narrowed and she spoke calmly, maybe too calmly. "Every time I look up and see something going on, some distraction. There you are. Right at the center of it. Do you need to take your test out in the hall?"

"Guilty until proven innocent, huh?" He hesitated, but not for long. Nobody likes to be spoken to like he's a damn child, least of all EJ, and he wasn't the kind of kid to stay quiet. He didn't miss a beat. "Just like Rashad."

I swear I could hear Ms. Webber suck in her breath as she tried to figure out how to answer.

It was awkward for all of us. Especially because EJ was black, just like Rashad, and Ms. Webber was white, just like Paul—like me and like Molly, too. I think EJ was hoping someone else would pipe up, but none of us did, not the white kids, nor any of the kids of color. We all just left him hanging out there until finally Ms. Webber found something she wanted to say.

"That's not— It's not— You just can't go conflating things like that." Then she pointed to the copy of the test she had in front of her. "This is for your benefit," she squeaked. "We don't have time to talk about this right now." She took another breath. "I'm sorry. I know there's a student from our school who is in the hospital today, but we don't have the full story. What I do know is that if we are going to be ready for these exams, we have to get down to business today. They won't wait for us. We have to be ready."

"Rashad," Molly said.

"What?" Ms. Webber said.

EJ looked at her, surprised.

"Rashad," Molly said louder. "That's his name. Rashad's in the hospital."

"I know that," Ms. Webber said.

"Yeah, well, *that student* in the hospital isn't here to take any practice tests today because he's, you know, beaten to hell," EJ said.

"Rashad," Molly said again.

EJ smiled. "Rashad," he said louder.

They both said the name again and looked around for others to join them, but the rest of us sat there in shock.

"All right, both of you, outside now!" Ms. Webber yelled. She was flushed straight down to the base of her neck. She stood up and walked EJ and Molly to the hall, and as they left they kept saying "Rashad, Rashad," until I couldn't hear them anymore.

And before Ms. Webber came back in, someone in the back whispered, "Paul Galluzzo."

The other damn name that was all over the news. I turned around to see who it was, but everyone had his or her head down. I was pretty sure it'd been a guy, and I found myself looking at Rahkim and Malcolm and realized I was looking at the only two other black guys in class. I was pissed. I was pissed someone had said it, because I was sure they said it so I would hear, and I was pissed I was taking it to heart, and I was pissed I'd just done the same goddamn thing and had assumed it had been Rahkim or Malcolm, but I was pissed that I was pissed, because I was also pretty sure it had been one of them.

And mostly I was pissed because I just wanted everyone to shut up about it. Didn't talking about it just make it worse for all of us? Did everything have to be about Paul and Rashad?

I was still pissed after school when I got to the locker room, changed, and headed out to the court. Guys were already shooting and warming up. I stretched and bounced up and down on the sidelines, keeping to myself. That wasn't new. I like to avoid the early shoot-around, the chaos of just throwing the ball up and having it bounce out because someone else's shot smacked it away. I liked to find my rhythm on my own. I got loose with a ball and worked on my handling, sprinting up and down the sidelines with shadow fake-outs, keeping the legs loose as I popped a zigzag pattern back and forth, working the day out, so I could just concentrate on basketball.

Easier said than done, though. I couldn't get my head in the zone—and found myself keeping an eye on English and Shannon Pushcart, and I knew exactly why—they were tight with Rashad. I watched English spin circles around Tooms, moving so quickly he could have been on skates on ice. Shannon, Nam, Dwyer, and Guzzo and most of the rest of the team chased loose balls that bounced off the rim like popcorn. Nobody else seemed pissed off, though. Was I the only one looking out at every goddamn interaction on the court through the filter of Rashad and Paul? I didn't think so.

Coach gathered us at the bleachers, and the fifteen of us stacked up side by side in the first three tiers, as if we were having our photo taken. He paced back and forth as he gave us a speech about how everybody was saying it was our year, the newspapers, people in the league, even TV sports news was covering us. But who was he kidding? He was going crazy about it too.

"Now I know what you're thinking, boys, you're thinking about the scouts," Coach now said. "Who is coming when? When's that guy from UNC coming, right, English? Or is it Georgetown?" He bent toward him and grinned.

English glanced up at Coach and nodded.

"But you got to block out the bullshit," Coach said, choosing English again, this time pointing at him. Then he stood up and continued to pace. "If all you think about are the scouts, all you think about is yourself. Then we don't win. Then nobody wins." He paused. "You listening?" he barked.

"Yes, Coach," we grumbled back, but he just kept on talking, not waiting for our answer.

"Every day is the same day. We are one team, and we stop the other team from getting easy shots, and we work them hard as hell on the other end so they give *us* the easy shots. We do that as one team and we do that every day. You hear me?"

"Yes," we said.

"I said *you hear me?*"

"Yes!" We all shouted now.

"You hear me?" he boomed.

"YES!"

"Bring it in."

We jumped out of our seats and circled him, dropping our hands into the pile.

"TEAM on three. *One, two, three.*"

"TEAM!"

"That's right, bring it back in here." We were all bouncing and swaying, loose bodies with blood on fire. We got our hands back in the pile.

"Media shit's gonna hound us every day. You let me handle that. You just ignore that shit. There's all kinds of pressure going on out there, at school, in your lives back home. You leave it all at the door of this gym. In this gym we're only Falcons, you hear me?"

"YES!"

"Pack it in closer!"

We did as we were told.

"You tell me whose house this is."

"Our house!"

"Who are we?"

"FALCONS!"

"Who?"

"FALCONS!"

"Who?"

"FALCONS!"

"Team on three. *One, two, three!*"

"TEAM!"

That is what I wanted to believe too. I'd walked onto the court and seen the team like this: seven black guys, five white guys, two Latino guys, and one Vietnamese guy. But now, after Coach's rally, after we got into three lines and began the weave together, passing and running, passing and running, five balls whipping through the air between all this, dodging in and away from each other, fifteen guys moving like the connected parts of one heavy-breathing animal, I thought that maybe leaving all the shit behind at the door wasn't such bad advice. And hell, it wasn't my problem, really, right? Couldn't I leave it at the door wherever I went? Maybe we all should have tried to do that. It wasn't any of our problem. It was a problem of the law, and the law would work it out—isn't that what it was for, for God's sake? To take care of us?

And as I hustled to the sidelines and jumped into a full minute of foot fire, shouting the countdown from sixty with Coach, I kept wondering: Wouldn't we have been better off thinking that way? *All of us.* What did we really gain by talking about this—Paul, Rashad, what happened—digging it up and making everyone feel like shit?

Maybe for this one practice we were all thinking only about the team: one unit, one thing, no parts, one whole, no problems, just one goal for one team, none of us thinking about race or racism, all of us color-blind and committed like evangelicals to the word "team," just like Coach wanted.

Maybe. But I doubted it. That's what I *wanted* to think, but it wasn't what was in my mind or gut. Instead I knew there was a problem, and I was beginning to think I was a part of it—whether I was in the damn video or not.

RASHAD

There's this dude named Aaron Douglas. Scratch that. There *was* this dude named Aaron Douglas. A painter in the time of the Harlem Renaissance. Mrs. Caperdeen, my art teacher freshman year, turned me on to him during a lesson about artists from that period. Now, I had already been into art, way before Mrs. Caperdeen's class. I've been drawing since I was like five or six. It came from hanging out with my dad after church on Sundays. Well, Spoony and Ma would be there too, but for some reason, when I think back on it, it always seemed like it was just me and Dad, probably because we had our own thing. Our own after-church tradition. He would drive the whole family to this diner downtown. Ma would order the eggs and English muffin, Spoony always got the French toast, and me and

Dad both got pancakes. Then Spoony and Ma would go back and forth trading corny jokes, which I was usually all about, except on Sundays. Sundays was when I butted out and let the two of them have their dry humor because me and Dad, we had pancakes, coffee (hot chocolate for me), and the newspaper.

Dad, of course, would be *really* reading the newspaper. Politics, current events, sports, every single story. But he'd pull the comics section out and hand it to me. As I'm sure you can tell by now, my old man doesn't do funny all that well. But me, I loved the comics. All of them. But there was one in particular that struck me more than the others, and the funny thing is, I'm not really sure why. It definitely wasn't the funniest one. As a matter of fact, most times it wasn't funny at all. Not to me, at least. It was called *The Family Circus*. A brilliant name for a comic strip, even though the family in the comic wasn't much like a circus. They were pretty normal. And the strip wasn't really a "strip." It was just one image. One scene. Not like the others, which were made up of a whole bunch of different boxes, each one telling more of the story. I know you know what I mean. Everybody knows what comic strips look like. But this one, *The Family Circus*, was just one picture, in a circle. Not even in a box like normal comics. And it was all about this normal white family. Four kids, two parents, and a grandma. And nothing ever seemed to be happening. Like I remember this one, where the oldest son, Billy, and his younger siblings are watching their grandmother talk on the phone, and it just said, *Grandma's phone is really old-fashioned.* That's it. See? No punch line. Not funny, and if anything, it's actually pretty lame. But maybe that's why I liked them. Maybe I was fascinated by the fact that it seemed like white families, at least in comics, lived simple, easy lives. That, and also the images—I loved them. *Loved* them. And every Sunday after church I would tear *The Family Circus* out to save.

By the time I got to Mrs. Caperdeen's class, and by the time she taught the lesson about Aaron Douglas, I had collected like a thousand *Family Circus* clips. I stored them all in a shoe box under my bed and would go through them sometimes, just to pick one out to copy-sketch. And after a while, I got better at drawing and started making my own family cartoons in the same style. I called them *The Real Family Circus,* and most of them featured a cartoon version of my father shouting at a cartoon version of my brother. But when I saw Mr. Douglas's work, well, *The Family Circus* kinda went out the window. Aaron Douglas was doing a different thing, on a whole other level.

Let me describe what his work looks like. Imagine *The Lion King.* But all the lions are people. Black people. So Simba and Mufasa, are, let's say, a black king and a prince. Now, imagine that you're looking at them through the thickest fog ever. So thick that you can't make out any actually feature on their bodies, but you can still see their silhouettes. So it could be any king. Or any prince. But you can still tell they're black. That's Aaron Douglas's work. And the first time Mrs. Caperdeen showed us a slide from his series *Aspects of Negro Life,* I knew the kind of art I wanted to start making.

And so I did. The only difference was that I framed mine in a circle, like *The Family Circus.*

And that's why I needed Ma to make sure she brought me my sketch pad and pencils.

I woke up early, and before doing anything else, before getting up and having a morning pee, or brushing my teeth, or spirometering, I turned the TV on, muted it, then grabbed my stuff and starting sketching on a fresh page. I wasn't sure what I was drawing.

That's not true.

I knew *exactly* what I was drawing. The only thing I could. I was going to re-create the scene, what had happened to me, what was playing constantly on the news, on the page.

First the outline. A teenage boy. Hands up. No. Erase. Hands down. No. Hands behind his back. Outline of a figure behind him. Bigger than he is. Holding him around the neck. No. Not that. Fist in the air. No. Not that either. Hand pushing through the teenage boy's chest. A building behind him. A store. Person in the doorway. Cheering.

After the rough outline I started shading, which was the tricky part. See, in Aaron Douglas's work, there's always this haziness. This ghostliness to everything. But then there's also lots of light. As if light beams just break through certain parts of the paintings. I like that. But in order for me to get that look with pencils, I have to do a lot of shading. A lot of licking my finger and smearing the pencil lead to make a lighter gray on some parts of the paper, then scratch the pencil over and over again on some other areas to make darker marks. Like I said, tricky.

Clarissa came in in the middle of me rubbing my wet thumb on the paper, adding a little light to a dark area.

"Hey, there," she said, bringing in breakfast. "How we doing?"

"I'm cool," I said, smirking. Clarissa set the food down. Pancakes and fruit cocktail. She glanced at the pad, the black and gray smudges probably seeming like a crazy mess to her. Then she shot her eyes at the silent TV.

"So you're an artist, huh?" she said, her focus now back on my work.

"Yeah," I said.

"I knew it."

I looked at her curiously. "Oh yeah? How you know?"

"I don't know. I could just tell." She could just tell? Yeah right. What she really meant to say was, *I want to say something, but I don't know what to say.* Instead she followed with, "Mind if I look?"

"It's just the beginning," I prefaced, handing her the sketch pad.

Clarissa, who by the way couldn't have been much older than Spoony, maybe early twenties, white, freckles, bright-red hair, looked at the start of my new piece.

"What you gonna call it?"

"Don't know yet," I said, shrugging. Sheesh. Even that hurt.

"Well, it looks like it's gonna be good. I mean, not good because I mean, this whole thing, this, I mean . . ." She went bright red but soldiered on. "I just mean it looks like it's going to be nice. Nice art," she finished, handing the pad back to me.

"You've seen the news," I said, letting her off the hook.

Clarissa glanced at the TV again. Then back to me. She sighed. "Yeah. And . . . I think it's bullshit." She put her hand to her mouth, probably realizing that maybe nurses shouldn't curse. Not that that was *my* rule, it just seemed like it was probably discussed somewhere in the training that you might wanna refrain from using foul language around patients. I liked it, though, and even thought about responding with a *hell yeah it's bullshit!* but figured that would probably be a little too much. "I think it's just so . . ." Clarissa couldn't finish her statement. I nodded to let her know I understood and that I was having just as much trouble trying to figure it all out too. But one thing we could agree on was the part about it being bullshit.

To cut some of the discomfort that now surrounded us, I flipped through the pages in the sketchbook to show her some of my more finished pieces.

"This is what a completed piece looks like," I said, holding the pad up.

The image was of silhouettes of soldiers. Maybe twenty of them in a line, marching. At the back were babies. Marching. And they progressively got bigger, older, and right in the middle was the ultimate image of a strong soldier. And then they started getting smaller again, becoming a baby again.

"Wow," she said. "It's beautiful. Why do you frame them in a circle like this? Why not use the whole page?"

"Because, well, the circle changes how you see it. Like, what are we looking through? A telescope? A peephole? The sight of a gun?"

"I see," she said. "But how come none of them have faces?"

"I don't know. Maybe they're there, but they're not. Like, ghosts. Or invisible people," I said, instantly thinking that sounded dumb, but hoping Clarissa would just think I sounded artsy.

She nodded, then glanced at the TV again. It was like a

magnet. My face was on the screen. "Well listen here, Rashad, the artist," Clarissa said, low. "Don't forget what I said about getting up and moving around. It's important." She wagged her finger at me playfully. "I'll come back and check on you later."

I worked on the drawing for a while, until my hand started to cramp up, which is just one of those things that happen when you work with pencil. Seems like some genius would've figured out how to make pencils out of rubber or something a little softer, even though that's probably a silly thing to even think. But when your hand starts aching in the middle of such a personal piece, there's no telling what you might think about.

I put the pencil and pad down and decided to follow Clarissa's instructions and get up. But not only did I decide to get up, I decided to get the hell out of that empty, boring, beige hospital room. Room 409.

I climbed out of bed, snatched the back of my robe closed, and ventured out into the wild—not so wild—world of the hospital. I hunched over like an old man, protecting, I guess, my ribs—they hurt more when I stood straight. I eased slowly down the hall, each step pricking me inside, as I looked around at the nurses and the doctors and the families standing around the beds of their loved ones in the rooms with opened doors. Phones ringing. Machines beeping. Doors opening and closing. Soda cans dropping in vending machines.

Conversations about next steps and tests and surgeries. At the end of the hall was an elevator that happened to open the moment I got to it. A doctor got off, and I got on for no other reason than that it was there, open, waiting for me.

I hit the "1" button, and down to the first floor I went. Once the doors opened again, I found myself in the busiest part of the building, the main floor where people were checking in, doctors and nurses zipping back and forth to the cafeteria, and most importantly, where the gift shop was. It was the only thing remotely interesting. So, destination gift shop was in full effect.

It didn't take long for me to realize that hospital gift shops have terrible gifts. At least that one did. I mean, really bad gifts. Oh, so sorry you're in the hospital having your legs amputated. Know what'll make you feel better? A snow globe with a unicorn in it. Oh, so sorry to hear about your cancer. But I've got just the picker-upper. A refrigerator magnet of a lighthouse that says SPRINGFIELD. Ain't no lighthouses in Springfield, but who cares!

I poked around, looking at all the snacks (they did have good snacks), weird doodads, and whatnots, trying not to make any moves that were too sudden. It was more of a step-step-step, swivel head to the left, then to the right. Repeat. Nice and easy.

The woman behind the counter didn't seem to be paying

me any attention and instead was flipping through the newspaper. She had to be in her sixties. I could tell, not because she looked old—she didn't—but because she had all those little moles all over her face that only old black ladies get. My grandma had them.

"Can I help you?" she asked, catching me off guard. I threw my hands up and backed away from the assortment of plastic flowers.

"Just lookin', just lookin'," I said, wound up.

She zeroed in on me, smirked. "Relax, kid. I've been here long enough to know that no one steals from a hospital gift shop. And if someone did, well, hey, I can't blame them. We should be giving this stuff away."

I put my hands down, embarrassed. "Sorry."

"Never apologize when there's nothing to be sorry for." She put her eyes back on the newspaper, licked her thumb, then flipped the page. I just stood there like an ass, until she spoke again. "But seriously, do you need anything?"

I almost apologized again, but caught myself. Not sure why I was all sorry sorry sorry, all of a sudden. "Nope."

"So you just came to see me?" she asked sarcastically. And before I could say no, she demanded, "Say yes."

I nodded with a big grin on my face and walked toward the counter. "Yes," followed by the truth. "Honestly, I just needed to get out of my room."

"Yeah, I hear ya." She closed the paper and extended her hand. "Well, I'm Shirley Fitzgerald."

"Rashad." I squeezed her fingers lightly.

Mrs. Fitzgerald and I talked a while, but I didn't tell her anything about why I was in the hospital. At least, not the truth. I told her I got banged up in a car accident.

"Were you wearing your seat belt?" she asked predictably.

"Yep, thankfully." I felt bad lying to an old lady, but I had to. This was the most comfortable I had felt in a while. Turns out the best gift in the gift shop was the fact that it didn't have a TV. No news. No fuss.

After we got through why I was in the hospital, I asked Mrs. Fitzgerald how long she'd been working there.

"I don't even know. Maybe three or four years. Lost track. Wait, let me think. Frank died . . ." She started running through the timeline in her head. "Yeah, four years. Mercy, has it been that long?" She put her hand to her neck and fiddled with the gold chain she was wearing. A ring dangled from it. "My babies are grown. My grandbabies, too. And my husband has gone on to glory, so this is how I spend my time. I volunteer here a few days a week, and on my off days, I go and volunteer down at the firehouse."

"What you do down there?"

"I fight fires, what you think I do?" she snapped.

"Oh," I said, stunned. I mean, she was *old*. Like, too old

to be hosing down blazing houses, that's for sure. "That's cool."

"That's a lie, baby," she said, grinning, and flipping the newspaper back open, fanning through it until she got to the comics. The rest of my time with her was spent with me standing at the register and her reading funnies out loud, and either bursting with laughter, or totally shit-talking about how lame some of them were. Eventually, my body, waist up, started broiling on the inside, and I knew it was time to make my way back to the fourth floor.

"Come back and see me, Rashad. An old lady needs a little company every now and then," Mrs. Fitzgerald said.

"I will."

Around four o'clock, I had visitors. But it wasn't my family this time. It was my boys.

"Housekeeping," a light voice came from behind the door, after a tap. "Housekeeping." Then came the idiotic snicker of only one person—Carlos.

"Don't come in!" I yelled.

"Oh, come on, Rashad. I know how much you *love* housekeeping," Carlos said, lowering his voice ten notches below its normal tone. He pushed the door open and English,

Shannon, and Carlos filed in, backpacks and all.

"Oh man," Shannon said, instantly becoming serious when he saw me lying in the hospital bed, my face swollen, bruised, bandaged.

"Dude!" English came right behind him, shocked.

"It's nothing," I said.

"Nothing?" Now even Carlos was serious.

"Come on, y'all. I've gotten it from my family already. So just chill. I'm fine," I insisted. Carlos leaned against the wall. English and Shannon took the chairs. Their eyes, caught between bad and worse, bounced from me to the TV. *The Rashad Show*, on repeat. I tried to bait them back in. "Tell me about the party." Carlos was the first to bite, of course.

"Yo, guess who almost got some?" Carlos asked, a clownish smile spreading across his face.

"Who, English?" I replied.

Carlos shot me a mean mug. "Really? Really, 'Shad?" He lowered the lids of his eyes until they were almost closed, then popped them open wide and bawked, "Me, man! That dog bark thing totally worked! My game was on a million, man, I swear."

"Who was it?"

"Sweet, sweet Tiffany Watts." Carlos closed his eyes and puckered his lips as if he was remembering some passionate kiss.

I glared at Carlos. "*My* Tiffany Watts?"

"Yep, cartoon-character-looking Tiffany." Now he wrapped his arms around himself and swayed. Asshole. My heart stopped. That cop didn't kill me, but the thought of Carlos getting with Tiffany might be the fatal blow.

Shannon couldn't hold it in anymore and burst out laughing. Then Carlos flashed a toothy smile.

"Sike, man. You know I wouldn't do you like that. I know her Daffy Duck–lookin' ass is the love of your life," Carlos teased. When dealing with a clown like Carlos, the key is to never let him see you flustered. Never let him think you take him seriously. It's the opposite, come to think of it, of how we were trained to deal with police. With your friends, you *never* put your hands up. I have to admit, though, Los almost got me with that one.

"By the way, she asked about you today," Shannon said.

"Word? What she say?" I asked, eager.

"Just that she and a bunch of other people were thinking about coming to visit you," Shannon explained.

"No," I waved my hand, as if I was waving off the thought of Tiffany coming. "No one can come. I don't want nobody to see me like this."

"You sure?" Shannon asked.

"Yeah, man. Please. Tell everyone I'm fine. But no visitors." I caught eyes with each of them to make sure they knew I was serious. I didn't need anybody else standing in front of me all teary-eyed, or sitting on the edge of the bed feeling awkward. I'd already had enough of that

When I caught Carlos's eye, he jumped right back into form. "Man, can I finish *my* story?! Damn!" he said, all indignant.

"Yeah, yeah, go 'head," I said, trying to rush him along.

"So, the girl I got a little closer to was, drumroll please!"

"Come on, man," I huffed.

"You wanna know or not?"

"I don't really care."

"Just give me a drumroll, bro. C'mon."

I shook my head and started patting on my legs, doing my best to ignore the pricking feeling in my abdomen.

"Latrice Wilkes!" Carlos blurted this out like a dude squatting behind a couch waiting to yell *surprise* to an unsuspecting birthday boy. "Latrice 'Silky' Wilkes."

Now, Latrice Wilkes was no slouch. As a matter of fact, she was pretty much one of the coolest, prettiest girls in our class. And "Silky" really wasn't her nickname. That's just what we called her among each other, and I have no idea why.

"For real?" I was honestly surprised. I mean, Latrice was way out of Carlos's league. "Okay, okay, well, then why was it an *almost*?"

"Because . . ."

"Because then Latrice saw English," Shannon interjected, with perfect timing.

"Whatever! It's because the cops came and messed my whole groove up," Carlos shot back.

I laughed. Hard. Well, as hard as I could without feeling like my head was going to explode, or my ribs were going to rip through my chest. Once I finally got it under control, I said, "Well, listen, if it makes you feel any better, the cops messed my groove up too."

None of them laughed. Not one of them. You could almost feel the temperature of the room drop, like the way light dims whenever a cloud floats in front of the sun. I was that cloud. So I changed the subject. "Anyway, what else is going on at school?"

"Same ol' shit. You ain't miss much except for the fact that everybody's talkin' about you," Shannon explained.

"Yeah, you finally popular," Carlos mocked. I couldn't figure out if he was trying to bring the mood back to a lighter tone, or if he was just trying to make up for getting crushed by Shannon. Or both. "This *might* even land you an actual date with Tiffany."

"Please, I don't need no broken nose to get a girl." The mere mention of it made the bandage itchy. I scratched it super gently.

"Take what you can get, bro. It's an easy layup," Carlos replied.

"Too bad you didn't have all this layup knowledge when you were trying out for the team, huh?" I owed him a good one for the *I almost got with Tiffany* joke. Redemption.

"Yeah, whatever."

Me and Carlos went back and forth because it's what we do, but neither one of our hearts was in it. The jokes lacked punch. No zing. Just . . . flat. Like *The Family Circus*.

"Forget all that, man. When you getting outta here?" Shannon asked. He stretched his legs, crossed them at the ankles.

"The doctor just left right before y'all got here. He said my nose and ribs are healing fine, but they're still watching me because I got some internal bleeding. He said it hasn't gotten any worse, thank God, and that after a few more days I should be good to go."

"Sweet," Carlos said. Meant it.

"Cool," Shannon said.

English didn't say nothing. He just stared at the TV like he was in a trance.

"English, you good?" I asked.

"Yeah, yeah," he said, snapping out of it. "I just . . . I don't know, man. This is crazy. You know that's Guzzo's brother, right?"

"Guzzo?"

"Yeah, big giant goony kid on the team. His brother is the asshole who did this to you. Paul Galluzzo. That's why they call Guzzo, Guzzo. It's short for Galluzzo," English explained.

"Wait, you tellin' me the ogre-looking dude on the team, that's his brother?" I asked.

"That's exactly what I'm telling you."

"Has he said anything?"

"Not that I know of. Coach Carney won't let us talk about it," English explained. "Says we gotta focus on the team and our season, and that's it, and to leave all this stuff at the door. Said he'd bench anybody who brought it on the court."

"And you can't afford to be benched, dude. Especially since scouts are checkin' for you, hard," I said.

"Yeah. But it's just nuts."

"Yo, what I wanna know is, what the hell happened," Shannon jumped in. "Since Carney's made it clear that I ain't allowed to ask Guzzo, let me hear your side of the story. I mean, English told us what Berry said, but I wanna hear it from you."

That was my cue. I knew English had already heard most of it from his sister, but I still gave the fellas the play-by-play, hoping that somewhere in it, it would make sense. But it didn't. I grabbed a bag of chips, reached into my bag to grab my cell phone, a random lady tripped over me, and the next thing I know I was getting pressed out by the officer. There really wasn't anything else to the story as far as I was concerned. The cop and the clerk thought I was stealing and wouldn't give me a chance to explain.

"Did you resist?" Shannon asked.

"Why would I resist? C'mon, man, you know I was shook. Ain't no way I was resisting," I said. "And when he got me on the ground, that's when he really started going in. Like, every time he hit me, I would move—who wouldn't—it *HURT!*— and then he'd tell me to stop moving. But I couldn't help it."

"Shit," Carlos said, his eyes full wide.

English was staring at the TV again, his face now becoming a fist, tight and angry. The room was stifling with a weird tension, this strange sadness, when finally Shannon spoke up. "English."

English didn't respond.

"English!" Shannon snapped.

"What?" he snapped back. And that's when I could tell this whole thing was getting to him. It was stirring him up inside in a way that I had never seen before. I mean, this was English Jones, the coolest dude on Earth.

English braced his hands on either arm of the chair, and for a second I thought he was going to throw it. But then he drew a deep breath and simply said, "We got practice. We gotta go."

He looked from Shannon to me, his eyes slightly glassy. He stood up. Shannon stood with him.

"Yo, what we gonna do about this?" Carlos asked, watching English and Shannon grab their bags. He ran his finger along his nose like he always did when he was thinking of something he probably shouldn't have been thinking of.

"I don't know. But I'm telling you, Coach ain't playing," Shannon said, flinging his bag up on his shoulder.

"Just leave it alone," I said.

"Naw, man, we gotta do something, 'Shad. I mean, maybe you can't do nothing, 'cause you in here. And maybe these two can't do nothing because of punk-ass Carney. But I'm not on the team." Carlos caught my eye and stopped me from cracking a basketball joke before I could even open my mouth. "So *I* can do something. *Somebody* gotta do something."

"Los, just don't be stupid," English warned, coming over to the bed and giving me five.

Carlos didn't respond. Instead he just asked me if I wanted him to stay. Carlos didn't have anywhere to be. He never had anywhere to be.

"Naw, I'm cool," I said. "I'm sure my parents and my crazy brother will be by here later."

"Word," from Carlos.

"We'll be back tomorrow," from Shannon, reaching out for my hand.

Only a nod from English. And then it was just me, the TV, and the shadows, fades, and outlines of my art again. I thought about the fact that English and Shannon wanted to do something but were afraid to break the rules. I understood. I did. But the look on English's face was a look I had never seen. He was struggling with it all. Maybe it was what happened to me that was eating him. Or maybe it was the fact that he felt like he couldn't do anything about it. And then I thought about what kind of ridiculous plan Carlos might cook up. I just didn't want him to put himself in some stupid situation where he got his ass beat too. Even though I hadn't had to put myself in any "situation" for that to happen.

I glanced at the TV. My face, again. Wasn't there anything else going on? I mean, there had to be something going on in the Middle East, right? Celebrity drama? Anything besides me?

I wasn't sure what to do about any of it, or if I even wanted anyone else to do anything on my behalf. The looks on my friends' and family's faces—it hurt me to see them that way. Especially knowing that it hurt them to see me this way. I didn't deserve this. None of us did. None of us.

I grabbed the remote, pointed it at the screen, and hit the power button to click it off. But it didn't go off. I clicked it again. Nothing. I slapped the remote in my palm a few times, because that's what you do to, I guess, activate the batteries. Clicked again. Nothing.

Now, split screen. Galluzzo's face, next to mine. Him in his uniform. Me in mine. But we were not the same. We were *not* the same.

I didn't deserve this. *Click.* Nothing. *Click.* Nothing. My eyes began to well up and my throat suddenly felt scorched, as if I had swallowed fire. *Click. Click. Click. Click.* Nothing. Fuck. *Click.* Please. Please turn off. *Please.* His face. Next to mine. I didn't do nothing. I didn't do nothing. His face. Made my bones hurt. A scrapy feeling in the marrow stuff. Fuck. *Click.* Nothing. *Click.* NOTHING. I couldn't take it anymore, and before I did something stupid like throw the remote across the room, smashing it into hundreds of plastic pieces that I wish were Galluzzo's face, I leaped from the bed in a panic and yanked the cord from the wall, which turns out was also stupid because it felt like giant hands that I couldn't see were ripping me in half.

But the TV was off. My face next to his, gone. Finally.

Tuesday

QUINN

On Tuesday morning, everything changed—*for real.* Spray painted in wide, loopy neon-blue letters like a script of stars so bright they glowed in the day, and stretched so large it covered the entire sidewalk at the foot of the front stairs, was a graffiti tag. A tag so huge every single student, teacher, administrator, staff member, parent, and visitor to Springfield Central had to step over or around, and could not miss:

RASHAD IS ABSENT AGAIN TODAY

Everybody was staring at it, taking photos of it, posing with it, and definitely talking about it. As soon as I saw it, I felt a ball of shredded nerves unwind and whip around my stomach. *Oh shit!* And my first thought was, probably just like everyone else's: Who'd done it?

At first you could tell the teachers were deliberately avoiding discussing it, but it was pretty much all we (the students) talked about between classes or at lunch. I say "we," but I was still trying to take Coach's advice and ignore all distractions, so when it came up, I tried not to engage. But it was frigging impossible. At lunch, kids were taking food from the cafeteria and heading out to the front steps, eating and talking while sitting near the giant graffiti tag, but I avoided that and looked for some of the guys on the team in the cafeteria. We'd always sat together at lunch, only in fragments, never the whole team together, but with the impromptu gathering out front, everything had shifted.

Only Guzzo, Dwyer, Hales, and Reegan sat inside—the four other white guys on the team. Guzzo looked up and saw me in line. He waved me over to their table, and although he'd ignored me all day yesterday, his interest now kind of ticked me off. See, that wasn't Guzzo's style. Usually, he'd let others call the shots. But today he was too insistent, beckoning me like he was some kind of Mafia boss and I was supposed to hustle right over to him.

And besides, once I had my sad, soupy Sloppy Joe on the tray and looked out over the rest of the cafeteria, I realized it wasn't just the basketball team divided up this way today.

Paul had once told me about how the city's demographics had changed over the last thirty years, and why that mattered for his job. "It's harder to be a cop here now than it used to be," he'd said, and his facts had been so particular I couldn't help but think of them now as I looked across the deserted tables in the half-empty room. Thirty years ago the city had been 84 percent white, Paul'd told me. Now, not counting Hispanics and Latinos who identified as white, Springfield was 37 percent white. Strange how some of that stuff just sticks to you, especially the shit that suddenly feels so real. Because right now, only about half the high school who had lunch fifth period sat in the cafeteria that day. The white half.

I would have stood there like an idiot, feeling those nerves in my stomach start to spin again, if I hadn't felt a push from behind.

"Hey," Jill said.

"Hey."

"Where you sitting?"

It was probably the first time since I'd been in high school that I'd ever been asked that question. I'm not a total fucknut. I know for some people, especially at the beginning of high school, where to sit and who you'll sit with is a big deal. Not everyone feels like they automatically belong. Not everyone feels like wherever they go they'll be welcome. But I did. I'd always just walked into the cafeteria and sat wherever the hell

I wanted. In fact, I did that pretty much anywhere I went unless the seats were already assigned.

"Um." I paused. "Not sure."

"Yeah, but you know what's weird? I want to go sit outside."

"Me too," I said, only realizing when she had said it that that's what I really *did* want to do. "But would that be weird?"

"I just *said* it was weird! But I don't think anyone out there would mind."

Huh. I hadn't thought of it like that. I'd been thinking of the guys inside. "No," I said, nodding to Guzzo's table. "Those dudes."

Guzzo probably realized what we were talking about, because he got up and walked over to us. "You two going to stand there all day? Come sit down." And once he had come over, it felt impossible not to follow him, so we did.

Dwyer, Hales, and Reegan got lost in a conversation about their fantasy basketball league teams while Guzzo pressed us. "Seriously," he said. "You two are spending a lot of time together."

Jill laughed. "You guys are all family to me."

"Quinn's not," Guzzo said, looking at me, but in an odd way. "Not really. Or is he?"

"I'm right here, man. No need to be all cold about it."

"I'm not the one who ran away from the barbecue."

"Jesus. Seriously? You're crying about that?"

He opened his mouth to say something more, but Jill interrupted him. "Guys, you've been at it since Friday. I've seen it."

This shut us both up. I bit into my hash brown, but it was so greasy, I just ended up shoving the whole thing in my mouth. While I chewed, Guzzo gave me that look again. "Quinn's the one acting weird."

"Come on," Jill said. "It's not only him. You are too. But why not? I would be too if I had been there and seen Paul whaling on Rashad."

"What the fuck?" Guzzo threw his plastic fork down on his tray. "Shut up about that." Hales glanced over skeptically, and Guzzo leaned in close to us. "Did you tell anyone else?" he asked her.

"That you were there?" she said. "No. Is it a secret?"

"Of course!" Guzzo said. His hand clenched into a fist. "You told her?" he said to me. "Are you fucking demented? Nobody should know about this. Not even my brother."

"What?" I said. "Man, we aren't in any trouble. We didn't do anything."

"You really are stupid," Guzzo said, picking his fork back up and pointing it at me. Red bits of Sloppy Joe dripped from the tines. "Don't tell anyone else we were there. The force, they're worried for my brother. They've given him some time so he can stay off the streets. There's probably going to be a lawsuit because there's always a lawsuit these days. Look, whatever, how the hell is he supposed to do what he needs to do if he gets sued for just doing his job?"

"Listen to you!" Jill exclaimed, leaning in now too, agitated. "You sound like our mothers. But tell that to Rashad's family. Rashad's *absent* today. Again. I mean, I know that guy too."

Guzzo looked disgusted. "You don't know him," he said, waving her off. "You just like thinking you know him because now he's a celebrity. A celebrity-victim, or whatever. That's bullshit." He gestured to the doors behind us. "You need to get outside before next period? Was that where you were headed before I called you over?"

I glanced at Jill. "Dude," I said to Guzzo. "Come on. It doesn't have to be like that."

"It already is like that, asshole," Guzzo said. He pushed his chair back and stood up. "*You* know. Paul was just trying to help someone inside the store. That's what he says. And then there's the whole stopping people from stealing thing." He was breathing heavy. Fighting to find words. "And, by the way," he finally said, pointing at me, "Paul's staying with us, you know. If you're curious. Remember him? My brother? The dude who fucking *raised* you. Feel free to drop by. I mean, you are like *family*. Isn't he, Jill?"

For once in her life, Jill didn't shoot back the last word, and Guzzo stalked off without looking back at either of us. I was about to get up too, because I was sick of it all—I hadn't started it, why the hell did I have to be in the middle of it? But as I pushed my own chair back, Dwyer grabbed my arm.

"Listen, man," he said. "You've got to fix this. We got to get the team straight. We've got scouts coming, man. This is too big. This is our life, man. Our futures. Don't be a dick about it. Like Coach said. Leave it at the door. All of it, you know?"

What he said stuck with me for the rest of the day. Yeah, I was thinking about the damn scouts too—of course I was! The kind of doors a scout's praise might open. The kinds of scholarships a kid like me needed when Ma was working night shifts over at Uline. I knew it was my future, and Dwyer's, and everyone else's, too. How could I not? It'd been on my mind in one way or another since I'd started working out with Paul—back when he was taller than me, not just bigger, flicking his wrists and teaching me how to sneak a crossover right in front of my opponent. Those hands. There was so much history slapping hands and saying yes to Paul.

As what Dwyer had said to me replayed again and again in my head, it began to say something else, too. Like maybe I was hearing what Dwyer was saying under his breath, between his words. He almost sounded scared, or not scared, but nervous. It wasn't Dwyer. It was fear. It seemed to follow me like my shadow these days, but I recognized now how it was trailing everyone else, too.

At practice, Coach had us running like crazy. Hales got so winded he puked in the trash can by the door to the hallway. "Boot and rally," Reegan yelled to him. He wanted to laugh but he was too out of breath. The rest of us crouched with our hands on our knees, or folded on our heads, trying to avoid cramps, and Coach paced in between us like he was a doctor walking through the asthma ward.

"Game ready," he lectured. "The team that makes its free throws when everyone is tired and strung out is the team that wins its games." Then he broke us into groups at the six baskets around the gym and told us to keep score. Ten free throws each, switching shooters every two shots. The score mattered. He didn't say it, but this was part of the evaluation to see who would be a starter. Who could get points on the board at the beginning of the game, and at the end of the game, when his legs were jelly and his lungs a fire collapsing. A scout might be the key to your future, but you had to be on the court, in a pressure situation, sticking it to the other team, in order for the scout to even see you. Then you had to make the shot. I missed my first shot, but it was the only one I missed. There were plenty of seven out of tens, some lower. Only English scored a perfect ten.

We spent another hour practicing some plays, putting them into action in little scrimmages, and then Coach sent us to the weight room in pairs. We didn't have to keep score here. Not for his sake, at least. Of course we kept score among ourselves.

Nobody could press or lift or squat nearly as much as Guzzo and Tooms and Martinez, so they always had their own competition, and the rest of us had ours. I paired up with English, and we started on the leg machines while the big guys hit the bench. He and I didn't say much at first, but as we moved around the room to different machines, we got into what was really on both our minds.

"Hey, man," I asked. "You know who wrote that graffiti?"

"Why are you asking me?" he said.

"He's your friend, man."

"He has a lot of friends."

"Come on, man. I'm just curious. I'm just asking."

"Nah. It can't be 'just asking.' It never is."

"Fine." I put another five pounds on either side of the bar for him, and then kept my voice low as I continued. "Guzzo's pissed. He thinks someone did it to make a statement."

English cocked half a grin as he lay down beneath the bar and began his set. "Of course. That's the point."

"No, but like, it's saying that Rashad is innocent, so that makes his brother guilty."

English put the bar back up on the rack and sat up. He looked at me like I was nuts. "Man, Rashad didn't do shit."

"Yeah, but what if Paul was just doing his job? Then no one's guilty." But even as I said it, I felt like I was Guzzo suddenly, or someone in the family, his family, and I wished I wasn't. "Ah, never mind. Let's just forget it."

"Forget it? Forget my friend is in the hospital?" English stared at me, pissed. "Since when is beating the shit out of somebody who hasn't done a damn thing *just doing your job*? Man, there's no way I'm going to pretend it didn't happen." He leaned back, looked at the ceiling, and pressed the weight back up. "I can't." He brought the weight down, and then up again. "I won't."

He lifted the bar again quickly, but on the eighth rep, he struggled.

"Look," I said, reaching out, ready to help him with the next rep. "I just wish this wasn't happening. I mean, for everyone's sake."

He fought to get the ninth rep more than halfway up.

"You need a hand?" I said, putting my fingers beneath the bar, helping him lift it slightly.

"Fuck no," he spat. I pulled my fingers back but kept them close. He pushed the bar up slowly, then lowered it and began the last rep. He grunted and got the last one up and onto the rack.

"Maybe he got out of hand?" I just had to say. "Maybe he was on drugs."

"On drugs? What are you? Seventy-five? Since when have

you ever gotten off your ass, let alone thrown a punch, when you were stoned, man?"

"Meth?"

"Only white people do that shit."

"Fuck you, man."

"No, fuck you, Quinn." He stood and pointed at me. "Why does it automatically gotta be Rashad's fault? Why do people think he was on drugs? That dude doesn't do drugs. He's ROTC, man. His dad would kick his ass. *You* do drugs, asshole."

"Just a puff here and there, man, come on. I don't *do* drugs."

"I've seen you smoking a blunt. Metcalf sold you that shit. Metcalf—a white dude, by the way. Man, that shit could have been laced with crack, or fucking Drano. You don't know what you talkin' 'bout."

"Look, man, I'm not trying to say anything bad about Rashad. I'm just saying that spray painting 'Rashad is absent again today' on the concrete in front of school is like, I don't know, extreme. He's not dead."

"But he *could* be. You have no idea. You have no idea, Quinn. The point is, he could be. Then what? Is that what it would take to look at this thing differently? You need him to be dead? Shame on you, man. I had no idea you were such a dick. You want to forget all this. Maybe you can. But I won't." He stood and caught his breath. "What do you know, anyway?

White boy like you can just walk away whenever you want. Everyone just sees you as Mr. All-American boy, and you can just keep on walking, thinking about other things. Just keep on living, like this shit don't even exist." He waved his hand in my face and blew a breath out the side of his mouth. "Man, I'm done with you." Then he sauntered off slowly, making sure I knew he was dismissing me, leaving me looking like the idiot I was.

When Coach called us back out to the court, I was now not just physically wiped, but mentally wiped too. I was getting a drink of water at the fountain and Guzzo came up behind me. He jabbed me in the back and I coughed up the water. He laughed. "Thanks," he said, grinning. "I mean it. I heard all that with English. Thanks for having Paul's back."

An unexpected wave of anger surged through me. That hadn't been my intention at all. I'd seen what Paul had done. I didn't think it was right. But I hadn't thought the spray paint was right either.

"Maybe somebody should spray paint something else tomorrow," Guzzo said. "Whaddya think it should say?"

"Don't," I said.

"What?"

"Don't be an asshole."

Guzzo slapped the wall with his open palm. "I don't fucking get you, man. One minute you're in there defending my brother and the next you are basically telling me to fuck off. You're demented." He stomped off to join the huddle at half-court.

Thank God Coach didn't try to get us all together in a rallying cry, because I sure as hell wasn't up for it, but neither was anyone else, probably. Instead he broke us into two teams of five and put the others on the bench, ready to sub in. I was on the same team as English, and before we began I pulled him aside.

"Look," I said. "I'm sorry, man. I sounded like an idiot." He didn't say anything back. "No, seriously. I'm sorry. I don't want to be a dick. I'm just trying to figure this all out. Rashad's your friend. But I get what else you're saying too. So—I'm sorry."

"Man, you have no idea how many times you've sounded like a dick. You think it was just today? Look," he said, passing me the ball hard. "Just don't miss when I give you the ball."

But I did. When we got into the scrimmage, I popped free and missed the first open shot. I got another chance on a fast break, and I could have passed, but I forced a difficult shot because I'd missed the last one. I missed that one too. Coach called me over. "Where's your head?"

"Up my ass," I blurted.

"What?" He grabbed my arm. "What did you say?"

"My head," I said. "It's up my ass. I don't know what the hell I'm doing."

"Maybe a couple suicides will wipe the shit off your face. Do them. Two. Along the sideline. Now. Go."

I didn't have to look at Guzzo to know he was smiling all smug, watching me out of the corner of his eye while he continued playing. I think English was maybe smiling too.

And for the first time since I could remember, as I sprinted up and down the court, I didn't have my father's voice in my head. I heard my own. I wasn't telling myself to *PUSH*, or to go *FASTER*. Instead I thought about the guy who'd just said all those things to English. The guy who hadn't meant to sound hurtful. The guy who was just trying to walk down the middle and not disturb anybody, basically give some meaning to what I'd seen in the street outside Jerry's. And here's what I realized I was saying beneath it all: I didn't want my life to change from the way it was before I'd seen that.

When I finished the suicides, I had to hold my hand against the wall to catch my breath. English was frigging right. The problem was that my life *didn't* have to change. If I wanted to, I could just keep my head down and focus on the team, like Coach wanted, and that could be that. Isn't that what I wanted?

Then why did it feel so shitty?

I had to squat down and touch the floor, feeling suddenly

nauseous, nauseous at the idea that I could just walk away from everything that was happening to Rashad, everything that was happening to Paul, everything that was happening to everyone at school, everything that was happening to me, too. I could just walk away from it all like a ghost. What kind of a person did that make me, if I did?

Those were Ma's words, and when I got home, I found myself, for the first time in a long time, also admitting that I wished she was home and not working. Of course, that made me feel like a goddamn kid, so I made myself feel like I was worth something by helping Willy with his homework. He was glad for it, but probably not as much as I was that he needed me and I could actually help him figure out his fractions.

Later, though, my mind drifted back to Rashad, and I totally blew dinner. It should have been simple. I'd made mac and cheese with tuna, peas, and hot sauce more times than I could count, but I overcooked the pasta and there was way too much hot sauce. Willy fanned his mouth after the first bite.

"Ahhh," he said. "Are you trying to kill me?"

I improvised by shredding some extra cheddar cheese into our bowls, and guiltily, I felt glad that he had his headphones on—though Ma would have killed him for that stunt at the dinner table—because my thoughts would not let up.

Now I was thinking about how, if I wanted to, I could walk away and not think about Rashad, in a way that English or Shannon or Tooms or any of the guys at school who were not white could not. Even if they didn't know Rashad, even if, for some reason, they hated Rashad, they couldn't just ignore what happened to him; they couldn't walk away. They were probably afraid, too. Afraid of people like Paul. Afraid of cops in general. Hell, they were probably afraid of people like me. I didn't blame them. I'd be afraid too, even if I was a frigging house like Tooms. But I didn't have to be because my shield was that I was white. It didn't matter that I knew Paul. I could be all the way across the country in California and I'd still be white, cops and everyone else would still see me as just a "regular kid," an "All-American" boy. "Regular." "All American." White. Fuck.

But then, after dinner, as I was helping Willy with the last of his math homework, I realized something worse: It wasn't only that I could walk away—I already *had* walked away. Well, I was sick of it. I was sick of being a dick. Not watching the damn video was walking away too, and I needed to watch it.

I borrowed Willy's headphones, plugged them into my phone, loaded up YouTube, and I watched it right there at the kitchen table. It was the shaky video taken from across the street at Jerry's and I was immediately back at Friday night, watching it happen all over again. There were two other videos too. I watched Rashad's body twisting on the concrete sidewalk. The video was taken from too far away. I couldn't hear what he was saying, I couldn't hear Paul. I heard the noise of the street just as I'd heard it that night, and I felt a zip line of fear rip right into the pit of my stomach. On Friday I'd been down the street, watching. But there, at the Formica table, I had a front-row seat. Close to Rashad and Paul. I could almost see myself hovering just beyond the frame of the shot. I texted Jill and told her how bizarre it was to see it.

> TUESDAY 9:43 p.m. from Jill
> FINALLY. NOW EVRYBDYS SEEN IT

We went back and forth a few times, and then I just got fed up.

> TUESDAY 9:55 p.m. to Jill
> HEY. CAN YOU TALK?

> TUESDAY 9:56 p.m. from Jill
> WHA?

> TUESDAY 9:56 p.m. to Jill
> NO. I MEAN IT. ON THE PHONE. TALK?

TUESDAY 9:57 p.m. from Jill
WHATEVER

TUESDAY 9:57 p.m. to Jill
LIKE, I NEED TO TALK.

She buzzed a second later, and I got up, slid the headphones across the table to Willy, and left the kitchen. We said our hellos and all that as I walked into the living room.

"I feel so gross," I said. "I keep telling myself it isn't my problem. But it is. It is my problem. I just don't know what to do."

"Yeah, but it isn't only your problem. It's everyone's problem."

"But I still don't know what to do. Like, tell the police?"

She paused, and I heard her breathe. "Maybe."

"Jesus." Telling the police meant telling Paul's friends. Meant Paul's friends telling *him* what I was doing.

"But everyone's seen it, Quinn. It's *all our* problem. But what *is* that problem?" Then it was my turn to be quiet, and I shuffled over to the couch and sat down. "What is it?" Her voice rose. "Excessive violence?"

"I don't know. Unnecessary beating. Uh . . . shit, police brutality?"

"Yeah."

"And, you know. The way it's all working out. It's more."

"Like who was sitting where at lunch?"

I looked at the carpet between my feet. "Yeah."

"And whose lockers they looked in first for spray paint cans?"

"Yeah. Shit, really? That happened?"

"That's what I saw. Three black students, boys, in a row. Then Martinez. They skipped me!"

"Fuck!" I let the air in my cheeks fill and then slowly blow out. "So yeah. Like all that."

"Like Paul's white and Rashad's black."

I just sat there staring at the door to the kitchen like a dumbass zombie trying to find some words.

"Paul says he did what he did because he was protecting some white lady in the store," Jill added.

"What?"

"Yeah. That's what my mom says. But, uh, really?"

"Seriously."

"You think it would have been the same if the lady wasn't white, or if Rashad wasn't black?"

"Seriously."

"Seriously, what?"

"Why is it taking me five minutes to say the word racism?"

"Maybe you're racist?"

"Don't joke. This is serious."

"I'm not."

"I'm not racist!"

She hesitated, and I sat there, stinking in my own sweat, needing her to say something. Eventually she did.

"Not like KKK racist," she said. "I don't think most people think they're racist. But every time something like this happens, you could, like you said, say, 'Not my problem.' You could say, 'It's a one-time thing.' *Every time* it happened."

I wanted to say something, but it was like my head just pounded and every word that came to mind just shook and fell back into my throat.

"I think it's all racism," Jill said for me.

"And if I don't do something," I finally mustered, "if I just stay silent, it's just like saying it's not my problem."

"Mr. Fisher spent our whole history class talking about it. If anybody wanted to talk about it more after school, he would. Me and Tiffany talked about it all day, so we went. There were a bunch of us there, and Fisher's helping us figure out what to do."

"I wish I could have gone. But I had basketball. But I have to do something!"

"Let's see what other people are doing tomorrow."

We said our good-byes, and I sat there on the couch, staring into the kitchen looking at Willy. His head bent down so close to the paper he was scribbling his answers on, the red headphones like beacons on either side of his head—it was like he was buried deep within his own little world. I felt like I'd been doing the same damn thing the last couple days— trying to stare so hard at my own two feet so I wouldn't have to look up and see what was really going on. And while I'd been doing that, I'd been walking in the wrong direction.

I didn't want to walk away anymore.

RASHAD

A s the story of sixteen-year-old West Springfield native Rashad Butler develops, the city seems to be split in terms of which side of the argument they fall on in this case. Was it about race? The abuse of power? Or was it just another case of a teenage criminal, caught red-handed? For those who are just joining us, we've been covering this story for a few days now. Last Friday, Butler was accused of shoplifting, public nuisance, and resisting arrest. The officer involved, Paul Galluzzo, is shown here forcibly removing Butler from Jerry's Corner Mart. Butler seems to be cooperating with the officer, but as you can see, he is taken to the ground. Warning: The rest of the scene is a bit graphic. We were able to catch up with Claudia James, the person who actually shot this footage from her phone."

"It was just like y'all saw it. That boy was being man-handled, and he kept saying that he didn't do nothing. He kept trying to explain. But the officer was just yelling, 'Shut up! Shut up!' And then slammed him. Then once he had him on the ground he started, like, punching and kneeing him in the back. He shoved his forearm on the back of the boy's neck. It was crazy."

"But had he been handcuffed?"

"Once he was on the ground, he was. I mean, how could he have been resisting?"

"But not everyone shares Ms. James's view. Some people feel that whatever it takes to clean up the community, so be it. Like Roger Stuckey."

"We don't know what happened in that store, so I'm not gonna sit here and just say this kid is innocent. He might not be. I'm a cabdriver, and I work nights, and the truth is, if that kid was trying to hail me down, and it was dark outside, I would keep on going."

"And why is that? Because of the way he looks?"

"I mean, listen, I've been robbed before. Right around here. And I just . . . I don't ever want to be robbed again. And he looks like the guy who robbed me. He was dressed just like him. These kids are crazy these days, and whatever it's gonna take to make the people who live around here feel safe, I'm all for it."

When I woke up, I followed the same routine as the day before. Well, not exactly the same. First I plugged the TV back in. Then I tried to turn it on, but the remote was still on the fritz. Sometimes when the batteries are getting weak, and smacking it against your palm doesn't work, you have to slide the back off and run your thumb over the batteries to turn them, and that makes them work. Sometimes. This time.

The TV came on and I watched for a minute. Everyone had opinions. The lady who caught the incident on tape seemed to side with me and thought the cop was wrong. But not everybody felt that way. There was a cabbie who straight up said he wouldn't pick me up if he saw me at night. That really pissed me off. I mean, I had heard Spoony talk about that for years. I never took cabs (the bus was cheaper), but he was always going on and on about how he could never catch a cab because of the way he looked. But I didn't look nothing like Spoony. Nothing. I mean, I wear jeans and T-shirts, and he wears jeans and T-shirts, so we look alike in that way, but who doesn't wear jeans and T-shirts? Every kid in my school does. And sneakers. And sweatshirts. And jackets. So what exactly does a kid who "looks like me" look like? Seriously, what the hell?

You would think I would cut the TV off, but I didn't. Maybe because there was something about having this moment in my life, literally hovering above my head, that served as some kind of weird inspiration for the picture I was making. So, as usual, I muted it, then dove into my art. Oatmeal for breakfast. Chicken burrito for lunch. Ginger ale. Art in between it all.

Clarissa had been in and out of the room, checking my vitals. Checking to make sure I was eating and using my spirometer. Checking to see how the piece was coming along.

"It's gonna be so good when it's done," she said, jotting down my blood pressure. She looked exhausted.

"You work every day?" I asked, shrugging off her compliment. It's not that I was trying to be rude. I just didn't really know if "good" was how this piece was actually going to end up.

"I have been. I usually work every other day, twelve-hour shifts. But I took on some extra work this week. Covering for a friend."

It wasn't hard to tell that that's just how Clarissa was. A for-real, for-real nice person. So when she brought the lunch in, I told her how thankful I was that she had been looking after me, and how happy I was that she had taken those extra shifts. My mother always raised me to be thankful. She always said, nobody owes you anything, so when you get something, be appreciative. And I was.

"I mean, I know it's your job, but you're really good at it. So, thanks."

Clarissa flashed a smile that slipped into an unexpected yawn. "It's my pleasure. Just trying to add a little sunshine," she said, lifting a hand to her mouth. She was so sweet, but man was she corny!

"I hear ya. Well, you're doing that. Every time you come in here, you brighten the whole room up. Maybe it's the hair."

The red hair up against her pale skin, like fire burning at the end of a match.

"Ah, yes. Ginger magic," she joked. "You know, I'm the last of a dying breed."

"What you mean?"

"I mean, gingers. Redheads. We're going extinct."

"Seriously? Like something is killing y'all?"

"Not exactly. It's like, not enough redheads are having babies with other redheads. So we're just not being born anymore." Clarissa laughed, then glanced up at the muted TV. Her eyes narrowed. "Check it out."

I looked up, reluctantly, and there on the screen was the police chief. So I unmuted. We listened. He didn't really say much except that they were investigating everything and that he had "the utmost faith in Officer Galluzzo's judgment" and that the officer was "a veteran with an immaculate record."

"Yeah, I bet," Clarissa said. Then, noticing me taking it all in, she added, "Hey, don't let the bastards get you down."

"Yeah."

"You know that song?"

"What song?"

"Don't let the bastards—" She stopped, grinned. "Never mind."

When Ma showed up, the TV was still unmuted. And the story was still *developing*. And I was still drawing.

"Knock, knock," Ma said, tapping the door frame. Clarissa had asked me if I wanted the door open or closed, and I told her open. It just seemed like a good idea to let some air in. Or maybe let some of the suffocating feeling of the room out.

"Hey," I said, now a bed remote expert, adjusting it so that I was sitting more upright.

"How you feeling?" Ma asked, coming in. She was alone.

"I'm fine. Just doing some drawing," I told her. "Where's Dad?"

She kissed me on the forehead, then sat on the side of the bed. "He couldn't make it. Something upset his stomach, and he was throwing up all night."

"Is he okay?"

"Yeah, yeah, he's fine," she said. She dug in her purse, pulled out an envelope, and set it on the side table. "This came to the house for you."

"Who's it from?"

"It's from Chief Killabrew." I nodded but didn't say anything. I figured it was a get-well-soon card, or something like that. Couldn't even read it because my mother was way more concerned with more pressing issues. "Have you eaten?"

"Yes, Ma, I ate. Breakfast and lunch," I said with a groan. I knew this was only the beginning of the mother questions. It's like all moms have a checklist that they read through to make sure their kids are okay.

1. *Have you eaten?* The most important one.
2. *Are you hungry?* Not to be confused with #1. And asked even if you say you've eaten.
3. *Have you pooped?* Just to make sure you're eating the right stuff.
4. *Have you bathed?*
   And if you're my mom,
5. *What are you drawing?*

I handed her the notebook. She looked at it and instantly started to get emotional, her eyes tearing up. She was blinking them back when a clip of Claudia James, the lady who taped the whole thing, came back on the screen.

My mother watched, still holding the sketch pad.

"You know, some people think the cop was justified. They say he was just doing his job," I said, darting my eyes from the TV to my mother.

She looked at me. Her face looked like it was made of clay. Like it could crack at any second.

"His *job*?" she said, the tears finally dropping. "You are not a criminal, Rashad. I know that. I know every word you said was true. You didn't deserve this. You're not a criminal," she repeated. I could feel the heat rising in the room. In her. I didn't know how she had been dealing with this at home, or if she and Dad had been getting into it, or what. But in that moment, the water in the kettle had finally started to boil in front of me. My mother was steaming.

"You're not some animal that they can just hunt. You're not some punching bag, some thing for them to beat on whenever they feel like it," she said, slapping my sketchbook down. She continued to lose her battle with the tears. "This is *not* okay," she said. It was the first time I had ever heard her say it—usually it was Spoony. "It's *not*. It's *not* okay." The TV cut back to the police chief. He said Galluzzo would be placed on paid leave until they got to the bottom of this. My mother clenched her jaw as the chief spoke. Then they flashed

Galluzzo's face on the screen. Ma's breath caught when she saw his mug on the screen. "That asshole," she growled.

Here's the thing: My mother almost never curses. I think I may have heard her say "damn," maybe once, but that's really it. She's just not that type. So to hear her say "asshole" let me know how angry she really was, that this thing was breaking her down inside too.

"I'm sorry," she said immediately, trying to get back to mom mode. She reached over and grabbed a napkin off my food tray to pat her face dry. "I'm sorry," she said again, forcing a crooked smile, which she was only able to keep up for about five seconds—yikes!—before crumbling into pieces. She was sobbing and panting, short and choppy, dabbing at her pouring eyes and nose with the napkin. It was like everything she had been holding in was now finally coming out.

I leaned forward and inched myself closer to her. Each small movement felt like a knife blade pushing into my side. But I didn't care, I had to get to her. Then my arms were around her, and now *I* was crying, my body burning on the inside, while I told her over and over again, "It's okay. It's okay. I'm gonna be fine." And as she pulled away to blow her nose once more, working as hard as she could to paint that half-full smile back on her face, I reached for the remote and (*please work, please work, please work*) changed the channel.

Spoony showed up about an hour later with Berry. My mother and I had calmed down and were watching *Family Feud*, laughing at some of the stupid answers people were coming up with.

"Name something you might find under your bed."

"A monster!"

"Naw, they don't hide under there no more. Or in closets," Spoony said, making an entrance as usual. "They hide in plain sight, with uniforms and badges." Spoony. Always an agenda.

"Hi, Mrs. Butler," Berry said, coming over to my mom with her arms out for a hug.

"Hi, sweetheart. Ain't you supposed to be in school?" Ma kissed Berry on the cheek.

Berry was in law school. Yep, law school. My dad always got on Spoony, asking him why he wasn't inspired to make something of himself since he dated such a smart girl. Then he'd say, "Well, at least you got enough sense to get a smart girl. I guess I gotta give you credit for that."

"I'll put in some extra work at the library this weekend. This is far more important," Berry said. Spoony gave me five, then he and Berry switched places so he could hug Ma, and Berry could hug me.

"Wassup, big man?" she said, touching her cheek to mine. Berry was the female version of English. Absolutely gorgeous. And so cool. And smart. Everything wrapped up in one girl. And she was everybody's first crush. Me, Shannon, and Carlos. We all loved Berry, and English knew it. We used to tease him so bad about her, and he hated it, but put up with it because that's just what we do. Jokes. But once Spoony started dating her, we cut all the jokes out, because even though Spoony wasn't anywhere near perfect, he was definitely a dude who got respect. I don't know why. He just did. It's not like anyone had ever seen him do anything crazy, but he had this presence about him. A confidence that made it seem like he wasn't scared of anything or anybody. So the Berry jokes were over, and she instantly fell into *big sister zone*. "How you holdin' up?" she asked now.

"Oh, you know me. Living a luxurious life," I said.

"Looks like it," Berry replied, but even though she was smiling, I could see the sadness in her eyes. I could see the sadness in everybody's eyes. My mother's, Spoony's, my friends', Clarissa's, even the lady on TV who filmed everything—Claudia's.

"'Shad, I want you to see something," Spoony said, easing Berry's backpack off her shoulder. He unzipped it, pulled out her laptop. "They got Wi-Fi in here?"

"I don't think so," I said, wanting to laugh at him. I don't know why, but I just thought that was so funny.

He put the laptop back in the bag.

"Here, just use my phone," Berry said, digging in her back pocket. She tapped the screen a few times, then handed it to Spoony, who handed it to me.

"Look at this."

On the screen was a picture of my school. And on the sidewalk was some writing. I enlarged the image and did a double take. RASHAD IS ABSENT AGAIN TODAY is what it said, spray painted in bright-blue loopy letters.

"What is this?" I asked, staring.

"There's major buzz about this thing, man. Facebook, Twitter, everywhere. People are pissed off. Kids your age. They're speaking up, man."

I stared at the picture. The letters, the tiny loop at the stop of the cursive s. So familiar. There was only one person I knew who did that. Carlos.

"English texted me earlier saying that some of the kids at your school have been talking about a protest. He sent me that picture," Berry said. "But that's not the only one." She reached for the phone and began swiping through photos, showing me picture after picture of RASHAD IS ABSENT AGAIN TODAY, tagged all over the city. I knew the first one was from Carlos, but not all the rest of them, because I didn't recognize the lettering, plus they were too loose. Amateur. I had no idea who those were from.

"There's even a hashtag," she said.

#RashadIsAbsentAgainToday.

I couldn't believe it. I had become a hashtag. I had become searchable. A trending topic. Another number on someone's chart. But to me, I was still . . . just me.

"A protest?" I thumbed the screen, going from picture to picture. It just seemed weird that there was so much fuss over me.

"Yeah, man," Spoony confirmed.

"A protest?" my mother repeated, her eyebrows knitting together. "I don't know about this. I don't want nobody else getting hurt."

A fierce look came over Spoony's face. "Ma, we have a right to protest. We have a right to be upset."

"I know that, Spoony. You don't think I know that?" Ma's voice rose. Spoony had no idea that *our* mom had just called the cop an asshole. He'd missed that. "You don't think I'm angry?" She glared at him, burned straight through his hoodie.

"I know you are. Sorry," he said, humbled. "I'm just so tired of this."

"I am too," Ma said, coming back down. "And I know protests can be good. Just like I know that not all cops are bad. I married one."

"I'm not sure Dad's the best example of a good cop," Spoony

said quicker than quick, the words sharp enough to cut.

Ma gave him a look. Not upset. But sad. Like she was sad that her son seemed so angry, so distrusting. And she didn't even say anything to refute his statement, didn't even argue with him, which to me was strange.

"Why not?" I asked.

Spoony looked from me to Ma before brushing the whole thing off with, "Nothing. Doesn't matter."

"Listen, I just don't want them to find a reason to beat more people. To kill people." Mom refocused the conversation, her eyes back on me. "And since apparently they don't trust us, I don't trust them."

"But Ma, all we want is to feel like we can be who we are without being accused of being something else. That's all," Spoony tried again.

"But do protests even work?" I asked. I mean, I was all for the idea. I really was. But the only time I had ever heard about any protests actually working was Dr. King's. That's it. Ain't never heard of no other ones making a difference.

"Do they work?" Spoony looked at me crazy, a *how I could even ask such a question* look.

Berry stepped in. "They're a piece to the puzzle. I mean, there are a lot of pieces, like reforming laws and things like that. But protests are what sends the message to the folks in power that something needs to change. That people are fed up," she explained. "We have a right to voice how we feel, and isn't that better than just doing nothing?"

Spoony and Berry tag-teamed me with the more political activism mumbo jumbo than I could stand, until at last, thank God, English, Shannon, and Carlos showed up. They all hugged my mom and Berry, and dapped up Spoony.

"Yo, you heard about the protest?" Carlos shot off instantly, picking up right where my brother and Berry had left off. "Hashtag RashadIsAbsentAgainToday."

I looked at him. He looked at me. Friendship ESP.

"So this thing is really gonna happen?" I asked.

"Dude, even Tiffany was talking about it in Mr. Fisher's class," English said. Mr. Fisher was a history teacher at the school. Kind of a weird guy, but still supercool. White hair. Jacked-up bowl cut. Weird cloth ties. Shirt tucked in tight jeans. But he knew all about history and would celebrate Black History Month in February *and* March. The only other teacher who was down for stuff like that was Mrs. Tracey, the English teacher. Shannon and Carlos used to always joke about how Mr. Fisher and Mrs. Tracey were probably dating, probably having gross sex after school on Mrs. Tracey's desk, on top of *Shakespeare's Sonnets* or something.

"For real?" I asked.

"Yeah, man. Fish is really supporting it. Like, he's helping us plan it and everything." English was gassed. "He kept saying how we are part of history. How this is part of history."

"Word? Is he giving out extra credit for it?" I joked, just to try to lighten the mood.

"'Shad, we serious, man," Carlos said. "Like, for real."

"Told you, 'Shad," Spoony said. "This thing is bubbling. People are sick of it." He looked at Ma, who seemed caught somewhere between mad and worried. "Ma, seriously, what if he was killed?"

"But he wasn't," she said, straight, the same way my dad had said a few days before when Spoony said the same thing.

"But what about all the others?" Spoony said. "Matter fact, how many of y'all been messed with by the cops?"

"Man, what? I've been pulled over so many times," Carlos said.

"Because you speed," I jumped in.

"Yeah, true. But at least three times, they've made me get out the car while they tore it apart looking for drugs or guns or whatever they thought I had. Then when they didn't find nothing, they let me go with a speeding ticket, but left my car a mess. Glove compartment emptied out. Trunk all dug through. Just trashed my ride for no reason."

"Man, I've been stopped on the street," English said.

"You have?" Berry sparked up.

"Yeah. More than once, too. Cops wanting me to lift my

shirt so they could see if I had weapons on me. Pat-downs and all that."

"Why didn't you tell me?" Berry asked.

"Because I already know what time it is. I'd seen it before, so it was nothing. Plus I didn't want you freakin' out."

"At least yours were only pat-downs. One time they had me facedown on the sidewalk on Overlook Street. Said they got word that there was a robbery and said the description of the person was five-foot-nine, dark skin, with a black T-shirt and black sneakers on," Shannon explained. "That could've been anybody."

"That could've been any kid I work with at the rec center. Matter fact, that could've been me!" Spoony chimed in.

"Exactly," Berry agreed.

And I wished the stories stopped there. I really did. But they didn't. They went on and on, story after story about not trusting police officers because they always seemed to act like bullies. And even though there were times when they'd been helpful, the bad times . . . were BAD TIMES. And it just seemed like they didn't . . . I don't know. Like, they see us. But they don't really *see* us.

"Okay," I said.

"Okay what?" Spoony asked.

"Okay. I'm down with the protest." I have to admit, I said I was down but I wasn't really sure I meant it. I was scared.

And it's not like they needed me to sign on. This wasn't really about me. This was bigger than me. I knew that now. But I wanted my brother and my friends to know, since the spotlight was on me, that I was in. That I would stand with them.

That is, if I could get out of the hospital.

"Name a word that rhymes with grain."
"Pain."
"Good answer! Good answer!"

Wednesday

QUINN

Willy was dragging his ass again on Wednesday morning, but truthfully it wasn't all his fault. I was kind of dragging my ass too, still dwelling on all the things I'd been talking to Jill about the night before. It's not like I was dreaming about it, it was more that weird state where your eyes are closed and you know you are thinking, and it feels like you are both asleep and not, like you're resting, but still thinking, kinda in control of your thoughts and kinda not.

Well, the daze carried right over into morning like I was sleepwalking, and when Willy and I finally made it down the steps to head off to school, it might as well have been a dream, because standing on the sidewalk a few houses down, having just lugged the garbage to the street, was Paul Galluzzo, staring right at me.

He waved to me and I waved back, automatically, out of habit. *What was I doing?* He jogged up to us, and I kept thinking, *All I had to do was turn and walk away, what the hell is wrong with me?* He looked like he hadn't slept in days. Maybe he hadn't. Maybe he'd been up all night too, thinking about what he had done to Rashad. Poor guy—yup, that was my first actual thought. Not Rashad. Paul. *Jesus.*

"What's up, Collins?" he said when he got to us.

"Uh, hey," I mumbled. All that normalcy was gone. He sniffled, and I wasn't sure if it was one of those things a guy like him did before he socked a guy like me in the face. I gripped Willy's hand.

Paul tussled Willy's hair. He glanced back and forth between Willy and me, and I focused on the grease stain on Paul's T-shirt.

"Hey," he said. "I thought we were going to practice some footwork?" He didn't sound angry, more like he was pleading. "I'm right here, man."

"Yeah," I said again, fishing for words. "Look, I know. It's been busy, and we have to get to school and all and—"

"Hey," he said, now with more force. "Don't bullshit me."

This made Willy jump a little, and Paul calmed down. "No, listen," he said, easy, like old times. "Little Guz's been telling me about all the chatter at school."

"Nah," I said, not sure what to say. "It's nothing."

"No," Paul said. "No, it's not. It's weird. I know it."

He hesitated, and I couldn't find a word to fill the silence. I just wanted to turn and run, but I had Willy holding me there like an anchor. Or maybe it was me? What the hell did I want him to say?

"You gotta hear my side of the story."

That was the last thing I wanted to do. "Uh, I know," I stuttered. "But—"

"No. Listen. You do." Paul clamped my shoulder with his hand. He raised the other one slowly and pointed close to my face, scabs still tattooing his knuckles. "Because you were there. I know."

Willy looked up at me. "What's going on?"

Paul sniffled again. His eyes were bloodshot, his hair a mess. He was wearing flip-flops, and I'd never seen him in those stupid things. He let go of me and stood back, his hands on his hips.

"Look," he said. "People tell a lot of fucked-up stories. People are talking about me. Well, I'm telling you this. There was a woman in the store. The kid took her down because she caught him stealing, I went in to protect her, and then he went after me, okay?" He wiped a hand over his head and then held his fist in front of his mouth for a moment. "What was I supposed to do? It's my job, Quinn. I was protecting the lady. I was just doing my job."

He reached out to me again but didn't grab me, just kind of touched my shoulder, like he wasn't sure what he was doing. I leaned back, and his fingers fell away awkwardly.

"I know," I lied. "I hear you."

"Do you?" Paul's face was all screwed up. "I don't think you do, Quinn. What the hell's the matter with you, man?"

"I know. It's just—" I couldn't find anything else to say. "I have to get this guy to school." I nodded to Willy. "Catch you later, though, right?"

Paul's look of disgust ripped a hole in my chest. "Are you serious, Quinn?"

I shrugged, and Paul narrowed his eyes.

"Yeah," he said, turning around and waving me off. "See you later."

But really, it sounded like he was saying *fuck you*.

And for the whole walk to Willy's middle school and then to my school, all I could hear was that lie in his voice. He didn't want to see me later. No frigging way. I didn't want to see him, either. But what was worse was that I couldn't believe he'd told me about what happened in the store. Or actually, it wasn't that I couldn't believe that he'd told me—it was that I didn't believe *what* he'd told me. Because even if Rashad did everything Paul said he did—*really?*

I saw what I saw on the street.

That was the real story.

■■
■■

I met Jill on the front steps by the tag. What had once been a non-hang at school had now become *the* hang at school. Everybody stood around the spray-painted slogan. The school maintenance crew hadn't washed it off, and what made it all the more powerful was that it was still true. Rashad had been in the hospital five nights, and he was still there. *Rashad was absent again today.*

On either side of the spray paint, kids passed out flyers. A black fist rose from the bottom of each sheet and called for justice. It was what Jill had been talking about. She was organizing, getting involved, and she was there, with Tiffany, handing them out. I didn't have Mr. Fisher for history like they did, but I knew who he was, and I saw him out there too—his bright white head bobbing through the crowd of students. Jill now told me in detail what was going down. A community group, a church, and some of the student clubs at school were planning a protest march on Friday. It would start on the West Side, go right by Jerry's, and wind its way through town to city hall and Police Plaza 1. The march through town would begin at five thirty p.m., approximately the same time Rashad had been arrested for petty theft, resisting arrest, and public nuisance—whatever the hell that meant. And just as I was thinking it, I heard someone else ask it: "Will Rashad be there?" Nobody knew.

At the bell, Jill and I took off in different directions. I tried to catch up with Tooms, but he ignored me and hustled ahead of me into our English classroom. When I walked into class behind him, Mrs. Tracey stood at the window, looking down over the front steps and the entrance to the school. Even when everyone had taken their seats, she remained by the window, and the rest of the class kept talking, waiting for her to go to her desk. But she didn't. In her hand, she held her copy of the novel *Invisible Man*. A week earlier she'd made photocopies of the first chapter, a short story Ralph Ellison published as "Battle Royal." That story—I'd never read anything like it. The violence. The all-out warfare. The *N* word all over the place. When it had been assigned a week earlier, I'd read it all twisted up in discomfort, like the actual reading of the story was painful, but now, as Mrs. Tracey clutched her book and looked down to the sidewalk, a kind of nervousness rose in me. I'd hated the way the old white men in the story had acted—watching black boys getting beaten, beating each other, for sport—and I'd put as much distance between them and me as I could. I wasn't them, I'd told myself as I read. White people were crazy back then, eighty years ago, when the story took place. Not now. But watching Mrs. Tracey stare out the window, a weight of dread dropped through me. Were we going to talk about the story again? After Rashad? Because after what had happened to Rashad, it felt like no time had passed at all. It could have been eighty years ago. Or only eight. Now it wasn't only the city aldermen. Now there were the videos, and we were all watching this shit happen again and again on our TVs and phones—shaking our heads but doing nothing about it.

Mrs. Tracey still didn't move from the window, and everyone began to fidget, looking at everyone else, and my eyes landed on the whiteboard. Her notes from what must have been her last-period class the day before were still on it. Active versus passive voice. I remembered the exact same lesson from ninth grade. I'd thought it was all a pain in the ass, but what had once been a stupid grammar lesson now formed a weird lump in my throat.

Mistakes were made, Mrs. Tracey had scrawled. And beneath it she'd written, *Who? Who made the mistakes?*

In my mind, I ran through the exercise I remembered from the time, rearranging the phrases, making something passive active, but this time I found myself changing the other words too, because I was clearly becoming obsessed—even if I didn't want to be.

Mistakes were made.

Rashad was beaten.

Paul beat Rashad.

Mrs. Tracey finally moved from the window and did something just as surprising. She sat down behind her desk. Usually she walked around her desk, or she perched on the front of her desk. But she never *sat*. Now, slumped behind it, she'd never looked so small, the whiteboard as big as the sky over her tiny, hunched shoulders. I thought she was about to begin the lesson, but she pushed the book away from her on the desk and began to cry.

I clenched my jaw tight and stared down at the floor, trying not to let her tears make me cry back in response. I just sat there breathing heavily through my nose.

She pointed to the window and dropped her head into her hands. "I don't want to see this happen to any of my students," she said, catching her breath. "I don't want to believe it still happens."

I gripped one hand with the other, hoping to disappear. I wasn't the only one. The room had never been so quiet. No one spoke or whispered. Mrs. Tracey just sat there, with her head in her hands. After a few last sobs, she apologized. "I'm sorry for my outburst—it's just—" And then the tears came again and she apologized again and continued. "Mr. Godwin thinks it's best if I don't assign papers for this story. He thinks it's best to just move on to the next unit."

Something felt off about that. Don't get me wrong, nobody wants to write a paper if he doesn't have to, but this time, it felt like we were getting cheated out of something. Everyone still kept absolutely silent, but I wondered what was going through Tooms's mind. He was nodding a slow, hesitant nod. An *I read you* kind of nod. I leaned back in my chair but couldn't actually go anywhere, because the damn thing was all one unit and I felt trapped. It was too damn small for me anyway. And as I was sitting there, shifting around in that tiny-ass chair-desk, I remembered Mrs. Tracey making fun of Mr. Godwin, saying she'd never follow what the department head or the administration wanted her to teach. But now, suddenly, when they actually did direct her, she was blaming them for not talking about the book.

And then I thought about what was right there in the text. Ralph Ellison talking about invisibility. Not the wacky science fiction kind, but the kind where people are looking at you but not seeing you, looking through you, or around you—like, why the hell shouldn't our classes be talking about what happened to Rashad? Was what happened to him invisible? Was he invisible?

I scribbled a note. *I might be an asshole, but I know this isn't right. Should we do something? The Invisible Man at Central High: Rashad.* I tore the note from my notebook, wadded it, and threw it at Tooms.

The crumbled ball bounced off his desk, into his chest, and onto the ground. He squinted at me. "Read it," I mouthed. He hesitated, but then he snatched it up and smoothed it out. He stared at the note for what seemed like forever, and then he looked back up at me.

"You with me?" he mouthed back.

I nodded.

Then, for the first time ever in any class I'd ever been in with him, Tooms spoke up without being called on.

"Battle Royal," he said, pulling his photocopy out of his folder. "For Rashad."

And he began to read. "'It goes a long way back, some twenty years. All my life I had been looking for something, and everywhere I turned someone tried to tell me what it was.'"

Now, Tooms is not a read-out-loud kind of guy, but he went right into it, reading clear and confident for the whole room to hear, and it made the most perfect sense reading the words Ralph Ellison had written years ago. Mrs. Tracey lifted her head, her face a mess, and something about her crying there in class made me so mad, like Rashad's reality meant now she couldn't talk about the story, or didn't know how—but there was Ralph Ellison, and Tooms, too, just telling us what we needed to do. I unfolded my crinkled pages and followed along as Tooms read aloud, ending with the final line of the first paragraph: "'It took me a long time and much painful boomeranging of my expectations to achieve a realization everyone else appears to have been born with: That I am nobody but myself! But first I had to discover that I am an invisible man!'"

When Tooms fell silent, I glanced back, and I realized he was looking at me. I nodded, and even though I'm not the kind of guy who likes to read aloud either—I hate it—the rest of the room just sat there waiting for something to happen, and even Mrs. Tracey was stunned, so I jumped into the next paragraph. The lines were the old grandfather's deathbed advice, talking about his life after slavery, his life still struggling: "'Learn it to the young'uns'" his final, "fiercely" whispered words. And it seemed like the words were calling right into the classroom. They weren't my words, they were Ellison's, but there he was reminding us all what had to be learned by the "young'uns."

Then it was my time to be surprised, because Nam picked up where I left off, and after Nam, Sonja read, then Latrice, and Alex, and soon it was clear the whole class was going to take a turn, because what would it say if you didn't?

Mrs. Tracey watched and listened. She didn't interrupt. The slurs and the violence from the dialogue ricocheted around the room. Some people skipped over them. Some people said "line of dialogue." Chloe looked up, tears streaming down her own white face, and said, "I don't want to say these words," and nobody judged. We just waited to see what she would do. Some people said it all word for word.

But here are the words that kept ricocheting around me all day: Nobody says the words anymore, but somehow the violence still remains. If I didn't want the violence to remain, I had to do a hell of a lot more than just say the right things and not say the wrong things.

Practice was better than it had been in a couple of days. Coach drilled us with a few plays, then made us run laps, then dropped the three-point contest on us. It was no surprise that I won, because I'd been hitting threes since I was a freshman—I used my legs to shoot like Paul had taught me. But I didn't think about him as I shot. I kept my head where it was supposed to be, in the moment, even when we scrimmaged. Coach was trying out different combinations of players, and although he didn't say it, he was evaluating who was going to be a starter for sure. At first I played against English, then I got swapped briefly, and when I went back in I was on his team. I was nervous, but a shooter has to shoot. I hit the first one I took on a pass from him, and on the very next play, we had a two-on-one against Tooms, and although English might have taken it to the hoop against Tooms, he kicked it to me for the easy basket. I got him later too when I dropped the ball around Guzzo. English and I had a rhythm going, and I knew that if we kept it up for the next few months, we'd both be breaking records. I mean, hell, why couldn't the scouts be here now? When English and I were playing so well together!

But no game is ever that easy. Ten minutes before practice was supposed to end, Guzzo and Tooms went up for a rebound, and Tooms knocked Guzzo in the face with his elbow. Guzzo bucked backward, spun, and stumbled down to one knee. Coach blew his whistle and we all stopped, but already Guzzo was springing to his feet and shoving Tooms. Tooms pushed him back, and Nam and I got in between them before either of them threw a punch.

"What the hell's the matter with you two?" Coach barked. He pulled us all apart, and for a split second it seemed like Guzzo and Tooms were going to go at it again, but Coach got each of them by the collars of their shirts. "There's no room for that bullshit here."

"He jacked me," Guzzo said. A line of blood dropped from his nose to his shirt.

"It was an accident," Tooms said.

"No, it wasn't," Guzzo shot back.

"Enough," Coach told them, letting go of their shirts. "Take it easy." He stared at Tooms. "It was an accident, right?"

"Of course."

"Bullshit," Guzzo interrupted. "Everyone has it out for me."

Coach rubbed his jaw. "All right, look. Enough of that." He looked around at all of us. "You think it's dumb when someone says there's no 'I' in team, but you stick one in there and you see how dumb that looks."

Guzzo took a step back, but Coach waved him closer. "Bring it in, boys." We all hesitated. "I said BRING IT IN!" he yelled.

So we piled in around him, and he stuck his hand in the middle. We followed, like we always did. "I get it. There's a lot of bullshit out there, and it needs to get resolved, but we're not resolving it in here. Not in practice and not on this court. We leave all that bullshit at the door. In here, on this court, we need to win games. That's all we need to do, and we need to work like one team or we're fucked. You hear me? We've got all kinds of people coming to see us. They start coming next week. Next week! You ready for that? The press, the scouts. When is the last time those guys from Duke were here? You hear me?"

A couple guys said yes, but the rest of us merely nodded. Guzzo leaned on my back, but I was looking across the circle at English and Shannon. I *got* what Coach was saying. I wanted to see teammates, but it got me thinking. Maybe right now all I saw were teammates around me, but once we stepped back into the real world, who did I see? Who did *they* see? Coach could keep shouting at us until we all parroted back what he wanted, but I knew English and Shannon answered because they had to, not because they wanted to. Tooms, too. And that's what I was doing too, because Coach kept telling us to leave everything else at the door, but I was thinking about it the other way around. How did the team stay a team back out the door? How did the team stay a team out in the street?

Guzzo's nose kept bleeding, right through all the yelling, so Coach told me to get him into the locker room and cleaned up. Then Coach blew his whistle, the scrimmage started again with new combinations, and the squeaking of sneakers and the ball on the court followed me into the locker room.

Guzzo jogged ahead of me, not saying a word while he washed his face and grabbed a couple paper towels. He walked around to a bench deeper in the locker room, sat, and held his head back.

I leaned against a nearby locker and crossed my arms. "He didn't hit you on purpose."

"Yeah, he did."

"Come on."

"People have it all backward. They do," Guzzo said. He wiped at his nose and then pinched it closed again. "Look," he said. "I'm sorry, but my brother did the right thing. He has to make tough calls. I'm sorry they're friends with that guy, but what are you gonna do? I mean, Paul—he was helping the woman in the store. He didn't do anything wrong. He was doing his job."

"But that's not how everyone sees it, man."

"Yeah, but that doesn't mean they're right."

"Yeah, but—"

"But what?" Guzzo wiped at his nose again and raised his voice. "But what? Whose side are you on here?"

"Come on, you heard Coach," I said. "No sides."

"No sides? Asshole, of course there are sides. There are two sides to every situation." His nose started bleeding again, so I got him another paper towel. He wiped at his nose again. It still bled. I got him another paper towel, but he just held it in his hand. "They could call you for a witness, couldn't they?"

"Maybe," I said. I was feeling paranoid about this, because ever since my conversation with Jill, I kept thinking that I had to do it. I had to let someone know. And then what, stand in a courtroom and point my finger at Paul? I couldn't even imagine doing that.

"I don't know how it works, though," I continued. "Anyway, everyone's seen the video. It was taken from a spot closer than I was."

"But if they called you, what would you say?"

I was silent. Before anybody would call me into some freaking courtroom, I'd have to tell somebody official that I was there.

"Whose side are you on?" Guzzo asked again, and when I didn't answer him, he continued. "Everyone's gotta get their heads out of their asses. We're not a team if Tooms or anybody else is going to clock me every chance he gets."

"No, man, the problem is assuming he's out to get you. He isn't."

Guzzo pinched his nose again and tipped his head back. "I don't need a fucking nurse," he said. "Get out of here. I know whose side you're on. And I'm going to tell my brother how you don't have his back. After all he did for you, man. Fuck you."

He stood, and I backed away. Even with a bloody nose, Guzzo could drop me in a heartbeat. "It's about doing the right thing," Guzzo said mockingly. "I hate all this politically correct bullshit. Nobody'd be spray painting *your* name on the sidewalk if Paul had grabbed you coming out of Jerry's." He punched a locker with the side of his fist. "Half the school's calling my brother a racist. He was just doing his job. People throw that word 'racist' around all the time now. Pretty soon everyone's going to start calling me a racist if I don't pass Tooms the ball. It's fucked up and you know it."

"Guzzo," I said. "You're not the victim. Your brother isn't either."

The look on his face went fierce, and I was glad as hell that Coach began bringing the rest of the team into the locker room. He called out to us, and we reluctantly joined him and the rest of the guys around the bench closest to the showers. "One more time—bring it in, boys," Coach said. "We're all in this together." He looked at Guzzo, then at Tooms.

"Sorry," Tooms said to Guzzo through his teeth.

"Galluzzo?" Coach prompted.

"Yeah, yeah," Guzzo said. "Me too." Then he pulled the bloody paper towel away from his face and wadded it into a hard ball. "We're good, right?" he said across the circle to Tooms. He smiled, sarcastically.

If the rest of us had melted away and Coach had disappeared, I think Tooms would have leaped across the bench and punched Guzzo straight in the face, for real this time. And I wouldn't have blamed him. But what the hell? Didn't that make me a traitor to my best friend?

"Hey," I said to Guzzo. "It's over."

Guzzo glared at me. "Damn straight," he said.

"That's right!" Coach said. "And we're a team, and we need to take care of each other. You know the rules. We take care of each other on the court and off it. We don't go to parties, and we help make sure no one else on the team goes to them either. No one needs to be stupid. We've got four months to show the world we're number one. No parties, and no protests, you hear me?"

Some of the guys nodded.

"I said, you hear me?"

"Yes," we yelled automatically.

"Mean it!"

"YES."

"Again!"

"YES!"

He stuck his hand in and we followed. "Okay. Team on three. *One, two, three.*"

"TEAM!" we all shouted, lying just to get the damn practice finished. Team. Maybe? Like the whole school is a team, the whole city is a team? But we weren't one just because we called ourselves one. We had to mean it to be it, and to be it maybe we had to talk about the tough shit out loud. Otherwise we'd just keep lying to each other all the time. Lying. Paul wasn't the only one.

DEAR CADET BUTLER,

I HAD PLANNED TO COME VISIT YOU, BUT IT WAS COMMUNICATED TO ME THAT YOU DIDN'T WANT ANY VISITORS. AND IN TOUGH TIMES LIKE THESE, I CAN TOTALLY UNDERSTAND YOU WANTING AS MUCH PRIVACY AS POSSIBLE, AND HAVE ENCOURAGED YOUR FELLOW CADETS TO ALSO RESPECT YOUR WISHES. NONETHELESS, I WANTED YOU TO KNOW YOUR COMRADES AND I HAVE YOU IN OUR THOUGHTS AND WISH YOU A SPEEDY RECOVERY AND RETURN TO THE PROGRAM. AND TO ENCOURAGE YOU IN THIS TIME, I'VE ENCLOSED A CARD WITH OUR CREED.

ALL THE BEST,
CHIEF KILLABREW

I AM AN ARMY JUNIOR ROTC CADET.

✶

I WILL ALWAYS CONDUCT MYSELF TO BRING CREDIT TO MY
FAMILY, COUNTRY, SCHOOL, AND THE CORPS OF CADETS.

✶

I AM LOYAL AND PATRIOTIC.

✶

I AM THE FUTURE OF THE UNITED STATES OF AMERICA.

✶

I DO NOT LIE, CHEAT, OR STEAL AND WILL ALWAYS
BE ACCOUNTABLE FOR MY ACTIONS AND DEEDS.

✶

I WILL ALWAYS PRACTICE GOOD
CITIZENSHIP AND PATRIOTISM.

✶

I WILL WORK HARD TO IMPROVE MY
MIND AND STRENGTHEN MY BODY.

✶

I WILL SEEK THE MANTLE OF LEADERSHIP AND
STAND PREPARED TO UPHOLD THE CONSTITUTION
AND THE AMERICAN WAY OF LIFE.

✶

MAY GOD GRANT ME THE STRENGTH
TO ALWAYS LIVE BY THIS CREED.

If you're wondering if I had been having nightmares, y'know, about that day, the answer is, no. I hadn't been. Not until Wednesday. Actually, it started Tuesday night after my friends and family left my room, and I decided to finally read Chief Killabrew's card. I couldn't figure out if he had inserted the creed as some kind of reminder to me that if I'm guilty to fess up, and that I was expected to never lie and steal, or what. Maybe he really was trying to encourage me. Maybe he was saying that because I was a cadet, there was no way I could be guilty. I don't know. I just know that it rubbed me in a weird way, because ROTC, especially to people like my dad, was the first step to the military, and ultimately into law enforcement. I mean, for all I knew, Galluzzo could've been in ROTC when he was my age. Was he "the future of America"? Was he upholding "the American way of life"? I guess it depends on who you ask. Maybe. And maybe it was these thoughts rattling around my head that sparked the nightmare.

I was back in Jerry's, but in the dream, the chips were located in the drink fridge. So I'm standing at the refrigerator staring through the glass, when I hear a voice coming from behind me.

"I know what you're doing," the voice said.

For some reason, I didn't turn around. I just looked into the glass to see the reflection of whoever was there. And it was him. Officer Galluzzo, like Goliath standing with his hand already on his weapon, sizing me up.

"I ain't doing nothing," I said, still facing the glass.

"I know what you're doing," he repeated, taking a step closer, the sound of his boots thumping on the vinyl floor. I knew I should've turned around, but I couldn't. I was frozen. But I could still see him through the glass, his mirrored image becoming clearer as he got closer and closer. Then I adjusted my eyes to see my own reflection, my own face. But I couldn't. I mean, my face was there, but . . . it wasn't. There were no eyes. No nose or mouth. Just blank brown skin.

And that's when I woke up, my heart pounding, my throat scratchy and dry. The dream seemed to last five minutes, but it had actually been hours, and it was now Wednesday morning. I reached over to the food tray beside my bed for the leftover cranberry juice from dinner the night before. In hospitals, juice comes in the same kind of cups as fruit cocktails and applesauce, the ones where you have to peel back the foil. Damn things are hard to open. My hands, for some weird reason, were weak, wouldn't work right. Maybe it was the dream. Maybe it was everything that was going on— the reality. Whatever it was, I struggled to pull the aluminum seal back far enough to take a sip of juice. And I *needed* it. My throat felt like I had eaten my blanket.

I pulled and peeled, until finally the stupid foil snapped

away from the plastic and cranberry juice spilled all over the place. Of course.

I snatched the wet sheet back. There was still some juice left, so I decided to get what I could. Right when I took a sip, there was a knock on my door. Now, I know it was probably just a regular knock, but at that moment it sounded like a bang, and I was so jittery that I spilled whatever was left of the juice on myself.

"Shit," I grumbled.

"Watch your mouth." My father was pushing the door open. He poked his head in—a strange thing that everyone does at the hospital for some reason—before entering.

"Good morning," he said, eyeing me as I dabbed juice into my gown, the burgundy blotches on my chest and stomach looking like blood.

"Hey," I said. "What time is it?"

"Just about seven."

"Why are you here so early?"

Dad closed the door behind him and came to the foot of the bed. "Wanted to catch you before I went to work. See how you were doing?"

"Oh," I said, kinda shocked. "I'm okay. How 'bout you? Ma told me you were sick."

"Yeah. Something didn't agree with my system. But I'm fine." He sat on the edge of the bed, which was different for him. Usually he sat in a chair on the other side of the room—as far away from me as possible.

"Cool." I wasn't really sure what else to say.

Dad sat there staring at the side table where my phone and the spirometer were.

"Listen, I, uh . . . ," he started. "I want to tell you a story. When I was a cop—" Pause.

Here's the thing. My father has three different ways to start a parental sermon about a whole bunch of *I don't want to hear it.*

1. *When I was your age:* always about how he was doing way more than I am when he was in high school. Let him tell it, he put the principal in detention.
2. *When I was in the army:* always came whenever I was tired. It didn't matter what I was tired from. If I showed any signs of exhaustion, he would hit me with how when he was in the army he wasn't allowed to be tired, and that if he even yawned they made him drop down and give them a thousand push-ups.
3. *When I was a cop:* always came whenever he was either defending cops or insulting teenagers.

"When I was a cop," he started. He reached up and loosened his navy-blue tie. Then he hiked his khaki pants up, just enough to show his tan socks, peppered with dark-brown diamonds. Office clothes are as boring as offices. Anyway, I braced myself and prepared to ignore whatever was coming.

"One time," he began, "I got a call that there were a few guys making a bunch of noise in the middle of the night, over on the East Side. You know how it is over there. Nine o'clock, that whole neighborhood shuts down. Now I was used to these quick runs. You drive up, hit your lights and your siren, and if the kids don't take off running, you just roll down the window and tell them to keep it moving. Never really a big deal." My father was still staring at the spirometer. As if he was talking to *it*, as if I wasn't in the room. "So my partner and I answer the call and head on over. When we pull up, there's a white kid in tight black jeans and a sweater and this black kid going for it. A backpack was upside down on the side of the curb, and these two were just throwing down, scrapping. The black kid was dressed like . . ." He looked at me, finally. "Dressed like your brother. Hair all over his head. A hoodie. Boots. His pants were damn near all the way down. And he was mopping this boy. My partner and I jumped out of the car and approached them, and before we could even give them a chance to stop fighting, I ran over and jacked the black boy up because I knew he was in the wrong. I just knew it. I mean, you should've seen how he was pummeling this kid. And he fought me back, telling me that I had it wrong.

He slipped right from my grip and ran for the backpack. I pulled my gun. Told him to leave it. He kept yelling, 'I didn't do anything! I didn't do anything! He's the criminal!' But now he's wheezing, like he was having a hard time speaking. Then he grabbed the backpack. By now, my partner's got the white kid. I tell the black dude to leave the bag and put his hands up. But he doesn't, and instead opens it. Puts his hand inside. And before he could pull it out, I pulled the trigger."

Holy shit!

"What!" I yelped. I had never heard this story, and I thought I had heard all the stories. I heard all the ones about the people he saved—the woman who had been beaten by her husband; the high-speed chase of a bank robber, who Dad eventually caught after running him off the road, movie-style. I had heard all the stories about how Dad had been shot at. And definitely the one about how he had been shot. I saw the bullet wound in his chest every morning when he got out of the shower, like a tiny crater or a third nipple, a symbol of near death. But I had never, ever, *EVER* heard this one.

Dad's Adam's apple rolled down his throat, then back up. Then he continued. "He was reaching for his inhaler. Turns out, he lived in that neighborhood and was walking home late, when the white kid tried to rob *him*. He was trying to fight the kid off, and when we showed up, his adrenaline went so high that he couldn't breathe. Asthma attack. So he had to get to his inhaler, but he was having a hard time telling me that. I just assumed he . . ."

"Wait. Wait . . ." I put my hand up, pushing the words back into my father's mouth. If there was ever a time that I needed, for once, to control a conversation with him, it was now. I only had one question. "Did you kill him?"

"No." Dad teethed his top lip. "But I paralyzed him from the waist down."

I just sat there, dumbfounded. My dad, *my dad*, had paralyzed an unarmed kid, a black kid, and I had had no idea. My dad shot a kid. I mean, to me, my father was the model of discipline and courage. Sure, he was stern, and sometimes judgmental, but I always felt like he *meant* well. But to that kid—and now my head was reeling—to that kid, my dad was no different than Officer Galluzzo. Another trigger-happy cop who was quick to assume and even quicker to shoot.

My father filled in the silence my lack of verbal response had created.

"You know, you were still very young, but Spoony remembers it all. The news. The drama. I'm not proud of it. It'll never stop haunting me, and I think it messes with your brother still too."

"It probably messes with that boy's—what's his name?" I asked, hard.

"Darnell Shackleford," he rattled off. It was clearly a name he couldn't forget.

"It probably still messes with Darnell and his family too."

"Right." Dad nodded, sadly. "Thing is, I had been in so many other situations where things had gotten crazy. A hand goes in a pocket and out comes a pistol or a blade. And all I could think about was making it home to you, Spoony, and your mother. It's a hard job, a *really* hard job, and you could never understand that. You could never know what it's like to kiss your family good-bye in the morning, knowing you could get a call over your radio that could end your life."

I could hear the struggle in his voice. Like, he really wanted me to understand this, and part of me did. Part of me could even appreciate knowing he thought of us every time he left the house. But still. "Then why did you choose to be a cop?"

"Believe it or not, I wanted to do some good. I really did. But then I realized after a while that most of the time, I was walking into situations expecting to find a certain kind of criminal. I was looking for . . ."

"For me?"

Dad reached over and picked up the spirometer and started inspecting it from every angle. He couldn't say it, and instead just finished the story. "So I quit the force." He took a deep breath, and I got the feeling that he felt both relieved and ashamed that he had gotten that off his chest.

"Look, all I'm trying to say is that not all cops are bad."

"I know that." I hadn't even noticed—mainly because of my nervousness—that the foil from the juice cup, I had taken it and rolled it between my thumb and pointer fingers, over and over again, until it had become a perfectly round pellet. A tiny, uncrushable thing.

"As a matter of fact, most cops are good. I worked with a lot of great guys, really trying to make a difference. You need to know that they're not all wolves."

"Dad, I do. But not all kids who look and dress like me are bad either. Most of them aren't. And even the ones who are don't deserve to be killed, especially if they don't have no weapons."

"But a lot of times they *do*, Rashad."

"But Spoony was telling me yesterday that most times, they *don't*."

"Spoony doesn't know everything." I could tell Dad was getting frustrated. "And neither do you."

"And neither do you." I couldn't back down from him. Not this time.

Dad stood up, smirked, and nodded. He looked at me as if it was his first time seeing me. As if I had just taken off a mask, even though I was practically wearing one with all the itchy gauze taped to my face. Maybe it was him who had just taken off a mask. He set the spirometer down on the side table and reached for my hand. "Listen, I gotta get going. Your mother said she was coming by later, and that she might be bringing a lawyer in to talk to you. She wants to press charges, so . . . yeah. Be on the lookout for her."

Press charges? My initial thought was that pressing charges was a bad idea. My second thought was that I would have to go to court, which I already wasn't too keen on. My third thought was just an echo of my first thought, that pressing charges was a bad idea, but there was no point in trying to talk my mother out of it. Even my father knew that.

"I'll be here." I stated the obvious. We shook hands, awkward and formal.

"Okay."

He headed for the door.

"Dad," I called. He turned around. "If I'm checked out by Friday, I'm thinking about going down to the protest. If I go, you should come."

He didn't respond. But as he left the room, something in his face dimmed.

Later, after an hour or two more of sleep, and an hour or two of working on my drawing, sketching and shading some, I guess, screwed-up self-portrait, I decided that it was time for another walk. I took Tuesday off from walking, but I knew I couldn't take another day off, because if I did, Clarissa would chew me out (in the nicest way ever). And the truth is, I wanted to get out of the room, this little closet room, with the beeping things, and the TV. If it weren't for Clarissa, my hospital room wouldn't have been much different than a prison cell. Not that I've ever been to jail, but based on what I've heard in rap songs, and what my dad always said about it (another one of his tactics to get us to do right was to talk about jail), it seemed pretty similar. An uncomfortable bed. Three meals. Loneliness, even when the visitors come.

So I got up, brushed my teeth, washed my face, closed my gown up tight—what's the deal with the whole ass-out hospital gown thing, anyway?—and left my room. I was going stir-crazy, especially after my father dropping that bomb on me. My dad. I mean, how could he have just . . . I couldn't even think straight about what he did. The other thing, though, was that I needed to make sure that if I was going to try to go to this protest—I hadn't really made up my mind yet, but I was definitely thinking about it—I had better practice walking.

Once I got through my door, the fluorescent white light from the ward hit me, stung my eyes. This time, the plan was to just do a loop. Walk all the way around until I was back where I started. I inched down the hall, my legs eventually returning to normal as the stiffness worked itself out. I tried not to be a creep, but it's really hard not to look in an open door, and most of the patients on the floor had their doors wide open for whatever reason. A woman sat in a chair, asleep, in Room 413. An older man sat on the edge of his bed, oxygen tubes hooked under his nostrils as he struggled to clip his fingernails in Room 415. A young girl playing on a cell phone as an older woman massaged the feet of a person I couldn't see lying in bed, in Room 417. And on and on I went. Peeking into the rooms of strangers. Peeking into their lives. Hearing people coughing and moaning. Seeing families gathered together, sometimes talking, sometimes not talking. I even saw a few rooms with TVs on, the news playing, everyone peeking into my life as I was peeking into theirs.

Once I finally finished the lap, which may have taken fifteen minutes—pathetic—I returned to my room to find two women in it, one I recognized and one I didn't. The one I didn't was looking sort of down, toward the floor. The one I did recognize was looking directly at the one I didn't. At first, I thought I was loopy, like I was buggin', so I stepped out to make sure I had walked into the right room. Room 409. R. BUTLER. That's me.

I stepped back inside hesitantly.

"Uh, hello," I said, then spoke to the woman I recognized. "Mrs. Fitzgerald?"

"Hi, baby," she said grandmotherly.

"What are you doing here?"

"Well, I was coming to bring you something, but when I got to your room this lady was in here. And I asked her if she knew you and she said, not really, so I decided that I would sit in here with her until you got back." Mrs. Fitzgerald's arms were crossed, and she was glaring at the lady. She was guarding my room. Shoot, maybe she really did volunteer at the fire department.

"Thank you," I said, easing farther into the room. I was happy to see Mrs. Fitzgerald, as I'd had no intention of trying to make that trek back to the gift shop—last time damn near killed me. So it was nice that she popped in to check on me. Then I turned to the other lady because, well, now Mrs. Fitzgerald had made the whole situation even more awkward.

The woman stood and extended her hand. I shook it. "Rashad, I'm so sorry for just barging in like this. I'd been meaning to come see you, but things have just been so busy, and I just, well, I just wanted to stop by and see how you were."

I had no idea what to say, so I just studied her face, trying to place her. But I couldn't.

"Oh, gosh, you don't know who I am!" she said suddenly. "My name is Katie Lansing. I'm the lady in the store who accidentally fell over you."

The woman with the navy suit and white sneakers. The one searching for a beer after a long week.

I reached for my bed and sat, suddenly feeling a little dizzy, my mind racing. Why had she decided to come see me? It wasn't her fault that all this happened—though that klutzy moment seemed to set this whole thing in motion. No, I take that back. It had nothing to do with her. It might've happened even if she hadn't tripped over me. And if not to me, maybe to someone else. Definitely to someone else.

"How . . . did you find me?"

"This is the only decent hospital in town—lucky guess. Plus, your name's on the door." She smiled slightly.

"Well, what can I do for you?" I still had no idea what to say.

"Yeah, what can he do for you?" Mrs. Fitzgerald totally had my back. I guess she could tell I was uncomfortable.

Ms. Lansing's face went serious. "Well, I guess I just wanted to say I'm sorry about everything that happened, I mean, that is happening." She blinked hard. I was getting used to the hospital blinks. "I saw everything. The way that officer . . . I just . . ." Now she started to get choked up. "I should go. I just mostly wanted to come by and give you this." She handed me her business card. "If you need me to testify, I absolutely will."

"Thanks," I said, suddenly thinking again about the fact that at some point, once I was out of the hospital and even after the protest, there was going to have to be a trial. I had to go to court. I had never been to court before, but judging from all the TV shows—which is all I really had to go off— it seemed almost as scary as going to jail. But maybe if Ms. Lansing came and told the story as it really happened, they'd believe her, and I could get out of there as quickly as possible. That was my hope. Not likely, but still . . . a hope. And for that reason, I was grateful for her business card, which I set on the side table. And then she was gone.

Now it was just me and Mrs. Fitzgerald. She sat with a plastic bag in her lap, and her right leg crossed over her left, exposing her saggy stockings, which were the same color brown as she was, so it looked like a layer of ankle skin was shedding from her body like a snake.

"So . . ." Mrs. Fitzgerald folded her hands on top of the plastic bag. "A car accident, huh?" *Uh-oh*, I thought.

"She told you everything?"

"She didn't have to. I knew who you were when you came into the gift shop. I read the newspaper, front to back, every single day. And I don't know if you know this or not, but you, my boy, are news." She glanced up at the TV. It was off, but the gesture was merely to acknowledge that it had been on, *everywhere*.

"Yeah, unfortunately," I huffed. "So why didn't you say something?"

"Say what? To hold your head up? That everything would be okay? Baby, I could tell by the look on your face that you ain't need none of that. Sometimes, when people get treated as less than human, the best way to help them feel better is to simply treat them as human. Not as victims. Just you as you. Rashad Butler, before all this."

"Yeah," I said, really grateful for that, though it had never really even crossed my mind that that's exactly what I needed.

"But there's still business to tend to."

"What you mean?"

"Well, there are still things that can't be overlooked. Like this protest I've been hearing about. You going?" Mrs. Fitzgerald asked, blunt. Old people never hold back.

"Planning on it. I think. I just gotta wait and see if I get outta here first."

She raised her eyebrows. "Ain't nobody holding you here. You can walk out whenever you want." I reached over and slid Ms. Lansing's business card from one corner of the side table to the other. Then I flipped it upside down and moved it back to its original spot.

"Yeah, I guess you're right. But I don't know. I just don't want to get out there and then have something go wrong with my ribs and then I gotta come back here for another week. Better to be safe than sorry." I ain't never been so careful in my life, but I had also never felt pain like that before either.

"No, it's not," she said, as if she'd been waiting for me to say that so that she could shut it down. "Not all the time." She glared at me for a moment, and then just as quickly her face relaxed. As if she was scanning me and then found what she was looking for. The chink in my armor.

"You scared."

"It's not that, it's—"

"It *is* that." The old lady cut me off. "Let me tell you something. I'm seventy-four. You know what that means? That means I was around during the civil rights movement. Means I remember all of that. The segregation. The lynchings. Not being able to do what you want to do, or go where you want to go. Or vote. I remember everybody looking at my brother, God bless his soul, like a criminal. An animal. Like he was scum or less than, just because of the way he looked. Skin like coal. Hair like cotton—" She paused and tongued the roof of her mouth, so I offered her water in a Styrofoam cup Clarissa had brought in earlier. I hadn't touched it. Mrs. Fitzgerald took a sip, and then she was off. "I remember the bus boycott, and the Freedom Riders, and all that. I remember the March on Washington, and I especially remember the ones down in Selma."

"You were there for all that?" I asked in amazement.

She took another sip of water, swallowed, then said, "No. I wasn't there for any of them." She got a fierce look on her face.

"Because I was scared. My brother took the bus trip down to Selma. He begged me to go. *Begged* me. But I told him it didn't matter. I told him that he was going to get himself killed, and that that wasn't bravery, it was stupidity. So he went without me. I watched the clips on the news. I saw him being beaten with everyone else, and realized that my brother, in fact, was the most courageous man I knew, because Selma had nothing to do with him. Well, one could argue that it did, a little bit. But he was doing it for *us*. All of us."

Mrs. Fitzgerald rocked forward in the chair until she eventually got back to her feet. "Now, I'm not telling you what to do. But I'm telling you that I've been watching the news, and I see what's going on. There's something that ain't healed, and it's not just those ribs of yours. And it's perfectly okay for you to be afraid, but whether you protest or not, you'll still be scared. Might as well let your voice be heard, son, because let me tell you something, before you know it you'll be seventy-four and working in a gift shop, and no one will be listening anymore." She set the plastic bag on the seat. "Brought some snacks. You gotta be sick of this hospital mess by now."

"What is it?" I asked, reaching for the bag.

"Just some chips. I didn't know what flavor you liked, so I brought them all. Except plain."

I sat back on the bed and thought about what Mrs. Fitzgerald said. Tried to imagine protesting in Selma, the March on Washington. Man. And I was worried about a regular street in my regular town. I thought about the fear, but I also thought about how I would feel if I didn't go, if I didn't, as she said, speak up. Maybe nothing would happen. But it was at least worth a try. I turned the TV on, and sat and watched the news, but this time I really *watched* it. Forced myself to see myself. To relive the pain and confusion and my life changing in the time it took to drop a bag of chips on a sticky floor. I pulled out my sketch pad and started drawing like crazy, but it was hard—stupid damn tears kept wetting the page, they wouldn't stop, but neither would I. So I kept going, letting the wet spread the lead in weird ways as I shaded and darkened the image. The figure of a man pushing his fist through the other man's chest. The other figure standing behind, cheering. A few minutes more, and normally it would've been complete. A solid piece, maybe even the best I had ever made. But it wasn't quite there yet. It was close, but still unfinished. I took my pencil, and for the first time broke away from Aaron Douglas's signature style. Because I couldn't stop—and I began to draw features on the face of the man having his chest punched through. Starting with the mouth.

Thursday

QUINN

I woke up a frigging hour before the alarm clock. My mind was racing. Ma was still at work, Willy still snored in the trundle bed below me, and so I got up and stood in the living room, staring out the window. Pink sunrise warmed the houses on the other side of the street, but it was still early enough that the dark blue-purple of night had not completely burned away. The whole neighborhood looked asleep. I headed for the front door, then down the stoop to the sidewalk. There was no one else out. Not a single car moved on my street or the two avenues at either end. Everything was still and quiet except for the swoop and chatter of a pair of sparrows darting in and out of driveways.

I was completely alone.

I looked toward the Galluzzo house. From where I stood,

I could see the American flag spearing up in its holder and hanging in loose folds in the air above the front steps, and a memory bit me—the day I stood beneath that flag in a cheap, itchy, dark suit that had once been Paul's and didn't fit Guzzo, but fit me everywhere except that the shoulders were too wide. I remembered Paul, squatting in front of me as I stood on the bottom step, patting my shoulders, trying to adjust the seam so it didn't fall forward over my arm. "Quinn," he'd said. "There are no words that will make you feel any better that he's gone, but know this—you need anything, I mean anything, little man, you come to me." And I remembered how miserable I'd felt, but also that— because Paul made sure I *knew* he was always going to be there for me—I felt relieved. Even though I didn't have my dad anymore, at least I had a version of his protection. I remembered how Paul, finally satisfied with the seam, had stood, turned toward the street, and held up his hand to block the sunlight from his eyes, and as he did, the shadow of his body fell over mine, blocking all the sunlight from me, too. I didn't have to squint. I looked out at the faces of the people along the sidewalk in front of us and I did not feel alone.

Something else dawned on me. When I'd stood under the flag and I'd looked up at Paul, who promised to take care of me, he had only recently graduated high school. I mean, he hadn't been much older than I was now. He'd probably been thinking the same thing I was this year: Where am I going to be next year, and what the hell am I going to do with my life?

What had happened to that guy? Who had he become?

Until this week, all anybody'd been talking about was the damn basketball scouts. I'd obsessed over it too: what I needed to do to set myself up for tomorrow, next year, and whatever the hell came down the road after that. But as I stood in front of my own house in the cool, violet morning, I had the crazy idea that I could be standing here thirty years from now looking back. In my history class, we'd talked about how some moments in history are moments people never forget. People could remember exactly where they were and what they were doing. I was three years old when 9/11 happened, so I didn't remember it like all the teachers in school did. But Ma did, because she knew what it meant for Dad. Adults were always asking each other: Where were you when it happened? Where were you?

Well, where was I when Rashad was lying in the street? Where was *I* the year all these black American boys were lying in the streets? Thinking about scouts? Keeping my head down like Coach said? *That* was walking away. It was running away, for God's sake. I. Ran. Away. Fuck that. I didn't want to run away anymore. I didn't want to pretend it wasn't happening. I wanted to turn around and run right into the face of it.

I took a deep breath as the breeze picked up, and as I stared down the street at Paul's house, I knew for damn sure what I was doing *this* Friday night.

I went back inside and began my usual morning workout, and as I was pumping through my squats, I had an idea. I ran into the kitchen and rifled through the junk drawers, looking for a black marker. I couldn't find one. I knew I didn't have one, but Willy might, so I crept through our room while he still slept and tried to find something that might work. Finally, in a green plastic box on the floor on his side of the closet, I found a big, black permanent marker. Then I dug out one of my plain white T-shirts.

On the front, I wrote: I'M MARCHING

On the back, I wrote: ARE YOU?

There were plenty of kids, black, white, and everyone else, who looked at me like I was a dumbass when I got to school wearing the T-shirt. And there were plenty of kids, black, white, and everyone else, who nodded or slapped hands with me. Even in English class, Mrs. Tracey looked at my T-shirt and smiled. "Me too," she said. And I was actually daring to think that the day was going down much easier than I thought it would when I saw Dean Wykoff walking down the hall between second and third periods. He stepped in front of me, one eyebrow raised, and read my T-shirt. I assumed he was going to give me one of his signature finger curls, that thing he does that's kind of like he's making fun of himself but also isn't and he actually expects you to come closer when he does it. As dean of students, he was also Dean of Discipline, and since I was "the model son" Quinn Collins, I'd never been called to his office before, and I thought, well, if this was going to be my first time, it was worth it. But he didn't give me the finger curl. He nodded, threw a little frown in, but kept on walking, not giving me a hard time at all.

Yes, there were some kids giving me the stink eye for wearing the shirt, but no one directly gave me shit until Dwyer found me in the hall after fourth period. He grabbed my elbow and pulled me over to the lockers.

"What the hell, man?" His freckly face was so close to mine he barely had to speak much louder than a whisper. "What are you doing?"

"What it says I'm doing."

Dwyer glanced around the hall. "I said don't fuck this up, not fuck this up even more. What the hell, man? You better not let Coach see that shirt. No protest, remember?"

"Dude," I said, yanking my arm out of his grip and stepping

back. "People should be able to go to the protest if they want. It's important, man."

He pulled up and looked down at me, giving me a face worse than Dean Wykoff had ever given anybody. "You're wack," Dwyer told me. "What the hell happened to you?" And then he split for class, leaving me to chew on that by myself. I didn't have the words for it, but I felt I had an answer to the question.

The rest of the day was a blur of distraction. Nobody was getting much done in class, and I had to hand it to Mrs. Erlich, because she trashed her trig plan for the day and wrote a bunch of facts and figures on the board, which I started copying into my notebook, fast.

> In 2012, in the United Kingdom, the number
> of people (regardless of race) shot and killed by
> police officers: 1

> In 2013, in the United Kingdom, the number
> of times police officers fired guns in the line of
> duty/the number of people fatally shot: 3/0

> In the United States, in the seven year period
> ending in 2012, a white police officer killed a
> black person nearly two times a week.

"I'm not much of a talker," she finished up. "You know that. But I know numbers. The numbers don't lie, kids. The numbers always tell a story."

Guzzo was nowhere at lunch, but even though he'd avoided me all day, I knew he'd seen me, seen my T-shirt. At basketball practice, though, he couldn't avoid me anymore. He showed up late, just as Coach blew his whistle and a chaotic warm-up came to an end. I tried to catch Guzzo's eye, but he wouldn't look at me. Coach had us run drills to get the blood pumping, and then we practiced four or five plays. The last play was designed specifically for English, and Coach called it "Fist." It was an isolation offense to run when another team played us man-to-man defense. We'd all form a column in the paint as English called the play at the top of the key, and then we'd scatter and make a wide box away from the net so English could take his man one-on-one to the hoop, because he could beat anybody off the dribble. And he did. Even though we knew the play, as we ran it, English beat us all, again and again. He was unstoppable.

And when it was finally time to scrimmage, Coach asked us to play hard, and he let the point guards call whatever plays they wanted. He struck a good balance—I was playing on the team opposite English most of the time, and even though Fist was designed for him, he didn't call it. He ran every other play, once, twice, he ran Gold three times, and then finally, after I'd sunk a three from my sweet spot, English calmly walked the ball up the court to the hash mark and called Fist. He blazed past Nam for the easy layup. We missed at the other end, and English didn't push the fast break. He slowed it all down, got to the top of the key, called Fist again, spun a circle around Nam, and another one around Tooms—who came in from the weak side to help—and swooped under the basket with a reverse layup. He did it a third time in row, and this time, when he put his fist in the air, he paused and said, "Rashad," and waved his fist like a flag before zigzagging a fierce line to the hoop, banging and slipping past nearly everybody. He yelled and slapped the backboard as he went up for the layup and nailed it.

We were glistening with sweat under the incandescent lights in the gym, all breathing heavy, even English, as he jogged backward to set up for D, and somehow, even though I was concentrating on the play, another part of my brain recognized how stupid it was to believe Rashad's name wasn't on all our minds—how interconnected all these things were in our lives, how we couldn't just separate basketball from the rest of our life, just like we couldn't separate history from the present, just like we couldn't have racism in America without racists.

My team pushed the ball up the court, and you could

already feel the nerves bouncing in our bodies. Nam kicked the ball down low as I made my cut to the far corner, but someone else got a finger on it, so it spun off course, and Guzzo and I chased after the loose ball. It had nearly rolled out of bounds, but he slammed into me anyway. We hit the floor, and what might have looked like good hustle was actually just us ripping at each other more than the ball itself, elbowing each other, until finally, the ball rolled away and the two of us wrestled on the floor. I slipped out of Guzzo's grip and got to my feet. His face was a twisted mitt of hate. He hated my guts, and I think he hated everyone's guts at that moment, but mine most of all, and I didn't blame him.

Coach blew his whistle, but Guzzo just stared dead at me.

We got back into the scrimmage, and I tried to shake it off, but I couldn't shake the snarl on Guzzo's face when he looked at me, any more than I could shake Rashad's name from my head.

The game started up again, and after only a few trips up and down the court I found myself going for a rebound against Guzzo, and it was like he had been waiting for this all day, because as I went up for the ball, I caught a flash of his elbow in the corner of my eye, and then I felt my lip explode. I fell straight on my ass, tried to stand, wobbled, and collapsed. Everybody was around me in seconds. Guzzo first. He had his hand out, helping me up, apologizing loudly, saying it was an accident. My whole head rang like the bells of St. Mary's after Easter Mass.

It was an accident, Guzzo kept insisting, and while I'm sure no one believed him, Coach let it slide and told me to go clean myself up. It was getting near the end of practice anyway, and I didn't want to hear any damn speeches or anything— especially more rules about not going to the march. I'd worn the T-shirt. Now I was committed. As I washed and got changed, my mind was on fire, and it would have been impossible to chant *team* if Coach had asked me to.

I was ready to go when the rest of the team came into the locker room. I slung my backpack over my shoulder, and on my way out, I found English. I told him we should just call the play Rashad, instead of Fist, something everybody in the stands would have to hear every time we ran the play.

"I know," English told me. "I'd already been thinking that."

We smiled and slapped hands.

I was out of the locker room and heading down the hall to the doors, when Coach called my name. I turned, and he called me back to him. He stood with his legs spread in his Superman stance by the door to the locker room, but twirling his whistle in one hand.

"Collins," he said when I got back to him. "I don't think you're thinking this through."

I shrugged.

He gestured to my shirt. "I want to remind you what I'm talking about."

I nodded.

"Yes, sir," I said. The tone in his voice was flat and deadening and frankly starting to scare me a little.

"This bullshit," he said, pointing at my chest again, "has to stop. You know the rules."

"Sir—" I began, but he cut me off.

"No excuses. I'm calling your mother about this too. You need to straighten your shit out, stay focused, and remember we have everything riding on next week and every practice and every game for the rest of the season. You hear me?"

I was about to speak, but he put his hand up.

"Actions speak louder than words, son." He bent forward, his eyes wide. "You've got too much riding on this, Collins."

He turned and walked past the locker room toward his office, and even though I hate when people call me "son"— like they have any frigging right to call me that—I couldn't go after him or tell him, or say anything to him, because I knew for damn sure he meant what he said and he was going to call Ma right then.

I got the hell out of there before anyone else slipped out of the locker room to give me a hard time, and I left the gym by the side door, like usual. I was about to pull out my phone to text Jill when I saw Guzzo leaning against the wall a few feet away, still in his basketball shorts and T-shirt.

"I've been trying to find you all day—" I started, but he didn't waste any time talking. He charged. He swung as soon as he was close enough, and I blocked it, but the force knocked me back into the brick wall. He swung again and I shielded my head, but he got me in the chest with his other fist, I lost my guard and he slugged me across the cheek. I spun and hit the ground.

I wasn't thinking clearly, the grooves in the concrete were moving in and out of focus, but I knew enough to know that my body wasn't being hit anymore. Mostly I was fine; he'd hit twice, and that must have been enough. Maybe he'd even scared himself, because if he'd wanted to, he could have ruined me right there, but instead he just hovered over me, calling me all kinds of names, telling me how awful I was for turning my back on him, on Paul, following the crowd and jumping on the Rashad bandwagon because it was the easy thing to do.

"First Jill gets all crazy and radical. And now you? What the fuck?"

I rolled over and tried to catch my breath.

"Don't let me see your face in our house again," Guzzo went on. "Don't even speak to me. We play ball, but we don't speak to each other. You got me?"

I sat up against the brick wall and gave a short nod. I

unzipped my coat and wiped the blood from my mouth with the T-shirt that said I was marching. At the sight of the shirt, Guzzo spat on me and slammed the door behind him as he stormed back into the gym.

I didn't want anyone making more of a big deal about Guzzo and me, so I hauled myself up and hurried away before anyone came out. I went the long way around, hit the Burger King, and leaned against the stall door in the bathroom with wads of toilet paper pressed to my lips until the bleeding stopped. I was all right. I could walk. I could see. I'd stopped bleeding. My cheekbone didn't feel broken. I didn't need to go to the hospital or anything.

Oh, shit.

I stood in the locked stall, staring up at the weak, flickering bathroom light, thinking about how I'd seen Rashad on the concrete a week before and I hadn't even known who he was. And now, not even a week later—what the hell? Rashad and I had been beaten up by brothers from the same family?

But even thinking that was off base, because there was no comparison. The beatings were no comparison. The reasons for the beatings were no comparison. I wasn't going to stand there and pretend I knew what life was like for Rashad. There was no way. We lived in the same goddamn city, went to the same goddamn school, and our lives were so very goddamn different.

Why? You'd think we'd have so much in common, for God's sake. Maybe we even did. And yet, why was there so much shit in between us, so much shit I could barely even see the guy?

It was like Jill had said. Nobody wants to think he's being a racist, but maybe it was a bigger problem, like everyone was just ignoring it, like it was invisible. Maybe it *was* all about racism? I hated that shit, and I hated thinking it had so much power over all our lives—even the people I knew best. Even me.

I wanted to figure out all that bullshit in between us. So now there was something else I wanted to do. I wanted to see the whole dude who lived that life.

I was frigging exhausted when I got home, but it didn't matter, because my fights for the day weren't done. Ma always had Thursday nights off. It was her first night home in seven days, and when I got in, I learned that, yes, Coach had called and warned her that something was going on between Guzzo and me. So there I was, looking like a crazy person, and there was Ma, looking at me like I was a crazy person, and at first she just fluttered around trying to make sure I didn't have a broken nose, or jaw, or loose teeth, or any of that, but when she finally accepted that the worst of it was a bruise on my cheek and a lip that looked like I'd tried to eat spaghetti with a steak knife, she finally sat down across from me at the little round kitchen table, leaned her head into one hand, and asked me what the hell I was doing.

Willy was at the table too, doing homework, and I looked to him. "See that?" I said. "Not 'What did Guzzo do?' What did *I* do?"

Ma frowned. Pointed to my bloody T-shirt. "Don't be coy with me, Quinn Marshall Collins."

"Ma!" Willy yelped. "Come on! Guzzo beat him up. Why are you getting on him?"

I stuck out my fist and Willy bumped it. "Thanks, man," I said.

Ma raised a half smile at Willy. "You can't play two against one on me. I'm immune. I'm your mother."

"But Ma!" Willy said.

She reached over and gently held his wrist. "Please," she said. "Let me speak with your brother." She turned back to me. "What are you doing with that shirt?"

"Letting people know I'm going to the march."

"You aren't going to the march, Quinn."

"Yes, I am."

"No, you are not. I'll miss work tomorrow night. We'll all stay home and we'll have a family night at home for once."

"Ma," I said. "I'm going to the march."

"Listen," she said. "After Coach Carney called, I called Rita. Guzzo told her why the two of you got into a fight." She sat back, folding her arms across her chest, accusatory. "I know this is all complicated, but think about what you're doing to the Galluzzos." She pointed to the shirt again. "What is all this? You're not marching!" She paused, rubbed her forehead, and when she was calm again, she continued. "Honey, I know you think you are doing the right thing, but you aren't."

"I think I am."

"No, what you are doing is thinking very selfishly." She got up and poured herself a glass of water and stayed standing against the counter. "You think you are taking the moral high road, but what does this all mean for the rest of your family, Quinn? What does it mean for me and your brother?"

"I'm kind of hoping you'll have my back."

"No, Quinn. Look," she continued. "Just step out of the way. Even if it's ugly at school, this isn't your fight. Why are you jumping into the middle of it?"

"I'm already there, Ma. I was there Friday night. Ma, I *saw* it. I'm right in the middle of it, which is why I can't do nothing."

She took a sip of water and stared at me.

"Have you seen the video, Ma?"

Willy turned to me. "I have."

"What?" Ma cried. "Why would either of you watch it? Watch the fool they're making Paulie out to be? Do you see what you've done, Quinn? You're just dragging us all into it with you."

"Ma," I said, pushing back my chair and standing. "You're already in the middle of it too. I think we all are."

She gripped the countertop. "I don't know how to talk to you right now." She paused, and then added, "What would your *father* say if he were here?"

She never invoked Dad. Even though the whole town whipped out their Saint Springfield cards whenever it was most convenient, Ma never did. Dad had been her high school sweetheart, her husband, and the father of her two boys, and so for her, that's what came first. He wasn't a symbol. He was just gone. Gone for seven years now, and Ma was frigging exhausted.

"I don't know," I said, working hard to keep my voice level. "But I know he stood up for what he believed in."

I walked across the kitchen and wrapped my arms around her. She put her glass down and hugged me back, her thin fingers holding on to me tight.

When Paul Galluzzo told me he was signing up to become a cop, he and I were practicing three-pointers in the Galluzzo driveway. I was in ninth grade, and basketball tryouts were one week away. Guzzo was still inside, changing, and before he came out, Paul tossed the basketball up and down in one hand and dropped his other hand on my shoulder. "Your dad," he told me. "Just thinking about him inspires me. I've been doing a lot of thinking lately. And I realize, your father was a hero. I want to be somebody like that. I want to be somebody who makes a difference too." He might have been the two hundredth person to tell me my father was a hero, but this was the strangest time, because it was the first time I'd heard someone say it and it didn't piss me off.

"Man, you already are somebody who makes a difference," I told him.

He laughed. "Nah, but I mean make a difference in the world. Like a real difference. Like your dad."

I did not want to be a hero. I did not want to make any of what had happened in the last week about me. There was a guy who'd just spent six days in the hospital because the guy who'd been *my* personal hero for four years had put him there. *Paul beat Rashad.* That was the truth. And if Ma was going to talk about Dad, so was I. She didn't remember Dad the hero, she remembered Dad the man—and so did I. I knew him too. He was a hero, not in the way people always talked about him—not the soldier, not the war hero—but because of the person he was.

Paul'd gotten it all wrong. Becoming a cop would not make him a hero—but what kind of cop he became could have.

I'd been thinking about that all day, but I didn't have the words for it until Ma brought up Dad. Everybody wanted me to be loyal. Ma wanted me to be loyal. Guzzo wanted me to be loyal. Paul wanted me to be loyal. *Your dad was loyal to the end,* they'd all tell me. *Loyal to his country, loyal to his family,* they meant. But it wasn't about loyalty. It was about him standing up for what he believed in. And I wanted to be my dad's son. Someone who believed a better world was possible—someone who stood up for it.

RASHAD

M y mother did eventually show up with the lawyer
she found Wednesday evening, but by the time
she got there, I was wiped, maybe from getting
up so early talking with Dad, or maybe from actually talking
with Dad, or maybe from talking with Mrs. Fitzgerald,
or maybe from all of it. I was beat. I tried to rally up the
energy because this attorney, a young woman named Maya
Whitmeyer, was definitely there to talk business, or law, or
whatever, but I just couldn't. I was so sick of talking about it.

"Son, can you at least just tell her the story, beginning to end?"
my mother requested. And of course, I did. Again. I rambled off
every detail, just like I had done with my parents, my brother,
and my friends. Ms. Whitmeyer took notes in crazy fast writing
and asked if the officer ever even read me my rights (the right to

remain silent, the right to blah blah blah), which, once I thought about it, I realized he hadn't. He just skipped to the part about me not having the right to be in that store. She then explained that this should be "open-and-shut," which was lawyer-talk for "easy." But we all knew that it wasn't that simple. These types of cases were never easy. We had all seen cops get away with far worse, so why would this be any different? I mean, I wasn't killed. True, I hadn't even touched the cop; the video footage showed it all. I even had a witness. Still, there was no such thing as "open-and-shut" in cases like these. But I appreciated the lawyer's confidence. I guess somebody had to be hopeful.

There were so many questions I had for the lawyer, like why, exactly, she felt like this was going to be "open-and-shut." But honestly, I was just too exhausted to even get into it. Before drifting back to sleep, I made sure to give my mother Ms. Lansing's card. I'd barely glanced at it when she gave it to me, but before I handed it to my mom, I checked it out.

KATIE LANSING
Archivist
Springfield Department of Records and Information Services

Under her name and title was her phone number and e-mail. Seemed like another office job to me. Anything that said "Department of" just meant the job came with a cubicle and benefits. At least that's what Spoony always said. I handed the card to my mother.

"This is the lady who was in the store. She was here today," I said.

"Here?" my mother asked, nearly leaping out of her seat. The lawyer did the exact same thing.

"Yeah. She came by to see me. She told me to tell you that she would testify."

My mother stared at the card, a huge smile coming across her face, then handed it to the lawyer, who scanned it, then nodded and murmured, "This is good. This is good." And that was good night for me.

Thursday morning I was awakened by Dr. Barnes. He had come by to let me know that my vitals had been stable for forty-eight hours now—Clarissa had been keeping track, and I had been keeping up with my spirometering—and the internal bleeding had finally subsided. I just needed to stay put for a few more hours and then he'd be discharging me. Well, once my parents got there.

Best news ever. I was so ready to go. I took a shower, making sure I didn't get the bandage on my nose too wet, and I had to wash my torso lightly—even the slightest pressure on my ribs still made me see white. But when I got out of the bathroom, I realized that the only clothes I had were the ones I had on when I got to the hospital. My mother hadn't brought me anything clean to wear besides fresh underwear—she brought eight pairs! Actual clothes seemed to slip her mind. And if she hadn't thought about it, I knew my father hadn't thought about it. And Spoony—forget about it. I reached into the bottom drawer of the side table, which was also a dresser, and pulled out the plastic bag stuffed into it. I picked at the knot in the drawstring—damn, it was tight—until the mouth of the bag finally opened. I pulled my clothes out. First my jeans. I gave them a shake and laid them on one of the chairs. They were filthy and there was a small hole in the left knee, the knee that hit the ground first. Next came my shirt, swatting it out of the tight ball it had been in for the previous five days, the wrinkles deep and seemingly permanent. There was blood up by the collar. I laid it on another chair. The jacket Spoony gave me was in the closet. I opened that door, looked at the sleeve ripped a good three inches in the shoulder seam. I didn't bother taking it out—no reason to yet. I felt exhausted again, so I sat on the edge of the bed in nothing but clean boxers and looked at my clothes all ragged and torn. My blood on the shirt, concrete dust dingy-ing up the denim. Clothes that I would probably never wear again.

"Hello?" Clarissa's voice came from behind the door, just before she poked her head in like usual. I didn't flinch. It honestly didn't matter. "Whoops, I'm sorry," she said, noticing that I wasn't dressed.

"It's cool," I replied, grabbing the gown. "Come in."

Clarissa came in as I snapped the gown shut. "So, I hear you're leaving us," she said, pushing in the breakfast tray for the last time.

"That's what Dr. Barnes said."

"Good," Clarissa said. She twisted her hair up in a bun and checked my vitals, I guess just as a final precautionary measure. It would've sucked if she heard something weird in my heart, or if my temperature or blood pressure was high, and then I couldn't go home. Luckily, everything was fine. "So what's the first thing you're going to do when you get out of here?"

Funny, I hadn't really thought about it. I just wanted to go home. "I don't really know. I guess try to see my boys. Put on some clean clothes," I said, smirking awkwardly. Clarissa glanced to the chairs where I had my dirty T-shirt and jeans spread out like some kind of strange art exhibit.

"Oh my . . ." She put her hand over her mouth. "You want me to put those back in the bag?"

"No," I said. "I got it." I grabbed the shirt and jeans as Clarissa held the bag open for me to dump them in. I didn't want her to have to touch that stuff. Then I tied the drawstring back in a knot and made the decision right then and there to put the bag in the trash.

"Well, I'm probably not going to see you, so you make sure you take care of yourself."

"Thanks for everything. Really." I sat back on the bed as Clarissa gathered up her equipment.

"But before I go, I wanted to ask . . . did you ever finish that drawing you were working on?"

"Yeah, I finished it yesterday." I slid my sketch pad off the dresser and handed it to her.

"Wow," Clarissa said, gazing at the paper, then glancing back at me. "Rashad, this is incredible. You should be proud." Then she looked a little closer. "Hey . . . this one has a face."

"Yeah."

"Why?"

"Because, well, whoever is looking at this scene, you, me, I don't know, that lady Claudia James, my friends, my family, Mrs. Fitzgerald—"

"Who?"

"This lady I met," I said. "Anyway, all of us looking at the scene see the person who has the hand put through his chest. The dude with his heart torn out. It's impossible to ignore him. He has a face. He deserves a face."

Clarissa looked from the drawing, to me, then back to the drawing. "Yeah, he does."

My mom and dad showed up a few hours later. I had texted my mother, reminding her to bring me clean clothes, which she did. I also texted English, Shannon, and Carlos to let them know that I was finally on my way home.

#RashadIsAbsentAgainToday is what they all texted back, along with,

THURSDAY 5:33 p.m. from Los
ABOUT TIME. I ALMOST HAD TO REALLY STEAL
TIFF. GIVE HER A SHOULDER TO CRY ON.

THURSDAY 5:34 p.m. from Shannon
DUDE IM SO GLAD UR OUT. SHIT IS CRAZY.
GUZZO GOT INTO IT WITH QUINN AT PRACTICE.
YOU KNO QUINN?

THURSDAY 5:35 p.m. to Shannon
WHO IS QUINN?

THURSDAY 5:36 p.m. from Shannon
HE'S ON THE TEAM. MEAN JUMPSHOT. U
MIGHT NOT KNO HIM. BUT GUZZO HIS BOY,
AND THEY WENT AT IT OVER THIS WHOLE
THING.

THURSDAY 5:38 p.m. from Los
IM COMIN OVER 2NITE AROUND 8 SOLDIER-
BOY. NO CRYING. I KNO HOW MUCH UVE
MISSED ME LOL

THURSDAY 5:39 p.m. from English
DUDE WE GOTTA TALK. SCHOOL IS INTENSE.
EVERYBDY'S PICKED A SIDE.

THURSDAY 5:41 p.m. to English
I KNO. COME THRU 2NITE. LOS IS COMING.
BRING SHAN.

And before I knew it, I was leaving the hospital, wearing a sweat suit, carrying nothing but my notepad. But before we left, I tore out the piece I'd drawn and set it on the food tray for Clarissa. Just to thank her again. I wish I could've seen Mrs. Fitzgerald one more time, but the truth is, when it was finally time to go, I was ready to get the hell out of there. I didn't want to make any extra stops.

Apparently, the lawyer my folks hired asked the media to give us some privacy, which was a good thing because we didn't have to dash from the hospital to the car through a mob of cameras and microphones. That would have been too much for me. Instead, it was just a few short, peaceful steps from the door to the car. I sat in the backseat as my dad drove through the city. Neither of my parents said much, which was weird. I had this strange feeling like they were uncomfortable around me, or around each other. Something was different, but I couldn't put my finger on it.

I cracked the window, the fall crisp seeping in, the familiar static of air pushing through a tight space. Through neighborhoods, down the crowded streets, First Street, Second Street, Third Street. Red light. My father put his blinker on, but there was no reason for him to turn. We lived straight ahead. But he made a left at Third and went around the block, coming back out to Main Street at Fifth, the whole time glancing at me weird through the rearview. But I knew what he was doing. He was dodging Fourth Street. He wanted to skip Jerry's, as if him not driving by it made it no longer exist. As if that's all it would take to help me forget. Maybe he was doing it for himself, but the way my parents were acting made it clear that this was something they had discussed.

I decided not to bring it up, and instead just sat quietly until we got to the house, where I went straight in my room, to be around all my things. All my faceless sketches taped to the wall above my tiny twin bed. But more importantly, I needed my computer, so that I could scour the Internet to try to catch up on my own life. You know how weird it is to hashtag yourself, to read posts and updates other people—most of whom you don't even know—make about you? It's strange. But I did it anyway.

#RashadIsAbsentAgainToday brought up hundreds, maybe a thousand posts. Some were just pictures of all these random places with that tag, just like Spoony showed me. I knew where the first one started. At least I thought I knew. But I had no idea where all the other ones came from. Other links connected to the hashtag were of the news clips. Turns out, I was only watching the local news channel (the hospital could only get five or six channels anyway), but I was being covered in all the newspapers, and even on cable news channels. What the . . . this was insane! There were clips of panel discussions, where preachers and community leaders sat around arguing for me. Defending me. I mean, not just me, but, y'know. And then there were some clips of people defending Galluzzo, everyone saying the same things: *He was just doing his job*, and *He's a good guy*, and *We don't know if that boy was stealing or not*. And there were pictures of people holding up pieces of paper with the hashtag written on it. Some of them just said ABSENT AGAIN. There was even one of somebody in a T-shirt, I couldn't see the face, but written on the front of the shirt was I'M MARCHING, and then the back said ARE YOU?

Besides all this, the wildest part was seeing all the pictures of me snatched from websites and social media pages. Some of them were of me dressed in my usual, everyday wear. Jeans sagged just below the waist, T-shirt, sneakers. Pictures of me throwing up the peace sign, some—the ones Spoony feared—of me flipping off the camera. Carlos and the fellas had been cropped out. These images would have nasty comments under them from people saying stuff like, *Looks like he'd rob a store,* and *If he'd pull his pants up, maybe he would've gotten away with the crime! Lol,* and *Is that a gang sign?* Other pictures were of me in my ROTC uniform. Of course, those had loads of comments like, *Does this look like a thug?* and *If he were white with this uniform on, would you still question him?*

Everything was a mess. The real world. The cyberworld. All of it. I wanted to turn the computer off, but it was like seeing a car wreck—you keep looking. And I kept digging. Deeper and deeper into the rabbit hole, finding pictures and comments about my family. People saying that my father was a dirty cop and asking why everybody cared so much about me when my dad shot a kid for the same reason years ago. *Oh, so just because Officer Galluzzo's white, everybody's mad now? What about Officer Butler! This kid is the son of a bad cop. Karma is a bitch!* I have to admit, that one stung the most. Rage started to surge through me, but instead of shutting my computer down, I decided to try to look up Darnell Shackleford. I hated knowing what I now knew about my father. That he had done this to someone, and even if he didn't mean to, he ruined an innocent kid's life forever. All because of fear and assumption. And even though my father lived with the guilt, I now had to live with it too. So as I clicked on the first image link to pop up, as I stared at Darnell's high school senior picture, the arms of his wheelchair peeking into the camera too, I made it clear to myself that this protest, this whole thing, was also for him.

English, Shannon, and Carlos got to my house around eight. My mother ordered Mother's Pizza for us and had Spoony pick it up on his way in. We sat at the kitchen table waiting as patiently as possible for Ma to pick her slices before we dove in, tearing the cheesy triangles from the pie as if we had never eaten pizza before.

"So what's been going on?" I said, picking off the pepperonis and eating them like chips. Seemed like a stupid question to ask, but up until that point we'd all been sitting there listening to Carlos ramble on about how he thought Silky Wilkes really liked him. "I know y'all didn't come over here just to let this dude talk about Latrice."

"Naw, it was for the free pizza," Shannon said with a smirk.

"Oh really?" from my mother, who was using a fork and knife to cut hers.

"Kiddin', Mrs. Butler."

"Man, seriously, we just wanted to catch you up," English cut in. "People have been on edge. Even me. A few days ago I got into it with that dude Quinn I was telling you about. He was kickin' all that 'Paul was doing his job' crap, while you were laid up in the hospital with your ribs busted. I mean, it's wild. But then today, that same dude got into it with Guzzo at practice. Then afterward the dude, Quinn, came up to me to say that we should just call this one play we have, it's like an isolation play for me"—I had no idea what he was talking about—"he agreed that we should just call it 'Rashad.'"

"What?"

"Yep. Coach Carney named it 'Fist,' but I called it 'Rashad' in practice, and I'm gonna call it that in the game, too. Quinn was with me."

"Are you sure that's a good idea?" I asked, feeling really weird. Plus, I didn't want English to get benched for something like renaming a play after me.

"Dude, at this point, I don't care. It ain't like people ain't thinkin' 'bout it anyway. It's on everybody's mind."

"Plus, 'Rashad Is Absent Again Today' caught on like wildfire," Shannon said.

I looked at Carlos, who was trying to shove a whole slice in his mouth.

"Wha?" he grunted.

"I know it was you," I said. "And for the record, you should've did it in a way where the paint dripped. Almost like vampire blood style."

Carlos chewed and chewed, then finally swallowed. "I don't

know what you're talkin' 'bout." He smiled. "But that's a good idea!"

Spoony shook his head. But not in the *my little brother and his annoying friends* way. In the proud way. "So this protest," he said, getting down to business.

"It's tomorrow at five thirty," English said. "We're starting at Jerry's and working our way down to the police station."

"Y'all are gonna miss practice?" I asked, concerned.

"Who cares?" Shannon said, nodding to me. My boys. My brothers. "You should know, 'Shad, that Tiffany has been working with Jill and they've been planning the crap out of this thing. Her and Jill have been the main students organizing it from our school."

"But it ain't just our school," English explained, quick. "It's all kinds of people. Other schools. Folks in the neighborhood. Different businesses."

"I called Pastor Johnson, and he said he'd round up some folks too," Ma added. I was cool with the pastor coming, but my mother being on board, that really got me. My father, well, I wasn't sure. He wasn't out there with us, was he? Nope. He was in his room, hiding.

Spoony leaned forward. "Fellas, can I make a suggestion? When we get to the station, we should have a die-in."

"A what?" My mother went bug-eyed, probably at the word "die."

"A die-in. It's basically when you lie on the ground as a form of protest. Sorta like how the sit-ins were back in the day. But when you lie down, they can't push you over, they can't do anything to you, really, because you are already on the ground."

"They could kick you!" My mother wasn't a fan of this idea.

"But they won't. Too many cameras." Spoony looked at Ma. "I promise. It'll be fine." She nodded, nervously.

"But once we lie down, then what?" I asked, because the way I saw it, putting my body back on the sidewalk wasn't my idea of a protest. It was my idea of a nightmare.

"Then we make the most powerful statement we can make." Spoony dug in his bag and pulled out a stack of papers. "We read every name on this list. Out loud."

Friday

QuinN

Okay, look. If I thought my sudden allegiance to honesty would make me feel confident, I was wrong. If I was an honest dumbass the day before, I was a freaking piss-scared dumbass on Friday. I'd talked my game, but now I had to follow through with it.

First things first. I called the police. I had to start from the beginning. I was there.

I looked up the right number and extension and I made the call in the kitchen, shaking, holding the window frame with one hand and staring out into the sliver of street I could see from there. The phone on the other end rang and rang, as if the damn thing was testing me, trying to get me to hang up. But I didn't.

"I'd like to make a statement," I said when someone finally picked up.

There was a loud sigh. "Okay. About what?"

"The Rashad Butler incident. I saw what happened, and I'd like to make a statement."

There was a long silence on the other end. It seemed as if he'd muffled the phone with his hand.

When he came back on, he was quick and curt and aggressive, and rattled off a litany of questions. "Look. Were you in the store? Were you inside when it happened? Did you witness what happened inside Jerry's?"

"No. I was outside."

The officer sighed again. "Okay," he said. "Look, we have so many statements."

"I was there. I need to report what I saw."

"Fine. I'll take it over the phone, and someone will call you back if we need more. Name and address, please."

I couldn't see the Galluzzo house from the kitchen window, but it was hovering nearby, as if it, or everyone in it, was waiting for me just beyond my view.

He took my statement but didn't ask any questions, and he hustled me off the phone. No, I hadn't been inside. No, I didn't know *exactly* what happened. But that wasn't the goddamn point. I didn't believe Paul's story, but even if I did, it didn't matter.

I know what I saw after that, and that was all that mattered.

Plans for the march were all over the news, and so were discussions about how to deal with it. Would they cordon off the sidewalks? Would they try to stop the march altogether?

Like usual, I walked Willy to school first, and as I doubled back around to Central High, I turned the corner onto Main Street, but then I stopped and nearly ran back around the other way. About four blocks ahead, slowly making its way up the street, was an enormous black vehicle—not a tank exactly, but it had six giant wheels, and its triangular metal nose looked designed to crash through concrete walls. One cop in all-black paramilitary gear stood in the lookout turret on top, and he surveyed the street as if he were looking for snipers.

"Holy shit!" I said out loud, as it dawned on me that it was heading straight for the high school! Was this the city's response to the protest? A tank? What the hell would come next?

I zipped my coat up to the neck, worried now that going to the march was more dumbass than I'd thought. It got closer—the only frigging thing in the road!—and I realized I was shaking. I couldn't move. As it rumbled by, the concrete seemed to quake, and I stupidly ducked my head, as if that would keep me from being noticed, and steadied my hands by grabbing the straps of my backpack. *Oh my God! I can't do this. I can't do this! Tanks? Freaking tanks are coming down the street. What the hell, are they sending in the army?* It chugged by in all the thunder of its machinery, but then there was something even louder, a jeering boo rising up out of the crowd of students gathered around the front steps of the school.

The police tank continued on, and if it had meant to scare the students, it did the opposite. By the time I snapped out of it and got up to the steps, kids were yelling after the police tank.

"This is what a police state looks like!"

"Serving and protecting who?"

"Don't shoot!"

I found Jill, who was still at it, passing out flyers with info about the protest. "Hey, Quinn," she said, handing me one.

"What the hell was that?" I said, thumbing to the street.

She kind of bounced in place, all excited. "They're going crazy. I hear they're gearing up for major riots. We're not rioting. We're protesting! We have a permit to march!"

I looked back to the street and shook my head. "I don't know—now that I saw that." I mean, it was one thing to have a conviction, but to be beaten up or killed for it—was it worth it? "But is it really the right thing to do if the police are bringing in tanks? That's frigging scary shit!"

But even as I was saying this, another part of my brain was shouting at me. Tanks? What about Dad? Talk about a man who died for his convictions. How many times did he re-up after 9/11? Three. I was old enough now to know he wasn't fearless. He'd probably been scared shitless every time he went back. He wasn't strong because he wasn't afraid. No, he was strong because he kept doing it even though he *was* afraid.

Jill looked to the corner where the tank had disappeared down Spring Street—the route we were supposed to march to get to Fourth Street and Jerry's. "I hear you," she said. "But I was talking to Tiffany, and she was telling me about the speech her parents give her younger brother all the time—the speech, she said, all boys of color get from their parents. Did you ever get that speech from your mother? Did you ever get a list of ways you had to behave if the cops stop you?"

"But this is different, isn't it?"

Jill waved out over the crowd. "And it isn't just guys who fear the cops, and families with boys. There's a whole movement for the girls too. Hashtag SayHerName. It's big. This is about *everyone* who fears cops."

I adjusted my backpack, pulled the straps tighter against me. "Jesus," I moaned. Jill gave me a look. "No," I said. "I mean, that's real. I'm saying it sucks that there even has to *be* that hashtag, you know?"

"Look, if there are people who are scared of the police every day of their lives," Jill said, determined, "I'm going to live in fear of them for at least one day to say that I don't think that's right."

I grunted.

"Quinn, come on." She pushed my shoulder. "You said you want to do something. This is the something. Join the march. Look, Paulie, Guzzo, my mom—they all hate me now. But it's like it says on the flyer—" She pointed down to the paper in my hands. A block quote from Desmond Tutu covered the top half of the sheet:

IF YOU ARE NEUTRAL IN SITUATIONS OF INJUSTICE, YOU HAVE CHOSEN THE SIDE OF THE OPPRESSOR.

Jill curled a soft smile and glanced at the crowd, and then back up at me. "This is like a real moment in history, Quinn," she said, not yelling, not shouting out over the crowd, but almost shyly, like she was sharing something that meant the whole world to her. "I want to make sure I'm on the right side of it."

I gazed out over the crowd of students around us. There were other white kids like me and Jill, and black kids like Tiffany and Tooms, and Latino kids and Vietnamese kids, and multiracial kids, and kids I didn't know at all and didn't know how they identified, and I thought about what English had said to me and how many times I'd been a dick without knowing it, and it made me wonder how many times I'd remained neutral in the past too, and what that meant. What did Dad do? He ran right into the face of history. I couldn't duck now, just because I was scared.

"I'm going," I told Jill. I tried to be cool about it. "I mean, I did wear that T-shirt and all."

She laughed. "All right then. Let's go together."

The school day was a blur of chaos. Nobody was paying attention to what was happening in class—even most of the teachers were just letting the day run, so we could all get out of the building. It felt like when the last bell rang the dam would break and a flood of people would pour out of school.

And it wasn't until I got out onto the sidewalk near the gym that I remembered that, in fact, not everyone was going to the march. As I looked around for Jill, I saw Dwyer cutting across the parking lot to the gym. He was hunched forward, not looking back, trudging his way to practice, and I wondered if there'd even be enough players there to run a play. They sure as hell couldn't run "Rashad." What would they call it instead? There'd be consequences for all of us skipping practice, I knew that, but that would be Monday. Today—yes, Ma—I was trying to *take some responsibility.*

I was marching.

I repeated it to myself like a mantra. I was marching. I kept saying it as I scanned the crowd for Jill, pumping myself up, because some people had told me racism was a thing of the past, they'd told me not to get involved. But that was nuts. *They* were nuts. And more to the point—they'd all been white people. Well, guess what? I'm white too—and that's *exactly why* I was marching. I had to. Because racism was alive and real as shit. It was everywhere and all mixed up in everything, and the only people who said it wasn't, and the only people who said, "Don't talk about it" were white. Well, *stop lying.* That's what I wanted to tell those people. Stop lying. Stop denying. That's why I was marching. Nothing was going to change unless we did something about it. *We!* White people! We had to stand up and say something about it too, because otherwise it was just like what one of those posters in the crowd outside school said: OUR SILENCE IS ANOTHER KIND OF VIOLENCE.

I found Jill, and we walked with a huge group of kids, making our slow march to Jerry's. By the time we got there, the street was a river of people—an enormous group already!— winding back from the corner store. They were chanting and waving signs. All the streets behind us were open, but the police had cordoned off the side streets along the march route ahead of us. We were stuck in a kind of tunnel. Fucking hell! Sure, they'd let us march from Jerry's to the police station— that was the plan—but if anything went wrong, we'd be trapped. Thousands of us. Noise already echoed off the walls of the buildings on either side of the street.

There were thousands of cops, too, or what might have been cops. They looked more like an army of Robocops—black paramilitary outfits, helmets, automatic rifles. Jill and I kept squeezing our way closer and closer to the front, and when we could see beyond the first row of marchers, we could see the first line of the police guard, too. With the row of police tanks, like the one I'd seen that morning, and the rank upon rank of infantry, I swear it looked a lot less like Springfield and a lot more like Kabul. But it was the corner of Fourth Street. I held my breath for a moment, feeling again what I'd seen there.

Jill and I scooted toward the edge of the street, closer to Jerry's. I could see the black canisters of tear gas in the belt loops of the cops. I pulled out my phone and start filming them. I didn't know if I was allowed to film them or not, but I filmed them anyway. I filmed the tanks, too. I filmed the guys who had their guns raised and aimed toward the marchers. Then I tilted the phone back to me.

"Hey, Will," I said into the picture. "This is for you. Ma's always telling us to take responsibility. That we have to live up to what Dad died for. We need to get good grades and go to a good college and take advantage of every damn minute of our lives because he died for us. I believe that. But I believe he died for this, too. If he died for freedom and justice—well, what the hell did he die for if it doesn't count for all of us?"

Someone was blowing a whistle up front and I hit stop. People shouted instructions through a bullhorn. Jill pointed, excited. "I think I see Rashad up there! I think he's here." We tried to edge our way a little closer to the front line, and with all the camera crews hovering, and people watching us on their TVs back home, I wondered if anybody thought what we were doing was unpatriotic. It was weird. Thinking that to protest was somehow un-American. That was bullshit. This was very American, goddamn *All-American*. I craned my head, trying to see Rashad. And seeing who I thought might be him, right next to his family and English, I couldn't help wondering how, years from now, Rashad would be remembered.

The kid at the front of a march. Speaking truth to power. Standing up for injustice. Asking only to be seen and heard and respected like the citizen he was. Would he be thought of as the "All-American" boy?

But as the march began, and we trudged forward, shouting along with the people around us, "Spring-field P-D, we don't want brutality!" I just wanted to see Rashad, the kid who went to school with me. Rashad, English's friend. Rashad, the guy walking along with his family, the son they were probably all just grateful was alive.

The march wound its way from the West Side back into Central. The streets swelled with bodies and chants, and as we got down to Police Plaza 1, the crowd started to fan out around the square. I followed Jill and joined a cluster right near the front. Whistles blew around the square and the chanting stopped, the marching stopped, and everyone began to lie down on the ground.

"It's a die-in," Jill told me, and I dropped like everyone else.

Somebody had a microphone and a PA speaker, and she started reciting the names that I quickly realized were of young, unarmed black men and women who had been killed by the police in the last year. I knew some of the names from the news, but many I didn't. So fucking many.

As I listened, I looked up into what should have been the dark, autumnal evening sky, but instead the haze of flashing police lights, streetlamps, giant spotlights, the headlights of cars, the kaleidoscopic reflection off the cold concrete and glass of Police Plaza 1, all obscured the sky. There were no stars. The moon was hidden somewhere behind the blinding glare, and it felt like the city itself was collapsing, pressing in, taking only the shallowest of breaths in the squeeze of lost space.

The list of names went on.

And as I heard them, my mind sort of split in two—one part listening, and the other picking up the ideas I'd been kicking around in my head all day: Would I need to witness a violence like they knew again just to remember how I felt this week? Had our hearts really become so numb that we needed dead bodies in order to feel the beat of compassion in our chests? Who am I if I need to be shocked back into my best self?

But Rashad lived. His name wasn't on the list, and thank God it didn't have to be for us all to be here in Police Plaza. I rolled my head to see if I could find him.

I learned that the night before a protest, it's impossible to
sleep. I didn't toss or turn, I just lay flat on my back staring
into the darkness, my mind darting from thought to
thought, from friend to friend, from brother to mother, from
hashtag to hashtag. And in the morning, I wasn't groggy or
grumpy, or even sleepy. I was sick. And it was a good thing
that I hadn't planned on going back to school until Monday,
because I spent what seemed like hours in the bathroom
shitting nerves. And pizza.

Once I finally made it out to the kitchen, my mother—who
had taken the day off—was sitting at the table in her robe,
sipping coffee, staring at the television.

"Good morning," she said. Then, noticing my hand rubbing
soft circles on my stomach, her voice went into instant worry.

"What's the matter?"

"Not feeling too well," I said, easing into a seat.

"Should I take you back to the hospital?"

"No, no, I don't think it's anything like that." I hoped.

Ma got up, pressed the back of her hand against my forehead, then to my neck. "No fever. That's a good sign," she said, relief in her voice. She grabbed the kettle off the stove, lifted it to make sure there was water in it, then set it back down. She turned on the flame. "I'll make you some mint tea," she added, reaching up into the pantry to grab a tea bag and a mug. "I bet it's just your nerves. You keep 'em buried in your belly. Got that from your daddy."

"What you mean?"

"I mean, whenever you get nervous, your stomach acts crazy," she said. "Your father has the same problem. He can eat anything. Seems like his gut is made of steel when it comes to food. But when he gets nervous, he's a mess."

I never knew this about my father, maybe because he never seemed like he was too nervous about anything. I mean, besides that story he told me about him shooting Darnell Shackleford, I had never even known my father to show any sign of fear. But this new information got me thinking. He was sick earlier in the week. Said something didn't agree with his stomach, so maybe the thing that didn't agree with his gut was . . . what happened to me. Police brutality. Maybe. Or maybe it was just seeing me in pain. Or maybe even knowing somewhere deep in the pit of his belly that I was innocent.

Ma set the tea in front of me, then sat back down. We both sipped from our mugs and watched the news. Everybody was talking about the upcoming protest, which was scheduled to start at five thirty. Clips of military vehicles rolling past as reporters talked about "hopes for a peaceful demonstration." Police officers already dressed in military gear. I had seen it before. I had seen it all the other times there were protests in other parts of the country, other cities, other neighborhoods. I'd heard Spoony talk about it, because he and Berry had taken buses to other cities to march. He had been tear gassed before and told me it was like someone rubbing an onion on your eyeballs, and then pouring hot gasoline down your throat. The words "riot" and "looters" were being thrown into the conversation too, my picture next to Galluzzo's flashing across the screen, the footage of the arrest, looping. Experts arguing, *This isn't the first time this has happened. But until we have an honest conversation about prejudice and abuse of power in law enforcement, it won't stop*, and, *Unless you've been a police officer, there's no way to know how difficult a job it is. Law enforcement isn't perfect, but there are more good examples than bad.*

"Is Dad coming?" I asked, holding the cup up. The steam snaked up into my nose.

Ma pursed her lips. "Baby, I don't even know. I woke up in

the middle of the night, realizing he wasn't in the bed. When I got up to check on him, I found him standing at your door, peeking in at you, like he used to do when you were a baby. I didn't disturb him. I just crept back to the room. I was surprised he even made it up this morning for work, let alone a march."

"I was awake. I wish he would've knocked," I said, also surprised—that he had been watching me in the first place. I wondered . . . maybe he was reliving what it was like to leave me every day to be a cop. What it was like to love something enough to do anything to come back to it.

"Yeah, well, you know your father."

"Did he say something about it this morning?"

"No. He just went to work early, didn't say much of anything. Kissed me as usual and told me to be safe, but that was it. So we'll see."

The smell of mint suddenly turned my stomach. Or maybe it was what my mother had just said, which made me imagine that Dad had given her "the talk." You know, *Never fight back. Never talk back. Keep your hands up. Keep your mouth shut. Just do what they ask you to do, and you'll be fine.* Dad's guide to surviving the police. Dad's guide to surviving a protest. Dad's guide to surviving . . . Dad. Whatever it was, my stomach started hiccuping again, jumping around like I was possessed by something nasty. I set my mug down on the table and ran back to the bathroom.

Once I made sure it was safe to leave the toilet, I needed to go lie down. Who knew that lying down for a week could make you so tired? But before climbing back in the bed, I got on my knees and reached underneath it, trying to grab a shoe box that I had pushed way too far back. Argghkk—that hurt. Once I'd finally swatted it close enough to grip, I pulled the raggedy box from under the bed frame and set it on the mattress. I popped the top off and started digging through the hundreds of pieces of torn newspaper. My *Family Circus* tear-outs. I don't really know why I suddenly had to see them now, except maybe they were a distraction I could really, really count on. I mean, I could've drawn something myself, but whatever was inside was what was going to come out, so it would've probably been another picture of someone getting slammed, or something like that. So *The Family Circus* was better. Easier.

It had been a few years since I had looked at any of them, and leafing through them transported me back to sitting across from my father, licking marshmallows off the top of hot chocolate, reading them for the first time. Man, that seemed like a lifetime ago. Even thinking about it was like thinking about someone else's life, not my own. I mean, the innocence of it all seemed almost silly now. To think that life could always be as good as breakfast with your family and sharing the newspaper with your dad, looking up to him, imagining that one day you'd read the whole entire paper and drink coffee too. To think that my life could be as perfect as Billy's.

I flipped through a dozen tear-outs, then another, and then I froze. Between my fingers was the one of Billy talking to his mother. It read, *First thing you need to know is, I didn't do it.* I put it to the side and pulled out another. This one showed the little boy standing at his father's bed. His father is just waking up, and the little boy says, *Put your glasses on, Daddy, so I can remember who you are.* And another that simply said, *Mommy, when am I gonna reach my full potential?* They were still boring. Still not funny at all. But I kept reading them, a simple and safe white family framed in a circle, like looking into their lives through a telescope or binoculars from the other side of the street. From a different place. From a place . . . not always so sweet. I laid back in the bed and continued pulling them from the box, one by one, until finally I drifted off to sleep.

But it was only a short nap because before I knew it, Spoony was knocking on my door.

"Li'l bruh, you gotta get up, man. It's almost time to go," he said, cracking the door, peeking in before pushing it wide open, just as everyone had done at the hospital. He was dressed in all black. Black hoodie. Black jeans. Black boots. A megaphone in his hand. Damn. "Get dressed," he said, followed by, "What in the world were you doing?"

I looked around at all the scraps of comic strips littering the bed. "Nothing, man," I said, sitting up. "I'll be ready in a sec."

I put on all black too—just seemed like the right thing to do—and met Ma, Spoony, and Berry in the kitchen. Berry was also dressed in black. My mother, she had on her usual mom jeans, sweater, a light jacket, and sneakers. Oh, and a fanny pack. She was ready. They all were. But I needed to go to the bathroom, one more time.

"Get it out, baby," my mother said, explaining to Spoony that I had been sick all day, like that was any of his business. But that's moms for you. Funny thing is, I didn't even have to go. There was something else I wanted to do.

In the bathroom, I stood at the sink, staring at my reflection. I brought my hands to my face and slowly peeled the tape and bandage back, revealing my nose. Still swollen. There was a knot on the top—a lump that changed the way my whole face looked. I turned my head sideways—bump looked even worse. I hated that damn bump, but I didn't want people to see me all bandaged up like that. Not because I was embarrassed. Well, I was, a little. But more importantly, I wanted people to see me. See what happened. I wanted people to know that no matter the outcome, no matter if this day ended up as just another protest and Officer Galluzzo got off scot-free, that I would never be the same person. I looked different and I would be different, forever.

When I returned to the kitchen, my mother instantly began

to tear up. My brother nodded, balled his right hand into a fist, and extended it toward me. "You ready?"

I bumped my fist to his. "Yeah, I'm ready."

I couldn't believe it. We couldn't even get all the way to Fourth Street because of all the people. So Ma parked on Eighth and we walked down to join the crowd, English, Carlos, and Shannon all texting me telling me that they were in front of Jerry's. We wove in and out of the herd—so many people, mostly strangers, but everyone there for the same reason. It was unreal. Lots of people held up signs. Police officers lined the streets, creating a kind of wall, containing us. There were these huge trucks, like road tanks, blocking us at either end, locking us into a seven- or eight-block rectangle. The newspeople were there as well, men in gray suits and blue ties, holding microphones in front of some kids I recognized from school.

"Stay close," Spoony said as we pushed down Fourth Street. He held my mother's hand, and I kept a hand on her shoulder as he and Berry led the way. I was glad they had done this before, because my heart felt like it had grown feet and was trying to run away from my body. As we moved through, eventually people started to recognize me, and the crowd began to split open, making a clearer path for us.

"I see Carlos!" I said to Spoony, raising my voice to be heard.

"There's English over there!" Berry shouted back, pointing to the right. And there they were, my friends—my brothers—standing in front of Jerry's, holding big white poster boards, RASHAD IS ABSENT AGAIN TODAY written in bold black marker. They went crazy when they saw us—Shannon waving us forward like we were the royal family or something, making sure to let people know to let us through. When we finally got to them, they each hugged me, then my mom. I looked out at the crowd. People, young, old, black, white, Asian, Latino, more people than I could count. It was straight out of an Aaron Douglas painting, except there were faces. Faces everywhere. My teachers, Mr. Fisher and Mrs. Tracey. Tiffany, who gave me a look, both happy and sad. Latrice Wilkes. Oh! My comrades from ROTC, and because it was Friday, uniform day, they were dressed head to toe. Some of the basketball players. Football players. Neighborhood people. Pastor Johnson, in a suit, but this time, instead of a Bible, he held a sign up that said, RASHAD IS ABSENT AGAIN TODAY, BUT GOD IS NEVER ABSENT. Katie Lansing was there. I didn't see Mrs. Fitzgerald, but I wouldn't have wanted her out there, even though I was sure she was tough enough to handle it. Even Clarissa was there, which was amazing. I waved to her, but the crowd seemed to think that I was waving to everybody, and so they all cheered for me, which was overwhelming. I knew it wasn't just about me. I did. But it felt good to feel like I had support. That people could see me.

The chant was a simple one. I'm not sure exactly who came up with it. It just sort of started in the middle and rippled through the crowd. "Spring-field P-D, we don't want brutality! Spring-field P-D, we don't want brutality!" We chanted it, no, we screamed it, at the top of our lungs, over and over again as we started marching toward Police Plaza 1. Spoony shouted it into the megaphone, and he wasn't the only one. Everyone was on the same page, chanting the same thing as we moved down Main Street. Me, Spoony, Carlos, English, Berry, and Shannon were in the front of the crowd, and all of a sudden, our arms locked and we were leading the way like—the image came to me of raging water crashing against the walls of a police dam. Marching. But it wasn't like I was used to. It wasn't military style. *Your left! Your left! Your left-right-left!* It wasn't like that at all. It was an uncounted step, yet we were all in sync. We were on a mission.

And as we approached the police station, standing on the steps outside Police Plaza 1 was my father. Spoony slapped my arm and nodded toward Dad, totally surprised. My brother raised an eyebrow at me. I raised one at him. "Whatttttt?" Then we both grinned at the exact same time. Ma, of course, was crying. Instantly. She had been doing a pretty good job at keeping it together, but seeing my father standing there waiting for us broke her. He jogged down the steps and met us with hugs. He didn't say anything. Just hugged and locked arms with us as we turned around and faced the crowd, still chanting, "Spring-field P-D, we don't want brutality!"

Spoony gave Berry the megaphone and she started chanting through the speaker, even louder than he had. He dug in his backpack and pulled out the papers, the same papers he'd showed us the night before at the kitchen table, as Berry slowly got down on the ground. She lay flat on her back, the megaphone still to her mouth, still chanting. Spoony followed suit. He nodded to me. My father looked on, uneasy, as me, Carlos, Shannon, and English all laid down. My mother leaned in to him and whispered something. The confusion slowly slid from his face, and he took his wife's hand and helped her lower herself to the ground. Then he joined us as well. And the people in front of the crowd followed suit, realizing what was happening. The die-in was beginning, and like dominoes, the crowd began to drop, each person, young and old, lying flat on the dirty pavement, the police officers all around us in riot gear, their hands on their weapons, afraid and perplexed.

"Ladies and gentlemen!" Berry shouted through the megaphone. "Ladies and gentlemen!" The chanting died down. "We are here, not for Rashad, but for all of us! We are here to say, enough is enough! We are here to say, no more!

No more!" Spoony gave the first paper to her. And into the megaphone, she began.

"This is a roll call! Sean Bell!" Then she followed with "Absent again today! Oscar Grant! Absent again today! Rekia Boyd! Absent again today! Ramarley Graham!" She paused, and at that point the rest of us knew exactly what to do.

"Absent again today!"

"Aiyana Jones!"

"Absent again today!"

"Freddie Gray!"

"Absent again today!"

"Michael Brown!"

"Absent again today!"

"Tamir Rice!"

"Absent again today!"

"Eric Garner!"

"Absent again today!"

"Tarika Wilson!"

"Absent again today!"

And Spoony kept feeding Berry the papers, one after another, as she continued to read down the list of unarmed black people killed by the police. And I laid there on the hard concrete, for the second time in a week, tears flowing down my cheeks, thinking about each one of those names.

QUINN AND RASHAD

Oh my God! He was right over there!
Closer than I'd been to him when
Paul laid into him. Much closer.
And Rashad was looking at me, too.

I locked eyes with a kid I didn't know, but
felt like I did. A white guy, who I could tell
was thinking about those names too.

All I wanted to do was see the guy I hadn't
seen one week earlier. The guy beneath
all the bullshit too many of us see first—
especially white guys like me who just haven't
worked hard enough to look behind it all.

Those people. I hadn't known any of them,
and he probably hadn't either. But I was
connected to those names now, because
of what happened to me. We all were. I
was sad. I was angry. But I was also proud.
Proud that I was there. Proud that I could
represent Darnell Shackleford. Proud
that I could represent Mrs. Fitzgerald—
her brother who was beaten in Selma.

I wanted him to know that I saw him,
a guy who, even with a tear-streaked
face, seemed to have two tiny smiles
framing his eyes like parentheses, a guy
on the ground pantomiming his death
to remind the world he was alive.

For all the people who came before
us, fighting this fight, I was here,
screaming at the top of my lungs.
Rashad Butler.
Present.

ZOOM OUT.

ZOOM OUT, MORE.
A LITTLE MORE.

THE PLAZA. FLOODED WITH BODIES.

BUT NO BLOOD.

NO LIGHTS AND SIRENS.
JUST
CRACKLING
VOICES.
NAMES,
RISING
TO THE SKY.

IN THE CENTER OF IT ALL,

THE BOY WHO REMAINS AND THE BOY BESIDE HIM.

TWO BOYS, IN FOCUS.
TWO BOYS, CLEAR.
A NEW TOMORROW,

AN ARM'S LENGTH AWAY.

Acknowledgments

From Jason Reynolds:
First and foremost, I'd like to acknowledge all the men, women, boys, and girls who have lost their lives as a result of police brutality. Your names, though too many for these pages, will always live on in our hearts and minds. Your untimely, unjust deaths will hopefully serve as the cornerstone of change for the growing generation. I'd also like to acknowledge the people of all walks of life, in all professional and social sectors, who have been fighting this fight. The protesters and community activists, the artists, the political allies, the teachers and librarians, the everyday folks who can't quiet the internal screams—we all have a necessary part to play. ALL OF US.

I'd also like to extend a separate but very important salute to the women of every civil rights movement, whether victim or leader, who always seem to get overlooked. You have always been on the front lines. You have always been the backbone. So this is to say, I SEE YOU. WE SEE YOU. THANK YOU.

Obviously, I have to acknowledge Brendan Kiely for co-writing this book with me. My respect for you is immense. It's a true honor to call you a friend. Special thanks to Alicia Lockard and Christopher Smith for research help. I definitely appreciate you both. And as always, a huge thank you to Elena Giovinazzo, my agent, for always believing in me, and to Caitlyn Dlouhy and Justin P. Chanda, my editor and publisher, for once again providing me with a megaphone.

Last but not least, I want to thank my mother and father, and their mothers and fathers, and their mothers and fathers, for giving me an impenetrable sense of cultural pride, an unwavering sense of responsibility, and a childlike sense of hope. I do believe we can do better, be better. But we can't hide behind fear. We can't tuck truth between the cushions of comfort. We have to deal with it, really confront it, so that our children can live with a lot less weight. We owe it to them.

From Brendan Kiely:
It is one thing to write a novel, but it is another thing to live the life, and I firstly want to acknowledge the families and individuals affected by police brutality. It is my hope that this novel will be a productive voice in the vital public conversation about the many injustices inflicted upon those lived realities. I believe that we need to face honestly the legacy and effects of racism in our country, and that white people like myself—whose privilege is the result of systemic racism—have a particular responsibility to help dismantle it. We all live here. There are no bystanders. We all have a role.

There are many people who have been doing the essential work to foster the conversation about the effects of systemic racism and to deconstruct that system. I'd like to thank in particular the educators and organizers who I've worked with directly and who have inspired me, including the folks involved with the People's Institute for Survival and Beyond, the Carle Institute, the White Privilege Conference, the Anti-Racist Alliance of Educators, my colleagues at the Calhoun School, and other independent schools and public schools; and teachers, librarians, and friends in New York, New Jersey, Connecticut, and Massachusetts—I love you and thank you and honor the change that you make in the world every day.

To my family—Maryanne Kiely, Tom Kiely, Niall Kiely, Trish Kiely, Heide Lange, John Chaffee, Joshua Chaffee—I love you all and I'm so deeply grateful for your love, encouragement, and support. Thank you all. And thank you especially Jessie Chaffee, my partner in all things in life, who teaches me about the expansiveness of the word love—this and everything for you.

Thank you Rob Weisbach, super-agent and super-friend, for your enthusiasm, intelligence, and your belief in me and my work. I hold our partnership close to my heart.

In the making of this book, I am extremely fortunate to work with the amazing folks at Simon & Schuster, in particular Caitlyn Dlouhy, an editor who works with such speed, intelligence, and care, I have to wonder if she didn't anticipate the whole story before it was written. Thank you for making this book more the book it wanted and needed to be.

Thanks to Katy Hershberger, the tireless publicist who seems to be three people in one, and to whom I am especially grateful because she introduced me to Jason when she first put us on tour together last year. And thanks also to Ruta Rimas and Justin Chanda, for believing in my work from the beginning and welcoming me into the S&S family—here's to many more years of partnership.

And most importantly, thank you, Jason. The process of making this book was inspiring and challenging, and I'm so deeply grateful to have worked through it together with you. Thank you for your friendship, because as we remind ourselves, it is always the friendship that matters most. Thank you for trusting me, working with me, and believing that with both rage and love we could write this book.